Praise for
New York Times and USA Today Bestselling Author

Diane Capri

"Full of thrills and tension, but smart and human, too."
Lee Child, #1 New York Times Bestselling Author of Jack Reacher Thrillers

"[A] welcome surprise....[W]orks from the first page to 'The End'."
Larry King

"Swift pacing and ongoing suspense are always present...[L]ikable protagonist who uses her political connections for a good cause...Readers should eagerly anticipate the next [book]."
Top Pick, Romantic Times

"...offers tense legal drama with courtroom overtones, twisty plot, and loads of Florida atmosphere. Recommended."
Library Journal

"[A] fast-paced legal thriller...energetic prose...an appealing heroine...clever and capable supporting cast...[that will] keep readers waiting for the next [book]."
Publishers Weekly

"Expertise shines on every page."
Margaret Maron, Edgar, Anthony, Agatha and Macavity Award Winning MWA Past President

DUE JUSTICE

by DIANE CAPRI

Published by: AugustBooks
http://www.AugustBooks.com

ISBN: 978-1-940768-10-6

Original cover design by Cory Clubb
Interior layout by Author E.M.S.

Published in the United States of America.

Visit the author website:
http://www.DianeCapri.com

ALSO BY DIANE CAPRI

CAST OF PRIMARY CHARACTERS

Judge Wilhelmina Carson

Carly Austin
Marilee Aymes
Frank Bennett
Michael Morgan
Senator Sheldon Warwick
Victoria Warwick (Tory)
Christian Grover
Fred Johnson
O'Connell Worthington
Pricilla Worthington
Carolyn Young
Alan Zimmer

Court Personnel:
Chief Judge Ozgood Livingston Richardson (CJ)
Margaret Wheaton (secretary)

Chief of Police Benjamin Hathaway

Wilhelmina Carson's Family:
George Carson
Kate Austin
Jason Austin
Mark Austin

For my Buddy, who is better than George, with all my love.
You're still the one.

DUE
JUSTICE

CHAPTER ONE

Tampa, Florida
Wednesday 4:15 p.m.
January 6, 1999

I GREW UP OUTSIDE Detroit, where the weak were killed and eaten. Still are.

Every morning during my high school years, my clock radio blasted me awake with morning news: *Five men killed last night in Cass Corridor. Two hundred homicides this year.*

Like sports statistics, only bloodier.

Somehow it never occurred to me to change the station.

Even so, murder was far removed from my suburban life. Eventually I moved to Tampa for sunny charm, Southern hospitality, smiling grocery clerks, polite neighbors, small-town feel.

And no crime. Okay, less crime.

But lessons learned young stick with us. All those Detroit homicides proved one thing to me: You never see the bullet that gets you, even when it hits you right between the eyes.

Of course, I didn't think about any of this until long after the time to duck.

Carly Austin ambushed me at home. I'd dashed home from work later than I'd planned. Preoccupied. Distracted. Too much to do, too little time to do it. And there she was. Waiting for me.

Her mere presence was a shock; she'd been ignoring me for more than a year.

I covered well; offered smiles, hugs. Asked her to join me for drinks. She feigned reluctance, but allowed me to persuade.

Twenty minutes later we sat outdoors on the Sunset Bar patio. I played with the pink flamingo swizzle stick in my iced Bombay Sapphire and tonic, moving the lemon twist around the cubes, afraid to sip because the alcohol would do what alcohol does. The swirling gin, yellow lemon and white ice mesmerized, passed the time.

Perfect late January afternoon. Warm and clear. Setting sun and rising full moon cast simultaneous glow on Hillsborough Bay, giving a mystical quality to my experience.

I knew it was the atmosphere that made me feel this way because I hadn't swallowed any gin. Yet.

Carly's visit was urgent in some way; she never came to me bearing good news or even minor trouble.

I felt my muscles tense with anticipation and anxiety.

Sought understanding. Gaze lifted. Watched my almost-sibling. What was the problem? Sure I could handle it, if only she'd tell me what it was. Too much drama. With Carly, always. If only she'd come tomorrow, when everything in my world was scheduled to be less tense. She had to know that today wasn't the best time to commandeer my attention.

Something was very wrong.

Again I noted the setting sun reflected glistening orange that flattered her copper coloring; but her clothes were wrinkled and dark circles under her eyes showed through her concealer. Lipstick smeared. Bright pink blush on pale cheeks made her look more like Bozo than Garbo. Even her curly red hair was dirty.

So not-Carly.

More gin. Definitely. But not yet.

I felt the familiar ambivalent emotions Carly always inspired. She was fiercely independent, but perpetually getting into some mess that I had to get her out of. I loved her, of course; she was the only sister I'd ever have. But I could strangle her sometimes. Gleefully.

Stubborn as an elephant, she couldn't be pushed. Believe me. I've tried.

While I waited for her to speak I flashed back to the first time we met. Gathered around the bassinet, watching. Instantly beloved. Tiny face, flashing blue eyes. Red ringlets framed porcelain skin. Mom cooed over Carly's little feet and perfect hands. Her brothers murmured in hushed wonder as they examined miniscule fingernails, perfect eyelashes. One of the boys, not quite ten and very clever, wanted to call her Curly, but his mother insisted on Carly, and his brother punched him in the arm whenever he refused to get it right.

No one noticed me, Wilhelmina, standing off to the side, already five foot six and still growing. Nothing about me was petite or cute, then or now. I was gawky and awkward. Even my earlobes were big.

The only things Carly and I had in common were red hair and double X chromosomes.

And her family.

My relationship with Carly was born in that minute. Conflicting feelings of awe, jealousy, irritation—and protectiveness. I've always taken care of Carly and she's always resisted. She thought she could take care of herself. Experience proved otherwise.

I like to think we've both matured in 29 years, but maybe not.

She was all grown up now, but still 110 pounds and 5'2". Carly's style was anything but cute. Sporting brightly polished artificial claws and perfect makeup, she was a proud glamour hound. "It's better to look good than to *be* good" is her personal creed.

Maybe she *can't* be good, or maybe she just doesn't try. Either way, the result is the same: whirling dervish in a small, perfect package.

I sighed loudly. Stopped playing with my watery gin and pushed it aside. As much as drinking would have helped, I'd need to keep all my wits about me to deal with Carly, and I was now dangerously short of time.

Too soon, my husband expected more than six hundred guests to attend an AIDS research benefit here in his restaurant. It's no secret that I hate these shindigs. Not my thing. At all. George might actually have been holding me captive when he extracted my promise to act as hostess. A thousand dollars a plate. Movers and shakers and poseurs showing up to see and be seen at what they considered their finest. I was hot, sweaty, and still wearing my work clothes.

"Okay, the suspense is killing me. I don't know what it is you have on your mind, but it can't be that bad." Realizing I was sticking my neck out, I asked, "What's up?"

As if she'd been waiting for me to ask, Carly said, "It's worse than anything you can imagine."

She said it quietly, with none of her usual bravado.

Impatience deflated like a bayoneted blimp.

"Hey, come on. I have quite an imagination," I joked. "Just because you haven't talked to me in a while doesn't mean I don't care about you."

The truth was that I cared too much. Always had. Never figured out how to toughen up my heart where Carly was concerned.

She smiled a little, sheepishly; seemed to take the edge off.

Carly slumped back in her chair and looked at the water. There were a couple of late afternoon sunfish sailors out, racing back and forth from Davis Islands to a spot 100 yards off the edge of our island, Plant Key.

About a year or two later, or at least it seemed that long as I imagined myself forced to greet senators and celebrities wearing nothing but my underwear, Carly finally started to talk. I resisted the urge to cheer.

"Did you see NewsChannel 8 this morning?"

"Why?"

More silence.

She picked up her white wine, took a sip, put it down, picked up the blue paper cocktail napkin, concentrating hard while she folded it into a fan. She never looked directly at me.

I wondered if my deodorant would hold on another eight hours. Maybe I could skip my bath?

"Did you see the news story on the drowning victim?" She finally asked, in a small voice.

Drowning victim? Are you kidding me?

Maybe he drowned, but I hoped he was dead before he went into the water.

Frank Bennett had the report. He'd said pieces of a body were pulled out of Tampa Bay before dawn. The largest portion, the part the sharks hadn't eaten, was found banging against the pilings of the Sunshine Skyway Bridge in Pinellas County. Hands and feet were bound together by clothesline and tied to heavy cement slabs. Face unrecognizable.

By now, she had shredded the cocktail napkin into tiny blue pieces and dropped them all over the deck. I remember thinking foolishly that she'd need collagen on those frown lines next week if she didn't relax.

I nodded encouragement to keep the words flowing because I couldn't fathom Carly involved in murder. The possibility didn't surface.

"Let me ask you a hypothetical question," Carly said.

That very second, I knew. She wasn't looking for sisterly advice. Not the usual boyfriend trouble or help with credit card bills. Carly was involved in something much, much worse. My body shivered with visceral certainty even before my brain acknowledged.

I should have stopped her right there. Should have cloaked us both with appropriate protections. I knew what to do. I knew how to do it.

But did I even try to dodge the bullet I saw coming straight at me? No. So how much smarter had all those Detroit homicides made me?

CHAPTER TWO

Tampa, Florida
Wednesday 5:05 p.m.
January 6, 1999

IT WAS LIKE WATCHING my own train wreck.

Gooseflesh raised on my skin.

Carly had set me up. I felt foolish for letting her get away
with it. And I was scared for her. She'd manipulated me, which
meant she knew she was in serious trouble. Why didn't she take
her guilty conscience to Tampa's best criminal defense attorney?
At least he would have been required to keep her secrets.

Masterfully played, though. Showed up here without
warning; protested my invitation to talk just strongly enough to
establish reluctance. Didn't volunteer information, but waited
until I insisted she tell me. Forced me to press her until she
relented.

I might not keep her secrets, but nothing she told me could
be used against her now. Under the law, she'd been interrogated
in violation of her constitutional rights. It didn't matter that she

knew she had rights; it only mattered that I hadn't warned her before she spilled her story.

She must have used the technique hundreds of times before. Like a dumb street criminal, I had walked right into her game before I realized we were on the playing field. Call me crazy, but I wasn't expecting to discuss murder in the moon glow.

No matter. I am the law; a role that suits like second skin, as Carly well knows.

Keeping score? Carly Austin, member in good standing of the Florida Bar, one; Wilhelmina Carson, United States District Court Judge for the Middle District of Florida, zero.

Maybe she saw my dawning understanding and figured I might actually strangle her, for she perched on the chair's edge, ready to run should the need arise. I'll admit, shaking her silly appealed. I grabbed my biceps instead.

Carly's words rushed faster.

"Hypothetically speaking," she said—my teeth clamped painfully onto my cheek—"What if someone might know the identity of that body? Would they be *required* to go to the police? Tell who they think it is? Even if they're not sure?"

She stressed the word *required* to emphasize her legal question. One that posed serious risks to us both.

And raised my temperature a good ten degrees. Hers, too, judging by her deeply crimsoned face. I appreciated the warmth.

Just like she'd done all her life, Carly put me in a hell of a spot, even if she were telling me the whole story, which I was very sure she wasn't.

Carly's usual style was to reveal only what she thought you needed to know. As a kid, she'd say, "If I tell you, I'll have to kill you," but that wouldn't have been a funny line at the moment.

Swiftly, my mind stepped through the logic.

Knowing the dead man's identity alone wasn't enough to scare her so badly. She'd have handled that small issue on her own. One phone call to the police chief or even an anonymous 911 tip. Simple problem with a quick resolution.

No, complications motivated her behavior.

Whether she was *required* to disclose information about the identity of this body depended on how she'd obtained the knowledge—and who was asking. Consequences chased her here. But why? She didn't kill the guy. Right? I was afraid to ask; she might tell me.

Report Carly to the local police for withholding evidence or be an accessory to obstruction of justice and face impeachment myself. Just great.

Eyed the watery gin, tempted to drink it anyway and let it take the edge off, if it could.

I said, "Let's recap. A drowning accident. Hypothetical bystander may know the victim's identity. Your question is: Does an ordinary citizen have a legal obligation to report unsubstantiated suspicion?"

"I don't know," Carly said quietly. "I mean, let's assume you don't know for *sure* who it is, but you have enough facts to suggest a realistic possibility."

"The easy thing to do is make the call, isn't it? Any decent citizen would volunteer whatever information he might have about the identity of a murder victim," I told her. "Think of the man's family, if nothing else."

She didn't notice that I'd slipped into personalizing her facts. As always, Carly was totally focused on Carly. She was crazy not to call this in. She could lose her license to practice law if she handled things the wrong way. She could end up in jail.

And I might be the one who had to report her. Neither one of us wanted that to happen. I ran my fingers through my hair and blew out a stream of frustration.

Old annoyance elbowed concern aside. Carly was in trouble; she should tell me about it and stop acting like a cross between flaky child and super spy. How could I fix her problem if I didn't know what it was? I love Carly, if love is a way to describe my feelings. And I'd do anything for her mother. But Carly doesn't make it easy. *Dammit!*

I watched as she calculated how much to reveal: keep me tethered, but not overplay her hand. Gamesmanship. Maybe she'd been AWOL from my life a while, but her methods sure hadn't changed.

"Carly?"

"Well, hypothetically speaking, suppose you had been spending a lot of time with a guy and he missed an important meeting with you and for a month after that you were never able to get in touch with him," she said, parceling out the information as if she were serving up expensive Kobe beef to a homeless woman.

My patience snapped. "I know a number of people I haven't seen in a month, but I don't believe any of them have been submerged in Tampa Bay all that time."

What the hell. I reached for the gin and drank about half of it. Even with mostly melted ice water filling the glass, I felt it hit my stomach with a jolt. I should have had lunch.

"Yes, but then stories started appearing in the paper about his disappearance." Carly looked at the water for several moments. Voice so quiet I had to lean closer to hear, she said, "And the last time I saw him, he told me someone was going to kill him."

The effects of the gin evaporated as quickly as they'd settled over me. Years of listening to clients' stories, sitting stone-faced in court while your theory of the case gets flattened by opposing counsel, then on the bench listening to all manner of ridiculous tales, I'd learned to appear cool and calm no matter what happened.

But appearing cool and being calm are two different things. My pounding heart and racing pulse gave me the real story.

I could feel my hands starting to shake, so I sat on them. I didn't need what her mother calls my "inner wisdom" to tell me Carly believed, absolutely.

She knew who he was; that he'd been murdered.

Maybe she even knew who killed him.

Oh, God, I prayed. But for what? To be wrong? To turn back the clock and let me erase this entire conversation?

Merely knowing the dead man put Carly closer to murder than I wanted either of us to be, closer than I'd felt when I lived in Detroit and anonymous people were murdered every day.

"Hypothetically speaking, who does the bystander believe the dead man is?" I barely recognized my own voice, and I wasn't sure Carly heard me.

I cleared my throat and said "Carly?" a little louder.

Noticing the change, she turned her head and looked at me directly, unblinking.

"Doctor Michael Morgan." She thrust a small piece of newspaper toward me. "Here."

She'd been holding it crumpled up in her hand. The paper was wet, the ink smeared with her sweat. I flattened out the creases. The story was short, from the *Tribune*, dated about two weeks earlier. No pictures.

DOCTOR MISSING

Once prominent plastic surgeon Dr. Michael Morgan has been reported missing. Dr. Morgan lives alone and has become a recluse in recent years following his conviction on drug possession charges eight years ago.

A few details followed, but nothing relevant.

I realized I'd been holding my breath. I sat back in my chair and tried to breathe normally; Carly continued looking straight through me.

Dr. Morgan was a locally prominent plastic surgeon. Legendary. A boy wonder. Some said a genius. I'd never met him, but I'd seen his resumé in my court files many times. Small town tax rolls listed entire populations in fewer pages.

Morgan had been published more than once in every major American medical journal, authored two textbooks and done plastic surgery on three-fourths of Florida's affluent citizens, males and females alike. He taught at the medical school; lectured on medical legal issues at the law school. In short, he was about as close to medical genius as they come.

Cold sober now, I tried but couldn't grasp the idea that Dr. Morgan had been so malevolently killed.

Here in Tampa, murder sells for about five hundred dollars. At least, that's the rate for carnies, drug pushers and street people. I don't know about doctors. But Michael Morgan? What could anyone have had against him?

I must have pondered too long. Carly rose, pushed her heavy rattan chair back from the table, and walked away. I figured she'd gone to powder her nose. We'd talk when she returned. Hash things out. Decide what to do.

But she didn't come back.

After ten minutes, I went looking for her. The hostess said

Carly had left the building. I hurried outside to check the parking lot. No luck. No one around. Not even the valet.

Hustled back into the house, through the restaurant and took the stairs two at a time up to our flat on the second floor. Ran through the den and to the window overlooking the driveway.

Watched Carly's gray sedan roll over the bridge from Plant Key to Bayshore Boulevard. It turned left, away from downtown, and I lost sight of her between the palm trees and traffic.

I stood there awhile, staring toward her vanishing point in the swiftly darkening twilight.

"Breathe in, breathe out; breathe in, breathe out," I repeated to make my hands stop shaking as I slowly descended the stairs.

How like Carly to get herself into disaster and dump it into my lap. I'd been rescuing her from herself most of her life, but this time she may have gotten into more than I could handle.

For the first time, I noticed bustling activity in the dining room. Temporary staff my husband, George, hired to serve tonight's fundraiser worked purposefully.

Carly was gone; I had no idea where. I called her cell, her home, and her office. Left messages. I could do nothing more tonight.

Police Chief Ben Hathaway, along with everyone else who might be interested in Dr. Morgan's disappearance, would be right here at George's restaurant for the evening anyway.

Besides, George was so nervous about this party that I had to do my part to make it a success. Rumors claimed Senator and Victoria Warwick and Elizabeth Taylor, the actress and AIDS activist, might attend.

Dr. Michael Morgan, and Carly's involvement with him, whatever it was, would have to wait.

If he was already dead, I couldn't bring him back to life.

Contrary to popular belief, judges know we are not gods.

CHAPTER THREE

Tampa, Florida
Wednesday 5:30 p.m.
January 6, 1999

I DRIFTED BACK TO the Sunset Bar, swallowed my gin and let the watery liquid relax me. The tension was chemically erased from my stomach and the rest of my muscles would feel it soon, too. Along with some heat. The January sun, near the horizon, no longer warmed. How much colder would the Gulf waters be this time of year? Well below comfortable body temperatures, that's for sure. Hypothermia kills, too.

George emerged from the kitchen, tossing words over his shoulder that I couldn't hear. He wore his usual uniform: khaki slacks, golf shirt, and kilted cordovan loafers, sans socks. Today, the shirt was bright yellow. It set off his deep tan and dark hair like neon. Despite all the kicking and screaming about leaving Michigan, he'd become a perpetually comfortable Floridian about twenty seconds after we moved here. It's culturally closer from Grosse Pointe to South Tampa than geography suggests.

He spied me, came over and bestowed a kiss, which I returned more desperately, wanting to feel something solid having nothing to do with cold water, dead doctors, and missing sisters in trouble.

Once released, he said, "Good, you're home early. Take a quick walk through the dining room to make sure everything's done?"

"Just sit with me for a minute. I'm sure Peter has everything under control."

Peter, George's maître'd', could run the place with his eyes closed. A charity fundraiser for six hundred people was no great challenge. He'd done it all before.

"I've had a crush on Elizabeth Taylor since I first saw *National Velvet*. I want to knock her off her feet." He wiggled eyebrows like Groucho Marx to force my smile. He's not clairvoyant, but seventeen years of marriage have given him a sixth sense of my moods. He knows which buttons to push.

"You act like all this is wildly important to you when you don't really care whether they have a wonderful time or not," I teased.

"Every event we have here is important to me." Then, he relented a little. "Just because I didn't vote for our democratic senator doesn't mean I want the *Tribune's* food critic or the *Times'* society pages trashing my party."

The *Tribune* or the *Times* find anything less than perfect? Unlikely as snowfall during a Tampa summer. George's chefs have won the Golden Spoon Award five times and *Florida Trend* magazine removed his restaurant from the annual Best of Florida issue because nothing could compete.

"Bring your drink. I'll keep your mind off Elizabeth Taylor." I leered, mocking him, and this time, he was the one who laughed.

We moved to my favorite outside table. Wicker rockers invited us to kick back and enjoy the view. Sitting outside, watching either sunrise or sunset over the water, is one of the best things about living on Plant Key. I don't care enough about the sunrise to get up for it. Now, if sunrise is the end of a perfect evening, well that's something else.

We sat quietly, words between us unnecessary. Maybe the best part of marriage is comfortable companionship every day. George has been the best friend I could ever have, although when we met I imagined lifetime romance and lust.

Got that, too.

Like most evenings, he chattered on about today's events at the restaurant and asked what had happened in my courtroom. Both of us too keyed up to relax, albeit for different reasons.

The sun disappeared at 5:49 p.m., one minute later than yesterday, one minute earlier than tomorrow. Normal Tampa sunset. No low clouds to create the spectacular effects we enjoyed in Michigan. No frigid January wind, either.

George jumped up to complete his preparations. Guess after seventeen years, I can't expect to compete with Elizabeth Taylor.

As promised, I moved through the archway into the main dining room for a final inspection. The former ballroom comfortably held about thirty round tables. Tonight, decorated in fuchsia and white, with red and green bromeliads, bird of paradise and other tropical plants that grew in carefully cultured gardens here on Plant Key. White tablecloths; fuchsia napkins.

Not the usual restaurant china, but Minaret's best Herrend, Waterford and sterling flatware. All came with the house when we inherited it from George's Aunt Minnie; now set flawlessly in ten place settings per table.

Something truly spectacular was the ice sculpture on the

head table. An eagle, its wings spread, and spanning more than four feet, majestically demonstrated the strength most AIDS patients lacked. Too bad the eagle would melt before morning; it's never cold enough to keep ice frozen in Tampa overnight. Something else to be grateful for.

I walked the length of both dining rooms; examined the flowers and the table settings. If there were flaws in the presentation, I couldn't find them. Nor had I expected to.

I flashed an "Okay" sign across the way; George surveyed everything personally and barely noticed my appreciation.

Everything about our home is astonishing to me still. Often, I marvel that we actually live here. George claims we can't be evicted, but is that true?

George's Aunt Minnie married into the grand old building and bequeathed it to her favorite nephew when she died. Minaret, as it's called, was built in the 1890's to house Henry Plant's family. Plant was constructing the Tampa Bay Hotel, now the University of Tampa, which he hoped would be a vacation Mecca for the rich and famous. He wanted to surpass his rival Henry Flagler's magnificent Palm Beach construction.

Henry placed Minaret to be admired like a sparkling solitaire presented on her private island.

Originally too shallow for navigation and devoid of landmass, Hillsborough Bay was dredged to allow passage of freighters into the Port of Tampa. Henry Plant persuaded the Army Corps of Engineers to build the landmass for Plant Key at the same time they created Harbour Island and Davis Islands.

Plant Key is marquis cut, about a mile wide by two miles long. Narrow ends face north toward Tampa and south toward the Gulf of Mexico. Key Bridge connects us to Bayshore Boulevard just north of Gandy.

The locals, and New York society, dubbed the enterprise "Henry's Ego," but like everything else Plant did, his island and his home surpassed all expectations.

Hard to fathom sometimes how much ostentatious wealth was accumulated and displayed in the days before income tax by those who were willing to live maybe just a bit outside the law.

How lucky can one woman get? I have George, Minaret, a job I love, and I never have to wear parkas. Life is good. Damn good.

Or it was.

An hour ago.

Before Carly's bombshell.

No time to dwell on that now. By concentrating carefully, I hoped to avoid thoughts of Dr. Michael Morgan, dead or alive, for the next eight hours. A foolish plan.

CHAPTER FOUR

Tampa, Florida
Wednesday 7:00 p.m.
January 6, 1999

WATER SPLASHED HARD AND fast into the enormous claw-footed tub in my bathroom like Yosemite's Illilouette falls. Gotta love modern plumbing. I poured avocado oil bath gel in the water and while it bubbled into snowy white mounds, located piano nocturnes on the player and lit two gardenia-scented candles.

Lowered gingerly into steamy water, head rested against bath pillow, stretched out my full five feet eleven and a half inches and wiggled ten toes. Eyes closed. Tried to stay in the present, blissful moment.

No luck.

Kept coming back to Carly, catastrophizing her situation. Mine, too.

Inactivity is hard for me. My karmic purpose must be to learn patience. Regardless of how I redirected my attention,

Carly and Dr. Morgan occupied my mind. The more I tried to push the problem into tomorrow like an earlier Southern mistress, the more the situation menaced.

Both Carly and I could end up not only unemployed, but disbarred. Or worse.

Scarlett O'Hara was an idiot; the Bay Body, as Bennett called him, would still be dead tomorrow, too.

The water had grown as cold as the Gulf.

I gave up the effort to avoid bad news, pulled the plug, wrapped myself in a robe, and turned on the television.

Again, the lead story was ongoing non-identification.

Frank Bennett recapped the few facts he'd previously reported, then said, "Dental records have been requested and may take several days to locate."

His next words gave me hope.

"One source close to the investigation told us the victim could be a tourist who disappeared last year after what survivors claimed was a boating accident. Our source also said authorities are evaluating evidence of a copycat killing."

Bennett aired old film clips next. I realized why the Bay Body seemed so familiar to me. An eerily similar killing had occupied the news media for months four years ago and repeated endlessly when the killer was convicted last fall.

Two possibilities, both chilling: a serial killer, or maybe the wrong man was convicted. I shuddered.

Bennett ran old interviews following the two prior deaths.

I noticed the lateness of the hour, pressed the mute button, and began drying my hair.

Bent over from the waist, head upside down, I glanced at the screen.

Senator Sheldon Warwick and his wife, Victoria,

disembarking from a plane at Tampa International Airport. I restored the sound and heard that the senator and his wife were in town for tonight's benefit. Kind enough to plug the fund-raiser and George's restaurant, which was nice. I didn't see Elizabeth Taylor. Was she there?

When they began the sports report, I pressed the off button and finished up my hair.

I was standing in my closet when George came upstairs, patted my bare ass, and said, "Cute as that is—"

I pulled the creamy cashmere shift out of its garment bag, and held it shoulder level while examining my reflection in the full length mirror. No shape, no style, no color. "It seems like a perfect opportunity for this."

"How about one of your cocktail dresses?" He suggested, continuing through to his bathroom and shower. The secret to a long marriage, I'd learned eons ago, was separate bathrooms and separate closets, but never separate beds.

I focused on makeup. By the third try, my eyeliner looked less like rick-rack on my eyelids, so I left it alone. After a few drinks, no one would notice. Or maybe I'd start a new style.

Raised my voice to be heard over the pelting water. "This one would get Victoria's attention. You know how status-conscious she is."

Senator Warwick's wife was infamous for drinking too much and engaging in rowdy behavior that embarrassed everyone. She threw heavy objects and connected more frequently than the Ray's best slugger. No police department in Florida had ever been politically stupid enough to charge her. But George despised negative publicity and he wanted Victoria to behave. I'd been charged with that task during the planning stages.

"But if you'd rather I wore something else," I called out, "I'd be happy to."

George said nothing, but I knew I'd snagged his attention.

So I put on the dress and admired. Fabric draped perfectly from neckline to hem. Covered but did not conceal. Soft as a bunny's tummy. I loved the dress; every woman present would, too. When it came to fashion, pleasing women was more important. Besides, the dress cost so much I'd be wearing it the rest of my life. Might as well start now.

George came around the corner wearing a shaving creamed face and nothing else.

"You know, that's always been one of my favorite dresses. You look great in it," he said with such mock sincerity, we both laughed. Tried to kiss me, but I ducked. "You smell great, too," he said.

George's fun-loving side has faded somewhat over the years, but a couple of martinis can still bring out the best in him. I ducked away.

"Who's attending this thing?" I shouted, returning to finish my makeup. Minimalism takes more time than you think.

He said, "All the usual suspects."

"Meaning Marian and the CJ?" I asked, referring to the guy who thinks he's my boss and his wife, who are not my favorite couple.

Although CJ is the Chief Judge of the U.S. District Court for the Middle District of Florida, Tampa Division, the title means he's a paper pusher, not that he gets to boss me around. One of these days, he was going to figure that out. Maybe I could hold my temper until that happened.

"Among others." George said.

I put down my hairbrush, entered the steamy bathroom and confronted him directly.

"What others?"

"All of the offspring, too. $1,000 a plate." He said as he ducked under the shower to avoid my outrage.

"*Eight Richardsons?*" I shouted to be heard over the running water.

"I couldn't invite Pricilla Worthington and not invite her brother." Attempting to placate me by naming a guest who actually was one of my favorite people. No chance.

Steam heated me up and wilted my hair. The dress felt scratchy against damp skin. I escaped into my dressing room to finish my ultra short hair. It doesn't take much; whatever shape it's going to have flows from cut, not effort.

When George shut down his shower, I asked, "Who is Pricilla's brother?"

"We've lived here ten years, Willa," he said, truly exasperated. "The CJ is Pricilla's brother. How could you not know that?"

Indeed.

How could I not know that?

Denial. Pure and simple.

"The interrelationships of Tampa society don't interest me." Indignation is often the best defense. "Who else is coming to this thing?"

With exaggerated patience, as if explaining to a simple-minded child, he said, "It's a Junior League function. Anyone and everyone willing to pay will be an honored guest." He had finished making a perfect bow of his black tie, patted my cashmere-covered butt, and left the room saying, "If you're really curious, there's a copy of the guest list on the desk."

Still thinking about Carly, I skimmed over the names, which only reinforced how boring this evening would be. Every person on the list could afford to pay a thousand dollars a plate, all right. But this wasn't Silicone Valley. People who had that kind of money around here had made it the old fashioned way—inheritance.

About midway down, on the third page, found the name I'd hoped for—*Dr. Michael Morgan and guest*. The discovery lightened my heart.

He couldn't be dead if he was walking around our dining room tonight, right?

Find him, prove Carly's suspicions wrong. Then, I'd find her.

I wrinkled my nose and fumed at George.

This is the part of being married I don't like—the compromise, the accommodation. A single tonight, I'd be out with real friends, or working, or just relaxing with the dogs.

Friends tell me the best part of being single is doing whatever you want, whenever you want. No holidays with the in-laws, whiskers in the sink, toilet seats left up, or refusals to eat zucchini. Most definitely no interminable evenings spent with insufferable bores to raise money for the worthy-cause-of-the-moment.

Like the CJ, for instance. Chief Judge Ozgood Livingston Richardson, Senior—"Oz," to his friends (which does not include me)—is 65 years old, going on 95. Actually, I think the CJ was born old. If he ever laughs, it's politely. He knows which fork to use at eight-fork table settings. He married a debutante back in the day when that was important. Each of his three children, two daughters with husbands, and "Junior," (as Ozgood Livingston Richardson, II, is not-so-affectionately known) are firmly ensconced in society, and they're all just as interesting as processed white bread. If any of them had ever had so much as a ten-word conversation, the listener had to be hearing impaired.

The CJ's wife is regarded by one and all as a fixture in Tampa. She'll tell you, each and every time you're introduced, "I'm Marian Wright Richardson, and I'm a fifth generation Floridian."

If you live in Florida, you recognize immediately how remarkable that is. You're lucky if you can find someone who was born here, let alone a fifth generation resident. This makes her children sixth generation, the equivalent of royalty.

The rest of us are expected to kiss the ring.

Repeatedly.

I dropped the list of party guests, puckered up, and went to do what had to be done.

CHAPTER FIVE

Tampa, Florida
Wednesday 7:45 p.m.
January 6, 1999

THE GUESTS WERE SET to arrive at 8:00, but I hoped to have
a glass of wine first. I wanted to think about gathering
information tonight on Dr. Morgan; from him directly or, if he
didn't show up, his neighbors. Keep Carly out of trouble. Me,
too.

Someone would know something.

George had closed the restaurant for the evening, dedicating
both dining rooms to the fundraiser. Extra valets for parking.
News coverage because of the guest list. These affairs are set for
weeknights by people who don't work—or maybe by those who
do and need an excuse.

Sunset Bar for a peaceful quarter hour before the deluge.
Maybe a good Cabernet would improve my mood. What
brightened my outlook immediately was the sole occupant of the
room: Frank Bennett.

Ten years ago, Frank Bennett was the new kid in local television news. His gimmick was to introduce each newscast with a piece of Florida trivia. You know, like "We're here at Disney World where Richard Nixon once announced 'I am not a crook.'" The idea was that the trivia would relate to the newscast in some way and, of course, distinguish him from all the other wannabes. And he put a "state pride" spin on everything when he could.

The bit was popular with viewers and helped land him in the NewsChannel 8 co-anchor chair.

Like all successful gimmicks, keeping it fresh was the problem. He started out writing the bits himself, from local history books and the newspaper archives. Now that he's a "star," a research staff does the work. Every night, 350,000 viewers tune in; much of that audience is due to Frank's youthful ingenuity.

"Hey, Frank." The traditional southern greeting, not to startle.

He smiled with obvious appreciation.

"I guess you don't share my husband's disdain for this rather simple dress," I said.

"I guess your husband doesn't understand how fabulous you look in it. If you go to work dressed like that, I may request a transfer to cops and courts." He actually winked at me.

"Frank, it's illegal to flirt with a judge," I said, with mock sternness.

But I kissed him on the cheek.

Frank's always had something of a crush on me; I'd never exploited it before.

"Run out of cub reporters?" I sat down across the table with my wine; he raised his glass in silent toast. When seated, Frank can look me in the eyes. Otherwise, we look like Boris and Natasha having a chat.

"One sign of old age is believing you can do everything better yourself," he said. Ran his palm over his mostly bald head.

"What's the latest?" I smiled, going for the perfect level of curiosity. At least he didn't appear to be attuned to my need to know. Or maybe he was just used to it. Journalists are fun at cocktail parties.

He frowned, gnawed the plastic stir from his drink. "I'm trying to figure out how a guy can get himself shot, bound to cement slabs, and stuck in the Gulf of Mexico. And leave no trace of his life. Doesn't seem possible, does it, Willa?"

Was he baiting me?

No. Thinking aloud.

I relaxed a little.

He didn't know.

But he would.

Frank Bennett would nail the Bay Body's story: Who was he? How'd he get there? Why?

Maybe Carly and I wouldn't be among the wreckage when Bennett figured it out.

And where was she, anyway? Still no response to my messages. Forced myself not to report her missing, too.

That thought, at the front of my mind since she'd bolted, kept popping up.

"I've never seen such a terrible body. Brutal. Bloated, half eaten. Beating against the Skyway for days. If he hadn't been shot before he went into the water.... How could no one know? Didn't he have any friends? Family? How does a man get that isolated?"

He stared, intently focused on my face, as if I could answer his questions.

I detached.

Remembered Frank had never married. No kids or family. Maybe this was a life crisis for him. I hoped not. If he made the story personal, he'd never relent.

"You've checked missing persons reports, I guess?" Soft suggestion. I sipped my wine to cover my duplicity. Dissembling is not my strong suit; I prefer the direct approach.

"Nothing's turned up in our search or the cops'. I've got resources they can't access. If he's a local guy, I'll know his name this time tomorrow if I have to question every citizen in the three counties."

Mired deeper by each failure to speak, I hoped he'd find Morgan before questioning Carly or me. Could I maintain silence during his inquisition? Keeping client confidences is easy. Keeping my own guilty secrets was nerve wracking.

Confident that Frank would identify the body quickly and Tampa police would solve the murder soon, finding Carly became urgent.

Party noises raised the volume inside the Sunset Bar. I glanced toward the parking lot.

Limos and private cars pulled up at the valet stand. Doors opened and bedecked philanthropists emerged, well-heeled, well-dressed. Flooded George's restaurant exhibiting genteel chatter.

Dozens of guests were strangers to me, but many I recognized. Lawyers, judges, business professionals, physicians whom I mingled with regularly and those I knew by reputation only. Carly Austin might be the only Tampa woman I knew who was not present.

Where was Carly?

I said, "Frank, I've got to do the hostess thing. But now you've got me curious. Keep me informed, okay?"

Understatement is one of my cultivated southern virtues. I smoothed my dress. Straightened my hair.

Frank rose, waved for a refill, and squeezed my arm gently. "I'll call you as soon as I can."

"Thanks," I said, not the least bit grateful, as I scurried away.

By the time I ran the gauntlet of arriving guests wondering how I could navigate the evening, the main dining room was two-thirds full. I couldn't see Kate, but I circulated through the tuxedoed men and designer-dressed women. Passing waiters in white tie served canapés and champagne, and the room buzzed, clanked, tinged, whooshed, and guffawed with steadily increasing noise. In another hour, we'd need to shout our whispers.

I made my way to the maître d' station where Peter examined engraved invitations and checked names of arriving guests. Dr. Michael Morgan had not checked in yet. But Police Chief Hathaway was here somewhere.

Pricilla and O'Connell Worthington crossed the threshold. Their appearance, a Tampa standard, was nevertheless startling. Both were well past 70. Formal. Regal. Inseparable. Beloved.

But there the similarity ended.

O'Connell's full head of wavy white hair and courtly manners suited his position as the chairman and only surviving named partner of one of the oldest law firms in town. Yet he is small and slight of stature, fit and strong for his age.

His wife, Cilla, had to be 5'10", at least. The flowing gowns she favors thwart accurate estimates, but her bathroom scale hadn't read less than 200 pounds for several decades. Freckles and pale skin suggested blonde hair might have been natural once. A sweeter woman never lived, but she was no beauty.

It wasn't the first time I've wondered what had originally attracted them to each other. Given the times, theirs could have been an arranged marriage. But I thought not. It had always seemed a love match to me. Their relationship inspired nostalgia for eras when value mattered more than beauty, if any had ever existed.

Cilla, gracious as always, took both my hands in hers. "Minaret is beautiful, Willa. George has done an amazing job here. This benefit is the most successful event we've ever held. He is such a dear to do all of this. And you, too, for putting up with us." Cilla was chair of the fundraising committee; she took her job seriously.

Engrossed, I opened my mouth to answer her, but we were rudely interrupted.

Christian Grover, Tampa's Clarence Darrow, and his current sweet young thing startled us all. Manners like a cockroach. Too much success; too many rewards for behaving badly.

"O'Connell!" He shouted from ten feet away, over the din, filling a freakish momentary lull. All heads turned to watch the show. Applause addiction is a hard habit to break; he'd never tried. The man is insufferable.

Grover's tuxedo fit him the way my birthday suit fits me, but with a lot fewer wrinkles. Arm-candy probably worked nights at Jason's Doll House after her afternoon high school classes. I smelled Clearasil.

His voice boomed louder than a Shakespearean actor, even as he closed the gap between us.

"You're not having ex parte communications with the judge, are you?" Not a joke. Not meant to be. Grover accused. Like

British humor, if you knew the context, it was a not-so-subtle insult.

I am a United States district court judge, appointed for life. I take my responsibilities seriously, whether my "boss" the CJ thinks so or not. Both Grover and O'Connell regularly appear in my courtroom and ex parte communications are unethical.

O'Connell, ever the gentleman, replied smoothly. "Why, Christian, please introduce us to your companion. I'm sure she, like Cilla, abhors discussion of business at social events."

I cast him a grateful smile. Some wag once said about O'Connell Worthington that you'd think a man with such a large name would be a bigger guy. Maybe. But if O'Connell lacked physical stature, he more than made up for it in what George's Aunt Minnie would have called breeding. He'd rescued me many a time.

"Actually, we were just discussing how many breast implant customers are in this room tonight. Why, I've never seen so much cleavage—it gives the term 'silicon valley' a whole new meaning." Grover's voice was smooth, snide, sure. And it carried to the rafters. Everyone around us was listening and pretending they weren't.

"I'm sure that's something upon which you have a great deal more experience, Christian," Cilla said calmly, deliberately not looking at the young woman clinging to him like cat hair. She turned to me and O'Connell, took our arms and said, "Oh, look, Senator Warwick is arriving. Let's go and say hello."

With that, she walked the three of us off leaving Grover and his date standing in our wake.

"Cilla, you are precious. And O'Connell, you're one lucky man. It's no wonder you've been married over 50 years." I patted her hand, kissed his cheek and told them I would see them later.

I couldn't deal with the Warwicks just yet. First I needed a break, a drink, and Kate. In that order. The only thing I could manage was the break. I escaped. Or so I thought.

CHAPTER SIX

Tampa, Florida
Wednesday 8:20 p.m.
January 6, 1999

THE WOMEN'S ROOM WAS tastefully decorated for those ladies experiencing a tendency to swoon, or whatever.

Plopped onto the floral chintz loveseat, gratefully slipped off my high-heels. Why hadn't I worn my Nikes?

Closed my eyes for a moment to discourage socializing by new arrivals.

Shut out the visual noise. Hearing now acute. Two quick flushes.

One set of awkward shoe-falls exited each stall. Standing at the sinks. Quick tap-water flow. Talking to their reflections while no doubt adjusting appearances. It's what we women do.

"How long have you had yours?" Giggle. Youngish. "They look great."

"About ten years." Weary. Mature.

"Have you had any problems?" Worried.

Perkier. "I love 'em! After my third baby, I had no substance. Dr. Morgan did them right in his office."

"I've only had mine three years. No problems, but the bad news has me scared to death." She didn't sound scared, let alone near death. Drama.

"I know what you mean. My husband is freaked." Both sets of double-tap soles headed my way. "I'm thinking about having them removed. You know, just to be safe. Christian Grover's my lawyer. He said these things are leaking and are poisoning my body every day. Every time I get a little bit tired, I'm scared I'm getting sick, you know?"

They passed me without so much as a nod in my direction on the way out. I confess. I looked at their chests and they, indeed, had lovely breasts. Dr. Morgan was an artist.

When I'd stayed in the ladies' room as long as I could hide out before becoming an official missing person, I went back to the party. Everyone who is anyone or wanted to become someone was there. Attempting to sort them out was exhausting. Confusing, too.

Focused instead on the ones I'd been assigned to watch.

CJ and wife huddled in obvious camaraderie with the Worthingtons. Cilla and CJ's wife posed like wives do when husbands talk shop. CJ and O'Connell Worthington had been law partners for 20 years until CJ was appointed to the federal bench years ago.

No family resemblance between Cilla and the CJ that I could find. Except maybe in their coloring. If George hadn't told me they were brother and sister, I'd never have believed it. A proper lady like Cilla from the same gene pool as the sarcastically dubbed "great and powerful Oz?" No doubt about it, I'd have to reassess my judgments about one of them.

While I'd been hiding, Kate arrived. Thank God.

She looked perfect in the royal blue beaded gown she's worn to every formal event she's attended for at least the past ten years. I smiled when I saw it. Kate is so reliably normal. One of the many reasons I love her.

I walked up and kissed her cheek. "Thank you for coming. You look lovely in that gown, as always. Your eyes sparkle as much as the dress."

"Why should I buy a new gown? This one looks good on me and its perfectly acceptable. I'm long past the point of trying to impress 'society.'" She eyed my dress pointedly. Sometimes I think she and George were separated at birth.

Kate asked, "Where is Victoria? Has she been here long enough to get into trouble yet?"

Kate behaved normally, I thought, meaning Carly had not dumped her troubles on her mother. For that, I was grateful. Kate should have only happiness in her life. Maybe I cherished her more than Carly because she was not my real mother.

We looked around for the senator's wife. There were small conversation pods here and there, but I noticed a particularly large group under the stairs near the entrance to the dining room gathered like flies at a picnic.

"Why don't we try over there," I pointed my head. "Likely our guests of honor, right?"

We moved toward the swarm. Forward progress was glacial. Elbows and pointed toes blocked our passage. Sometimes painfully.

Eventually, we were close enough to see Senator Warwick, his wife standing next to him.

"Kate, look at that dress. She looks fabulous." I whispered close to Kate's ear, but needn't have worried about being overheard. The din was as loud as a rock concert.

Victoria, a woman of some years as they say, displayed herself in a full-length emerald lamé gown bearing a "V" neckline that plunged almost to her waist, exhibiting way more than a bit of cleavage.

"I heard she'd had surgery. I thought they said facelift. Apparently, it's something lower she had lifted." Kate whispered back with extraordinary cattiness.

"Christian Grover said breast implants stuffed this room," I replied, grinning.

"Christian's a pig, but he's usually right," Kate responded. "Have you ever noticed how humans are creatures of selective attention?"

When Kate gets into her Zen, or whatever it is, she's a little too Eastern for me to take her seriously. "What?"

"Attention focused on any thing creates that thing, Wilhelmina."

"So, I've created these implants through my imagination? They're not really here? We're not being invaded by an alien species of Amazons?" I teased her.

"Don't mock me. You know what I mean. You're so often in your own world that you don't see what's plainly visible." Sometimes she still acts like my mother. I like it.

The crowd stepped back a little and we could now observe its nucleus.

Senator Warwick, speaking loudly enough to be overheard, holding forth on what he proposed to do if the good voters returned him to the Senate in the fall elections. He was talking to O'Connell Worthington and other members of the party who had gathered around him closest. The liberals were adoring fans— conservatives resembled sharks to chub.

"Something has got to be done about the product liability crisis in this country. A number of our best corporate citizens have been put out of business by these frivolous product liability suits. When I return to the Senate, I'll make sure America can compete in the global economy without fear of bankrupting its businesses."

"Blah, blah, blah," Kate said.

Preaching to the choir, though this wasn't a political rally.

His wife looked glassy-eyed. She might have been drinking before she arrived; George's staff would not have served her.

Kate noticed Victoria's condition, too.

"Duty calls," she said, squeezed my arm briefly, approached Victoria and led her away.

I turned to thread my way out when Christian Grover's voice rose to challenge.

"Come on, Senator. That's a lie."

The collective gasped.

Warwick replied, "So you claim, Grover. You're not exactly objective."

Grover pressed on. "Maybe. But you are wrong. Statistics repeatedly show very few successful product liability awards to victims in this country. Corporations make billions of dollars selling defective products knowingly, intending to injure consumers. Big business owns you, Warwick. Don't dress this up like an altruistic crusade."

Polite cheers greeted Grover's comments, too.

An uncomfortable battle was joined. The atmosphere hung now with hostility. I searched for George and spied him across the wide ballroom, willing him to look my way until he did.

Warwick punched below the belt in reply. "I suppose you're handling those seven-hundred lawsuits pro bono?"

George assessed the situation at once; reached us in half a second; spirited Grover and his date away.

Crisis averted.

Red meat off the table; the swarm dispersed like magic.

Now what?

What I wanted to do was find Carly. Not an option. George would kill me if I left now. The second best option could be here in the room if Dr. Morgan had checked in. How to find out without making a fool of myself was the next issue. Maybe the solution was to ask a fool?

Tampa's not Savannah, but it's a southern town and we have our share of eccentric characters, many of whom were present and accounted for.

The medical community was prominently represented tonight. AIDS was their issue, after all. Several Tampa physicians and their spouses were in attendance. I saw Dr. Marilee Aymes, for many years the area's leading cardiologist and still the only woman cardiologist in town, standing alone near the entrance. A few moments later, her most recent escort approached her with a champagne glass in each hand. Marilee qualifies as eccentric, but she's certainly no fool.

Speculation around town is that Dr. Aymes is a lesbian and she brings virile young male escorts to all the social events to convince people otherwise. The evidence typically cited in support of this theory includes her extremely short haircut and brassy manner.

Tampa women are not abrasive, at least the socially successful ones aren't.

Dr. Aymes's graduation from medical school in 1960, when she was the only woman in her class, must have meant she was a little odd. That she wears a tuxedo to black tie affairs fuels the rumors.

Besides that, everyone will tell you, she smokes cigars, as if that clinches it. Tampa has never been on the crest of the fashion wave. Smoking cigars here is still something the men retire to after dinner with their port, while the ladies socialize. Oh, the tourists smoke cigars, and you can find trendy cigar bars in Ybor City open until the wee hours. But ladies? My dear, it just isn't done.

I saw Grover and Fred Johnson, Grover's partner, himself another prominent plaintiff's attorney here in town, deep in conversation with Dr. Carolyn Young. I certainly didn't want to get involved there, so I joined Dr. Aymes.

She ignored her escort; he looked like he'd stepped into the room from a Chippendales calendar.

"I wonder how much of her body is real?" Marilee said, pointing her unlit cigar toward Dr. Young. "I've heard she's actually sixty-five years old."

Dr. Young looked thirty-five, if that.

"You laugh. From here, I can tell those breast implants are at least five years old, the nose has been done more than once, and there've been some collagen injections around the mouth recently. Botox too, probably. Just think what I'd discover if I had my glasses on and was close enough to actually see her." She puffed on her stogie like George Burns while she talked.

"Marilee, you can't possibly tell all that from thirty feet away, can you?" I asked her, wiping mirthful tears from my eyes.

"Those breasts look like cereal bowls sitting on a flat board. That's what happens when implants get hard. As for the nose, you can see how small it is compared to the rest of her face. There's no way she was born with that nose. In fact, if you give me a minute, I can probably name the surgeon. It looks like a signature nose to me."

Covered my mouth, trying not to make a spectacle of myself by guffawing. But I couldn't help it. I could barely get the words out, but had to ask. "The collagen injections?"

"She probably had them done last week. Look how plump the lines are between her nose and her mouth. And when she's laughing, there's not a sign of crows' feet. Probably injected there, too."

She was precious. Tears streamed down my cheeks now, my carefully applied makeup a thing of the past. "Couldn't she be young? A natural beauty?"

Dr. Aymes snorted. "She could be. But she's not. How old do you think she is?"

My voice squeaked. "Thirty-five?"

"Try fifty-seven. Look it up. Date of med school graduation is a matter of public record."

Dr. Aymes took another glass of champagne from a passing waiter. At this rate, she'd be more drunk than Victoria Warwick, but I was pretty sure she'd be more fun, too, if we could change the subject.

CHAPTER SEVEN

Tampa, Florida
Wednesday 9:15 p.m.
January 6, 1999

MARILEE PUFFED ON THE unlit cigar. Asked, "And why do you think she's talking to those two sharks?"

"Grover and Johnson?"

"She does explant surgeries for their clients. Breast implant 'victims,' they claim. About $5,000 a pop. Then she talks the women into reconstruction surgery for another $5,000."

"How many of those can she do?" I asked, not laughing now.

"I can't get an operating room for my cardiac surgeries two days a week because she's doing explants. And that's just at my hospital. I know she's on staff at three others where she does the same thing. I'd say she does 25 a week. Add it up. Those two guys are going to make her a wealthy woman, and they're just a couple of her sources."

I'd been seeking an opening to ask her about Dr. Michael Morgan. Tampa is a very small town in many ways. Marilee practiced medicine here for years. I was sure she'd know him; might know who'd want to kill him, too. How to bring it up?

Before I could ask, George joined the conversation. He heard the tail end of Dr. Aymes' comments about Dr. Young.

"You mean to say that Dr. Young is charging $200,000 to $250,000 a week to do reconstructive surgery on breast implant patients? What insurance company would ever pay for that?"

George doesn't particularly care for Dr. Aymes; says I shouldn't be seen with her. After all, what would people think?

Marilee was too involved in her subject to notice. "That's just it. The insurance companies won't pay for it. There's no scientific evidence linking breast implants to *any* health problem. The lawyers pay for it."

"But where do they get the money?" He said, disbelieving. "I know those guys have made a lot of money in their lifetimes, but come on."

"I don't know, George." Dr. Aymes snapped. Annoyed. George questioned what she told him as absolute fact. She wouldn't be interrogated. Or disbelieved. "You're the banker. How do people normally finance a business deal?"

"I'm not sure, Dr. Aymes, I haven't been in banking for quite some time. But speaking of banking, Willa," he said as he turned smoothly to me, "I promised Bill Sheffield you'd speak with him briefly. Would you excuse us, Dr. Aymes?"

I couldn't think of a quick reason to refuse and found myself propelled. "See you soon," I said, and meant it.

George mumbled "What a most disagreeable woman. How preposterous."

He can be as stuffy as my father sometimes. I was still smiling. Marilee had provided more laughter than I'd felt since Carly ambushed me.

We joined Bill Sheffield, a local stockbroker, and his wife just as the rest of his group were moving away. They discussed the status of investments and the Dow Jones; I listened with half an ear while my mind wandered.

I heard Bill suggest that George consider stock in medical products companies.

"The breast implant mess has devalued the stock of a number of companies that are otherwise very sound, George. I have no doubt this crisis will blow over and those stocks will increase again. You can buy MedPro, for example, at $3.00 a share right now. It's a local company and I think it's going to turn around. It went public at $7.00 and it'll definitely go higher."

"I'm investing in technologies right now. Last week I bought DataTech and it's up fifteen points already," George responded, the first volley in a lengthy set.

I tried to pay attention, but Carly's employer was not mentioned again and my mind wandered.

Ten minutes later, both Mary Sheffield and I were long past any ability to feign interest. She opened a conversation about the next Junior League Show House, which I found only slightly more interesting than watching paint dry.

Spied a more interesting conversation near the Sunset Bar. Again, I escaped.

Chief Hathaway and Frank Bennett were doubtless talking shop. I approached, slightly obscured behind a passing waiter.

"How long will it take to make a positive I.D.?" Frank asked Chief Hathaway.

Ben replied, "The body's in bad shape. Finger prints are impossible. Searching medical and dental records will take a while. Too long, maybe."

"Are you sure it's the tourist, at least?"

"In fact, we're pretty sure it's not."

Frank saw me lurking, invited me to join them, and caught me up. "Sorry for discussing business at a party, Willa. But I was asking Ben about the victim we discussed earlier. I've got to have something to report at eleven besides Elizabeth Taylor's no-show."

I said, "You're kidding, right? You're not going to say that."

Ben ignored our nonsense, looked thoughtful for a few seconds and instructed Frank. "There's no point to upsetting everyone until we get a little more information."

Frank acquiesced. "Can I quote you that it's not the tourist, at least?"

"Not yet."

"Can you give me something on the missing Dr. Morgan, at least?" Frank never gives up.

Ben asked, "Isn't he here, Willa? I saw his name on the guest list and Peter told me he'd checked in. I marked that case closed."

Relief flooded through me in palpable waves.

Morgan wasn't dead after all.

Carly was ok.

I was okay.

I told them the truth. "I've never met Michael Morgan. But if Peter said he's here, I'm sure he is."

Just then two waiters walked by ringing chimes to signal that dinner was served; I was grateful for the excuse to move on.

By the time everyone was seated for dinner, I was ready to call it a night.

Kate was seated at the senator's table, as were George and I.

Elizabeth Taylor's place remained empty—a no show, as Frank said. The meal passed uneventfully.

The senator gave a short speech thanking everyone for their contribution to AIDS research and reminding them of the work ahead. Privately, the senator was campaigning. I heard him tell Kate that it was a critical time for foreign policy and free trade, and the party needed him on the Foreign Relations Committee for another term.

Elections were several months away, but early money is like yeast: its necessary to raise the dough to get elected. From the looks of the crowded room, I guessed he'd made the same pitch to all of them and several thousand packages of yeast would be contributed to his campaign in the next few days.

There was no question that the Republican candidate posed a serious threat to Warwick's reelection, but I wondered whether the campaign contributions made to Warwick's campaign would really support free trade or just his ego.

The party ended and everyone was gone by midnight.

Left George to close up, trudged upstairs for bed.

Called Carly again to tell her the good news: that Dr. Morgan had been here tonight, alive and in person.

Still no answer; I didn't leave another message.

George and I usually like to dissect these events and rehash the various conversations. But tonight, I collapsed into deep slumber long before he came upstairs.

Even though I consume mystery novels like candy, I was new to the investigator game. I had learned what I needed to know about Dr. Morgan without having to inquire. No one acted guilty, whatever that means.

So I missed my best opportunity to investigate everyone who had a reason to kill Michael Morgan.

In the long run, it would have saved me a lot of pain if I'd figured that out.

But ignorance is bliss. I had the last sound sleep I would have for a while.

CHAPTER EIGHT

Tampa, Florida
Thursday 9:10 a.m.
January 7, 1999

ON THURSDAY MORNING, WE slept late and had the after party chat over breakfast and coffee that we hadn't had the night before. We shared laughter and outrage and he gloated awhile before we kissed and left for work.

I didn't tell him about Carly just yet. George thinks I have a blind spot where Carly's concerned. He calls it my Mighty Mouse Routine. I'm always saving the day for her, he says, and he views it as an unnecessary extravagance. He thinks Carly is old enough to take care of herself.

That's not the only thing he's wrong about.

The good news about Dr. Morgan would resolve Carly's issues and then I'd give George the whole story without having to argue about how I'd handled her this time.

That was the plan.

For about thirty minutes after I reached my desk, it seemed the plan would work.

One of the greatest things about my job is no obnoxious phone calls. George, Kate, and select family can reach me on a private line. Otherwise, my secretary takes messages and my judicial clerks talk to the callers. It's one of the many advantages of being a federal judge. A state court judge is elected; they have to talk to everybody.

The point is, Carly could have returned my calls on my private line, my cell, or my home phone, but she hadn't. I'd heard nothing from her since yesterday. Not an unusual occurrence. But just now, damned inconsiderate. And worrisome.

My secretary brought in the message slips for calls I'd received through regular channels. I flipped through them quickly: CJ at 7:45 a.m. *Ha! As if.* In addition to making my own hours, my lifetime appointment means it's not necessary to kowtow to a little guy who thinks he's the boss. Gleefully, I crumpled it and tossed it into the trash can. *She scores!*

Four more slips. A reminder of my hair appointment, Kate, President of the Women's Bar Association, and, at the bottom of the pile, Carly.

She'd called yesterday. Before she appeared at Minaret.

For some reason, I felt a bit better knowing she'd tried to reach me first. Seemed not so desperate, maybe.

Asked my secretary to schedule an appointment with the chair of the Women's Bar Association, confirm my hair appointment, and make a date for late lunch with Kate.

Studied yesterday's pink slip reflecting Carly's call. No further clues revealed themselves. Wondered aloud, *"What's going on with you, little sis?"*

Remembered the last time we'd met before yesterday afternoon. We'd argued then, too. The issues were not dissimilar.

While I was still in private practice, I'd volunteered my time to teach a law school course. Despite her two brothers and me all being lawyers, Carly decided to go to law school. Or maybe it was because we were lawyers. Anyway, Carly threw caution to the wind and took my class four years ago.

Even if she hadn't been my "little sister," I'd have thought she was one of those rare students who understood the subject and demonstrated a desire to excel.

She became a colleague that year and I found myself working with her to make sure she understood the basics of cross examination, jury selection and evidence.

After she graduated, my personal relationship with Carly, always strained, finally achieved an uneasy truce: Carly began to look on me as an available, if not overly desirable, mentor. For a time. Too briefly.

She joined the prosecutor's office; called now and then with a particular question or issue. An almost easy peace descended.

Abruptly, she was asked to resign.

She wouldn't tell me why. Following unsuccessful attempts to find out, culminating in one really nasty screaming match, I got the message that it was none of my business.

She asked me to write a recommendation when she applied for a house counsel position with a small medical device manufacturer a few weeks later.

That's one thing about Carly; no matter how offensive she's been to me, she continues to act as if she has some sort of God-given right to keep coming back for more favors.

Of course, I gave her what she wanted.

Maybe because of what she thought of as her disgraceful

termination, and maybe because she was still jealous of my relationship with her mother, until yesterday, I hadn't heard from her in over a year, when she was in trouble again.

Maybe George is right. Maybe our relationship is seriously co-dependent. I need to rescue her as much as she needs the help.

Knowing that doesn't change it.

My thoughts started to wander down the well-trodden path of my feelings for Kate, who had been my mother's best friend and like a mother to me since Mom died when I was sixteen.

I jerked myself back to the present.

No point in going over that ground again.

Wherever my relationship with Kate's daughter had gone wrong, rehashing history wasn't going to change it. The only reason to relive history is to avoid making the same mistakes. Otherwise, you're just wallowing in the past—an indulgence I know from experience won't get me anywhere.

If I had back all the hours I've spent trying to figure out how to make Carly stop acting like a spoiled child, I'd be at least three years younger.

I picked up the phone and dialed Carly's office number.

"Good morning, MedPro," the receptionist answered the phone. I asked for Carly Austin and was put through to her office. Carly picked up on the first ring.

"Carly, its Willa."

"Judge Carson! I'm so pleased you called me back."

"Did you think I wouldn't?"

Some hesitation. Then, cryptically, "I'd like to see you for an hour or so. Would it be possible for me to meet you somewhere?"

I felt the frown lines between my eyebrows, and consciously tried to relax them. I remembered Dr. Aymes's comments on age lines. No point in getting needles punched in your face before you have to.

Carly sounded cheerful, almost normal. Not the nervous, timid woman who sat across the table from me yesterday. She'd always been confident and self-assured. Even when she was fired by the prosecutor's office, she hadn't seemed cowed. Yesterday, she did. Now, she didn't.

Confused, I wanted to strangle her and put us both out of my misery. "Look, about Dr.—"

She jumped in. "Let's talk when I see you, shall we? How about your office? Maybe three o'clock? Thanks."

My protest fell into empty space.

Annoyed, I dialed Frank Bennett. If they'd identified the body, I could put Carly's mind to rest this afternoon and bow out completely. He answered after the first ring.

"Frank, Willa Carson here."

"Willa! How nice to hear from you. What's up?" Frank has a nose for news, obviously. I'd never called him before. The direct approach wasn't always best.

We talked about the fundraiser, Senator Warwick, and George's disappointment that Elizabeth Taylor no-showed last night. Frank was covering the Warwick campaign, and asked if I knew when the senator would be in town again.

Finally, I worked into the real reason for my call.

"Frank, since our talk last night about that body they pulled out of Tampa Bay, I've been curious about something, and I haven't seen anything on your newscasts about it."

"What's the problem?"

"You said something about the guy being dead already when he hit the water—" I tried to sound tentative, unsure. Not easy for me.

"Yes?" He volunteered nothing. Rather unlike Frank, I thought. Maybe he'd been told to report anyone asking questions about the body. I wished I'd thought of that before I called him; too late now.

"I was wondering how you knew that?"

"Don't tell me you've been missing some of my reports?" He teased me.

"I guess I must have," I said, stifling impatience.

"A bullet to the front of his head blew the back of his skull off. There's not much chance he survived that. And the coroner's report said no water in the lungs, which means he didn't breathe in the water and die by drowning." He explained patiently, but seemed to be asking questions at the same time.

I was tempted not to answer the unspoken, but I didn't want Frank poking around in my life trying to find out why I wanted to know about this particular crime.

"Well, that explains it then." I told him. "George and I were having a conversation at breakfast this morning and he said the police couldn't possibly tell whether anyone had drowned or been killed before they were found in the water. I told him I was sure that even more complicated things had been determined forensically, and I would just call you and ask."

Tsk, tsk. A marital squabble. And too much for my pretty little head. Frank Bennett knows I'm not so vacuous, but he accepted the explanation, no doubt for his own reasons.

Then, he said, "While I have you on the phone, Willa, let me ask you something."

"Okay." Wary.

"I looked around last night, but I never found Michael Morgan. I talked to Peter, and he said he didn't actually see Morgan come in. Are you sure Morgan was there?"

My good mood vanished. Neck hairs tingled.

Even tone, slow cadence, total control. "Like I said last night, Frank, I wouldn't know the man if I saw him."

"Well, ask George, will you? Right now, I'm assuming he's still missing."

"Sure, I'll ask," I said. And I meant it. I didn't say I'd reveal George's answer.

We rung off with the appropriate farewells, and I made a mental note not to ask Frank anything else about the case before checking all other sources.

Frank Bennett had been an award-winning journalist for too long. Instincts would bring him back around asking questions, and I hoped I hadn't already sparked his curiosity too much.

I couldn't figure out what to do next without talking to Carly first, so I spent the remainder of the morning revising proposed orders drafted by my clerks, preparing matters scheduled for tomorrow, and reviewing next week's trial calendar.

Every ten seconds or so, questions about Dr. Morgan and the murdered man refused to stay in mental storage, questions Carly would answer this afternoon if I had to sit on her to make her tell me.

At one o'clock, I left to meet Kate at the Tampa Club for lunch, happy that I'd put on something besides chinos and a chambray shirt this morning.

I walked briskly to the Barnett Bank building, took the elevator to the 42nd floor and then skipped quickly up another flight of stairs to The Tampa Club. I had joined The Tampa Club when it first opened because I wouldn't join The Captains' Club.

The truth is, the "C Club," as it's known, would not admit women until a few years ago. When they started to admit women and invited me to join, I refused. I'm pleased to report that many other women did the same and now the "C Club" is having difficulty making ends meet.

On any given day, you can still find the old rich and long powerful at their club. I guess not getting my dues and membership fees hasn't put them into bankruptcy and, in the meantime, all the women who want to be on the inside are still on the outside.

If you won't come in after you're invited, what more can they do?

That's the trouble with Ghandi's method of political protest; it's so easy for the targets of peaceful resistance to miss it.

As I feared, Kate was already waiting in the Grill Room, the club decorator's idea of a cozy, paneled enclave on the southwest corner of the building. I kissed her cheek.

"I'm sorry to keep you waiting."

Kate kissed me back, and said, "Don't worry, dear. I enjoy the view of the Bay from here. It's almost as nice as the one from Minaret. And I haven't been waiting long. Just long enough to order this glass of Chardonnay. Why don't you join me?"

I took Kate's suggestion. Crisp Chardonnay and Greek seafood salad accompanied our lively discussion of George's party.

"I was looking forward to seeing Jason. It's been too long since my oldest son came to see me. I'm disappointed that he wasn't there."

"I was disappointed, too. He called, but I didn't get the message until this morning. He left for Romania earlier than he expected because of Senator Warwick's trip to resolve the financial situation over there. He apologized. Said he'd call next week."

Leave it to Jason to disappoint his mother through a message to me. By tacit consent, we ignored the fact that Jason hadn't been coming to the fundraiser to see his mother, but rather to support the senator, who is also his boss. Kate has a soft spot for all her children, each for different reasons. Jason she loves as her firstborn and she avoids his shortcomings, just like she does with her other son Mark, and Carly. And me, too, for that matter even though technically I'm not her biological child.

"Well, it was a lovely evening, even if I did have to spend it with the Warwicks. And speaking of Victoria, did you know that her mother has been very ill recently? They think she has Lupus."

"You're kidding! Mrs. Mendel is about the healthiest woman I've ever known. When did this happen?"

Kate smiled. "About the same time Christian Grover signed her up as a plaintiff in the breast implant litigation."

"You mean Mrs. Mendel has breast implants?" I couldn't believe it. "What for?"

"Apparently Dr. Morgan implanted her years ago after she had a mastectomy for precancerous fibroid tumors. Of course, she never told anyone. It used to be that people kept their medical conditions to themselves. Now, I think she's planning to be a guest on one of the talk shows."

This last was meant to be facetious. I think.

Kate's right, though. Health concerns used to be private matters, particularly health concerns over breasts and other semi-sexual body parts. These days, it seems everything is public knowledge.

We exhausted this topic and I was trying to figure out a tactful way to bring up Carly when Kate saved me the trouble.

"You know, I really wanted both Jason and Carly to come last night. It's been a long time since she's seen her brother."

"It would be even nicer if they could both be in the same room without snarling at each other. And you don't have to give me the 'disapproving mother' look, either. Jason isn't the only one Carly doesn't talk to. Have you heard from her?"

I could tell from Kate's expression that she hadn't, and she was trying to come up with some acceptable excuse besides the truth—Carly doesn't talk to any of us. I wouldn't hurt Kate's feelings for anything in the world. So I said, "You know I love Jason and Carly as much as if they were my brother and sister, but they're not perfect."

"No, and neither are you and Mark, as much as you both like to think so."

This wasn't going well. I tried another tack. "Carly called me this morning and left a message. If I talk to her, I'll invite her to Minaret, and you can come over, too."

This got the result I wanted. Kate promised to come, and she was happy. I do love Kate. She's been a great mother to me since my mom died. I love my dad dearly, but he's never around. I haven't seen him in a year. So it was important to me to keep the peace with all the Austins.

We finished our salads, ordered cappuccino and a sinful dessert, and parted half an hour later.

I went back to my office and dictated a few orders on yesterday morning's motions, looked over tomorrow's case load and took care of a few other odds and ends. It was almost 4:30 when I remembered the call from the CJ. While I could have ignored it completely, there was no reason not to return his call and I asked my secretary to place it. CJ hates getting calls through a secretary.

Margaret came back to tell me that the CJ was gone for the day. She'd left a message and he'd likely call in the morning. I smiled to myself. This game of wills I'd been playing with the CJ was humorous. He calls me in the morning because he knows I don't come in before nine o'clock; I call him in the afternoon because I know he leaves early. My amusement evaporated when I realized I'd need the CJ's support to avoid the Justice Department's public integrity unit if I didn't get this thing with Carly resolved soon.

It was then I realized Carly had never showed up for our appointment. I'd worked right through.

I picked up the phone and called her again. Her secretary said she'd gone out about one o'clock and never returned.

I should call Chief Hathaway, report what Carly had told me and forget it. Not knowing the extent of her involvement kept me quiet. I couldn't throw her to the wolves, even though it made me a dog in the road: just a matter of time before a speeding truck flattened me, too.

Margaret reminded me that I was expected at the Federal Rules meeting ten minutes ago. Too late to cancel, and too late to spend time catastrophizing. I'd have to leave that for later.

But I determined to find Carly and shake the whole story out of her.

Then, I'd fix it, like always.

Or so I thought.

CHAPTER NINE

Tampa, Florida
Thursday 5:00 p.m.
January 7, 1999

THE FEDERAL RULES SUBCOMMITTEE of the local chapter of the Federal Bar Association, a committee I've been on for a number of years, was scheduled to meet this month at the offices of one of our newer members, Charles Smyth. Instead of taking the time to get my car, I asked Margaret to call another committee member for a ride. It really hadn't registered with me where the meeting would be held until we arrived at the Landmark Tower offices of Able, Bennett & Worthington, where Smyth is a junior partner. Able and Bennett are dead. Elliott O'Connell Worthington is the senior partner here.

The Landmark Tower building, the most expensive office space in Tampa, sits at the corner of Florida and Jackson and takes up an entire city block. It is one of the newer "A" buildings in downtown Tampa, and it's the most architecturally interesting. The building is over forty stories high and topped by a white lighted dome. The dome's lights are changed to red and green for Christmas and red, white and blue for the Fourth of July. It's easily seen for miles around after dark, and finding your way back to town is not as difficult as it used to be before the building went up.

The walk to the front door is lined with grey granite pillars and in the lobby sits a larger than life size, multicolored metal sculpture of Don Quixote on his horse. This was the first time I had ever been in the building and it certainly had all the indicia of high-priced real estate.

The offices of Able, Bennett & Worthington were on the top four floors. As the elevator whizzed up, I was reminded of my lunch. After a 35 second ride, the elevator doors opened onto the lobby—less than one second per floor. I stepped out into the lobby the same way cartoon characters leave an out of control carousel.

I've been in some extravagant law offices but it's not an exaggeration to say that the lobby of AB&W, as it's known around town, was the most ostentatious lawyers' lobby I've ever seen. The floor was granite in three colors, with "AB&W" inlaid under foot. Windows at right angles gave one the feeling of standing on air outside, 420 feet above the ground. Glass walls allowed a floor-to-ceiling view of the Port of Tampa, Harbour Island, Davis Island, Plant Key and the Bayshore on the south side and the city, the University of Tampa and north Tampa opposite. The office was furnished in museum-quality antiques, the likes of which George's Aunt Minnie would have been proud to own.

The receptionist was a statuesque blonde Barbie look-alike selected for her acting ability. She played the receptionist part perfectly. When we entered the lobby, she greeted us both by name, said we'd been expected and someone would be out to escort us to the meeting shortly.

After about sixty seconds, Smyth's secretary, another exceedingly attractive and briskly competent greeter, escorted us to the meeting in the main conference room.

When we arrived, the meeting was already in progress and we slipped in quietly and sat down. A review of the last meeting's minutes was being concluded. While the familiar recitation droned on, I took the opportunity to look around. This room had a spectacular view of north and east Tampa. The conference table was made in the same shape as the building, of grey granite and various shades of wood inlay. The firm logo was again inlaid in the center of the table. The chairs were mahogany leather and the walls were lined with grey, granite-topped cabinets upon which were perched china cups and crystal glasses in patterns I recognized.

Oil paintings of the firm's named partners lined the long wall opposite the windows and above the paintings in large brass script were the words "The Founder's Room."

The decorating budget for this room alone must have exceeded the cost of a private college education.

After the meeting adjourned, Smyth said, "Mr. Worthington wants a few moments with you, Judge Carson, if you can stay."

"I have a transportation dilemma. I caught a ride over. If I don't leave now, I'll have to walk." Everyone knew walking around downtown Tampa after dark wasn't a wise choice.

Smyth said, "We'll get one of the firm's cars to drive you to your garage. This way, please."

I followed Smyth to O'Connell's office.

Winding through the corridors, Smyth delivered a running tour. Each wide hallway was lined with original work by artists

I'd admired in places like the Smithsonian and the Metropolitan Museum. Vases and antique pottery was displayed in alcoves under spotlights.

Smyth said, "The firm believes in investing in art. One of our partners is quite knowledgeable. He travels to New York galleries and auction houses. Our collection adds significantly to the firm's net worth." He sounded like a docent. Was the entire firm populated by the law office equivalent of Stepford wives?

"That's a rather unique practice isn't it?"

"Unique for Tampa. Firms in major cities invest in art. Here we are." He knocked on a large mahogany door, grasped the crystal doorknob and pushed simultaneously.

O'Connell stood to greet me and dismiss Smyth while my mouth hung open.

The opulence was awesome.

O'Connell's personal office was on the southwest corner of the building, the best view the building had to offer. He had floor-to-ceiling windows overlooking Harbour Island, Davis Island, Plant Key and the Bayshore. I could see our Minaret clearly in the distance. The floors were hardwood, with antique Persian rugs under the desk, the coffee table and the conference table. Navy and burgundy leather upholstery covered most of the room. On the credenza and several of the walls were pictures of O'Connell and Cilla at various milestones: their wedding, their children's weddings, their 45th anniversary party and last year's awards banquet where O'Connell was named Lawyer of the Year. The opposite wall was O'Connell with the governor, O'Connell with our Senators, O'Connell with our last four presidents.

"Wilhelmina, I'm so pleased you were able to stop in for a few moments. Can I get you a cup of coffee or a glass of wine?"

I told him I would take a glass of Cabernet and watched him open the door that concealed a wet bar. The wine rack held a selection of red wines, about twenty bottles. The white wines were in the wine refrigerator visible below. As he opened the bottle, I told him how impressed I was with his offices.

He handed me a Baccarat balloon glass, about two-thirds full of Stag's Leap and motioned me onto a sofa. While he remained standing, we were eye to eye. "I didn't realize you hadn't been here before. We've had these offices about four years. One of the first firms to lease space in this building. It's been a pleasure putting it together." We raised our glasses in a silent toast. To what?

"How much space do you have, O'Connell, and how many lawyers have you got?" I might not be a practicing lawyer anymore, but I still know how success is counted in the business.

"We have four floors here, 42, 41, 40 and, just recently, 39. We added ten new lawyers last year, bringing our total to 85." The open pride was uncharacteristic, but unmistakable.

"I had no idea you had so many lawyers in your office. Twenty percent growth in one year must make you about the fastest growing firm in Tampa. What's your secret?"

He smiled, smoothly conspiratorial. "Since you're not in competition with me, I'll tell you. We're strictly a litigation firm. We've been involved in some of the largest litigation in the country over the years. In 1991, when it all started, we were hired by one of the large manufacturers to defend breast implant cases. We've been on their national trial team since then. That's really fueled our growth."

"Didn't that company go into bankruptcy a year or so ago? That impacted your business significantly."

"Fortunately, no. By that time, we had also picked up the

defense of another large manufacturer, even larger than the first. I'm sure you've heard of them—General Medics. Because of trial team experience and ground floor work with the first company, we were able to take an increased role with the new client immediately. That assignment has led to additional work from the second company, and others, and the result is what you see." He spread his left arm out, indicating the office, the view, everything.

"Well, I'm sure you're the envy of all your colleagues. In fact, didn't I hear that some of the firms involved in breast implant litigation have gone out of business?"

He nodded. "We've been fortunate, but it's impolite to say so."

I set my wine glass down, and leaned forward, "Tell me, just because I'm interested. With all the experience you've had defending breast implant cases, what do you personally believe the problem is?"

"There's still a debate among the experts over that subject, and I'm certainly no expert." He looked away.

"I know that, but I also know that good lawyers, such as yourself, learn a great deal about the cases they're defending. I always had my personal opinions, unrelated to what I could prove or not prove, about the facts in my cases. Surely you must have some opinions of your own based on the work you've done." Seeing his reluctance, I added, "Which wouldn't, of course, be admissible at trial."

He paused with his wine glass held out as if he were about to make a formal toast. His voice took on the stentorian quality he used in opening statements and he started to walk around the room, still carrying his wine glass. "On a personal level, and not as lawyer to judge, I'll tell you that I think this is the greatest miscarriage of justice that has happened in this country since the McCarthy hearings. There is no evidence that breast implants, or any form of medical grade silicones, cause any type of health-related problem whatsoever."

"If that's true, how did we get to the point where there are more than 200,000 claims filed by women around the world?" I was challenging him, and it was clear he didn't like it. He began to get red in the face and his tone took on a sterner quality. I was grateful not to be one of his junior lawyers.

"If my car is wet, does that mean it's raining outside?" He expected an answer.

"Of course not. There could be any number of explanations for a wet car."

"Exactly!" He said, as if I was an exceptionally bright student. "That's the evidence that's been admitted in trials in these cases and upon which juries have been allowed to conclude that a sick plaintiff with breast implants means that breast implants caused the illness. No reputable scientist believes that. And on the basis of evidence no scientist accepts, one very reputable company is in bankruptcy and others have spent literally millions of dollars defending themselves."

"Then how did this all happen?" I asked, almost afraid to push the point, he had gotten so excited. The hand gripping his wine glass was white-knuckled. I carefully moved outside the path of breaking glass.

"It happened the way all of these goddamned products cases happen. The plaintiff's bar is so organized these days that they can make a mountain out of any molehill."

"I'm not sure what you mean," I said.

The vein over his temple was bulging now, pulsing rhythmically. "Well, they get together and contribute one-hundred-thousand dollars or more to a fund to begin litigation in a given area. Then they let it be known that they're the experts with the money and they're planning to launch an attack. Smaller scale plaintiffs' attorneys come along and contribute smaller sums of money until a war chest is developed. They advertise for plaintiffs, stir up public opinion and before you know it, you have Mount Everest created out of an anthill. Look at Bendectin or Phen-Fen. It's disgusting. No evidence to support those cases at all. None."

He was practically shouting at this point. I guessed this was a speech he had given many times before. Maybe he was practicing for the next Defense Research Institute meeting, or his presentation to General Medics' board of directors. Any good trial lawyer can turn on indignation in a moment, and turn it off just as quickly. We're all actors at heart.

I had the impression, though, that O'Connell's current display of anger was not completely acting. It was time for me to take my leave before the old gentleman had a heart attack and I had another death to deal with. That old law school brain-teaser came back to me—can words alone, if they lead to death, be murder? I turned the conversation to safer topics for a few moments and then said I needed to get back to my office.

We walked to the lobby and O'Connell asked the Barbie to have the chauffeur drive me back to the federal building. He thanked me for coming and escorted me to the elevator, once again the perfect gentleman.

When I got to the curb at the corner of Florida and Jackson, it was already dark. The only car parked there was a navy Lincoln Town Car and the driver, dressed in a blue blazer with the now easily recognizable AB&W logo on the breast pocket, was standing on the curb. He opened the door for me and asked

"Where to?" During the short drive, I asked him if he liked his job. Like every cab driver, he was loquacious.

"Yes, Ma'am. I retired from First National Bank here in Tampa five years ago and Mr. Worthington was our lawyer. I mentioned to him that I'd like to have part-time work and he put me on the payroll. The only thing I do is keep this car clean and drive people around town and back and forth to the airport. If there was an easier job in the world, I'd be ashamed to get paid for it."

"Sounds good to me," I told him.

"It's the only job in town like it. And I get to drive any kind of 4-door full size car I like. I get a new one every year. This baby's only three weeks old. What do you think of it?"

I said I thought the car was very nice and that he did, indeed, have an enviable position.

The traffic lights on Florida Avenue are timed, but we hit all the red ones, getting in more quality time together.

"What kind of car did you have before this one?" I asked.

"Oh, man, a beautiful Cadillac de Ville. Black. Prettiest car I've ever had the pleasure to drive. I was sorry to see that one go. I wanted to keep it, but the boss, he said Mrs. Worthington's car was getting old, and she wanted that one. So I gave it to her and got me this one instead."

He dropped me right next to my Mercedes CLK 320 Convertible I called Greta, and I thanked him for the ride.

On the way home, my reverie was about the reasons I was no longer working for a firm like Able, Bennett & Worthington.

About a year before George and I moved to Tampa to get off the "up and coming" merry-go-round. I looked around me and saw the partners in my firm and George's corporate superiors living the life George and I would be living in ten years, and I didn't like it. One of the senior officers at the bank owned five homes, each mortgaged to the point that his $350,000 annual salary fell far short of his payments and his private school tuition obligations for three children. The year he asked one of the bank's secretaries to drive him back and forth to work because his lease car was over the mileage allowance and he couldn't pay the ten cents a mile surcharge, I realized just how precarious his position was. His salary easily exceeded hers by fifteen times, yet she could afford to buy a car, and he couldn't afford to rent one.

Another bank officer divorced his wife of twenty-five years to marry a service clerk thirty years younger than he. To say the divorce was costly is putting it mildly. His ex-wife was not just bitter, she was vicious. On any given day, he could be seen eating his two-dollar lunch of hot dogs and cottage cheese in the cafeteria, while telling anyone who sat down next to him just how many more alimony payments he had to make before he'd be able to afford hamburger. When his new bride promptly had twins and quit her job, he stopped eating lunch all together.

The stories were so typical, after a while they weren't even interesting. There was the junior associate in my firm whose husband was in business school. Not only couldn't they make it on his $75,000 salary, they lived on credit card debt that would feed an entire third world country for a year. When they wanted to take a vacation, they counted up their available credit balances to see if they could drive somewhere. A mid level partner, living in a three-story Victorian home in Indian Village couldn't afford a car and had to take the bus to work; another mid level partner had to borrow money to pay the deductible on his health insurance for his newest baby; a third, more senior partner took a loan to pay for more equity in the firm.

All around me, people were working harder, earning more and having less. They were required to work a staggering number of hours just to earn salaries that (while in the top one percent of all salaries in the country) didn't buy even a modicum of time and peace of mind. So I got off the merry-go-round. When Aunt Minnie died and left us Minaret, we simplified our lives, moved to Tampa, cut back on the dollar hunt. But sometimes, like today, when I saw how successful some of my colleagues were who hadn't dropped out of the race, I wondered if I'd made the right choice.

That evening over cocktails, I told George about my visit with O'Connell Worthington and the splendor of his offices. "It's been pretty well known for quite some time that O'Connell has had a significant reversal of fortune," he told me as he was turning the page of today's *Investor's Business Daily*. "Five years ago, his house was in foreclosure and he'd been posted at the Club for failure to pay dues on four or five occasions. Now it's quite a different story and I'm glad to know what the explanation is. There've been some very wild stories around town about the source of his wealth. I like O'Connell. I'm glad to learn his financial reversal is due to good old American hard work and nothing else."

Nothing else that marrying money didn't cure, at any rate. That's what I thought at the time.

CHAPTER TEN

Tampa, Florida
Thursday 7:20 p.m.
January 7, 1999

LATER, I CHANGED INTO a canary-yellow sweat suit and
made myself a drink. I went out to our balcony and sat with my
feet propped up, lighting up my first Partaga of the day. It was
after dusk, but not dark. The sky was filled with reds and
oranges. Tomorrow would be another beautiful day. I was still
sitting there, contemplating what to do about Carly's problem
when George came out to join me. I was glad to see he'd brought
a larger than usual glass of Glenfiddich.

"How do you feel about room service tonight?" he asked me
as he sat down in the rocker next to mine. "I can order up some
poached salmon over greens with raspberry vinaigrette and fresh
sourdough rolls. What do you say?"

"Sounds good to me," I answered him, still contemplating.

"I'll give you a silver dollar for your thoughts. They look
valuable."

"I was just thinking how really unfortunate it is that the police department never closes." Then, I told George, my partner in all things, about Carly's visit.

"What is it about you that brings everyone with a problem to your door?" The question was rhetorical. It was far from the first time I'd been asked. Nor the first time I'd asked it of myself. For a long time I felt as if I walked into every room with a large sign around my neck that said "bring your problems to Willa." In every crowd, at every party, in every organization I joined, it seemed I soon became the "mother" of the group. Messy divorce? Problems with your children? Out of money? Weight problems? Drugs, alcohol, gambling? Ask Dear Willa a/k/a Mighty Mouse.

Now that I know myself better, I know I wear my philosophy on my sleeve. You see, I believe all problems can be solved. It's that simple. And most people don't. Most people just want to wallow in it, but they don't want it fixed, especially if the fix requires the acceptance of personal responsibility and personal change. On some level, I like solving problems, other people's problems anyway.

I accepted that was why Carly had come to me in the first place. Not because she had any special affection for me. It's just that I've always been the problem solver. And she certainly had a problem. Where else would she go?

But this time, George was as distressed by Carly's situation as I had been, maybe more. If I try to mother everyone who comes along, George takes in strays, any stray, as long as they're a stray. Because Carly had been estranged from the family lately, George was particularly protective of her.

"Don't you know someone to whom you could entrust this information in confidence? It seems the sort of thing that needs to be disclosed, but I certainly wouldn't want Carly to be arrested just for having suggested the possible identity of a dead man," he said. George still believes in all American institutions.

"I think I'd have to give some reason for my suspicions. Since I never learned why Carly was asked to leave the prosecutor's office, I'm not sure that if I disclosed her name, she wouldn't become a suspect. I can't risk that."

George and I debated the ethics and the practicalities for another hour before concluding that perhaps the tried and true "anonymous phone call" was the best way to go. Since it was scrupulously important, at least to me, that I not be involved, George volunteered to make the call from a pay phone in the local supermarket. I was amused and surprised. Until he suggested it, I wasn't really sure George knew where the local supermarket was, and cloak and dagger is clearly not his style. I'm not sure he even knows who James Bond is. George really is a sport.

We agreed on what he would say and how he would say it. I told him it was important to keep the call to less than three minutes so that it couldn't be traced. After we got everything worked out, he went downstairs to drive himself to the phone.

I waited for what seemed like forever. By the time George got back, I'd already finished three more drinks and smoked two more cigars. One a day is my usual self-imposed limit. I saw his car pull up in the driveway and I poured us both another drink. George is not a man meant for intrigue and I knew that he would be at least as shaken as I was.

"Well, what happened?" I pounced on him as soon as he walked in the door.

"It went as well as can be expected. I called the downtown branch instead of 911. I know all 911 calls are taped. I disguised my voice and I said 'I think the body you found yesterday morning in Tampa Bay is Dr. Michael Morgan'."

"Did they act like they believed you?"

"They asked me to repeat the information. After I repeated it twice, making a total of three statements in the very same words, I hung up. I think the whole call took about two minutes. Then I got back in my car and drove directly here."

"Were you followed?"

"Christ, listen to you! I don't know whether I was followed. I've never been followed in my life except in a funeral procession. I'd have no idea how to find out. Did you see anyone else come up the driveway behind me?"

I told him I hadn't and we both tried to calm down. At the moment, it appeared this was the most we could do. I had called Carly twice after George left. No answer. For all I knew, she could have moved or changed her number. In any event, we'd given the authorities the information we had and, with luck, we wouldn't have to deal with it further. I made a mental note to look up whether obstruction of justice was an impeachable offense first thing tomorrow morning. I was sure I knew the answer, but pretending I didn't gave me some hope.

We had the dinner George had suggested earlier sent up to our dining room and, although neither of us said anything, I knew we were both waiting for the evening news. At 11:00, we turned on the local broadcast. Frank Bennett carried the major stories, including the unidentified body. He recapped the prior reports, the reasons the police had for the conclusion that the victim had been killed before he was dumped in the Bay. The only new information came at the very end of the segment.

"This spot," Bennett said, "just in the middle of the Skyway Bridge, is where the body was found. But there's no evidence to suggest the victim was dumped from the bridge. In fact, it's almost certain that anyone stopping along the bridge, even in the early morning hours, would have been observed by passing motorists.

"Police Chief Ben Hathaway told NewsChannel 8 he believes the body was dumped way back here at the Port of Tampa, and unusual currents related to last week's storm washed the body toward the bridge. This is Frank Bennett, reporting live from the Sunshine Skyway."

Neither Frank, nor any of the other channels carried any information regarding the identity of the man. In fact, by eerie coincidence, none of the journalists even speculated on whom the man might be.

George and I went to bed and had a very uneasy night. Every time I woke up, he was already awake. When the clock finally read 5:00 a.m., there was no way I could continue pretending to sleep, so I got up. George was, finally, snoring. I got Harry and Bess, our two Labradors, and went down to the beach for our morning run. For once, I was in the office well before the CJ or anyone else.

I was just thinking it might be nice to take a nap, when I realized it was past time to take the bench. Although judges kept me waiting often enough when I was in practice, I try not to keep a room full of lawyers, at a gazillion dollars an hour, waiting in my courtroom. It's just my little way of reducing the cost of litigation.

I slipped my arms into my robe, zipped it up, took a deep breath for patience and stamina, and walked straight through the back door onto the bench.

As I feared, the court reporter was seated, the bailiff at the door and the room full of charcoal pinstripes and red ties.

Everyone jumped up at my abrupt and unannounced entrance: well-dressed jack-in-the boxes. I motioned them to be seated.

I looked around for any women lawyers who might be in the room and, predictably, saw none. Few women lawyers have federal court cases. Federal courts handle larger, more sophisticated disputes and crimes. Unfortunately, in Tampa as everywhere, relatively few women have a practice including the magnitude of claims typically brought in federal court. Whenever a woman appears in my courtroom, I always call her case first, just so I can give her the preferential treatment I never received as a lawyer. If they catch me at it, I'll find some believable way to deny it.

Calling the court to order is an old-fashioned custom required by the United States Code. But since I was already seated, I just nodded to the clerk to skip it and call the first case; first come, first serve, just like McDonald's.

On Fridays, I hear motions from ten until one. It's perceived to be a waste of judicial time and not worth the energy by most of my colleagues. I'm the only judge in the Middle District who schedules oral argument regularly. On any given Friday, I may hear up to twenty different motions. My colleagues are right about one thing: it takes a lot of time and energy to prepare for these oral arguments and they usually don't change my mind. The Chief Justice of the Supreme Court is wrong about something else—the quality of argument is generally much higher than judges like to admit.

I saw Christian Grover sitting in the back of the courtroom carrying on not-so-quiet conversation with other lawyers waiting their turn. His motion was number four on my docket, but since I detest his style and because I didn't want to give him an audience for the morning, I put his matter at the end. I could tell he was wildly annoyed and he began to speak louder and louder, just to challenge my authority. I made him wait until 12:45, when I finally allowed my clerk to call his case.

"*Jones v. General Medics*, Case No.: 95-57-Civ-T-23E," the clerk called out.

"Ready, Your Honor" O'Connell Worthington, himself. I hadn't seen him come in.

"Ready," Grover said, unable to summon the courtesy to call me Judge. I tried not to smile. It was so easy to tweak him these days. I'm told there was a time when he wasn't so self-important, but that was long ago in a galaxy far away. Since then, Christian Grover has been President of the State Bar, President of the American Trial Lawyers Association, President of the Florida Trial Lawyers Association, and on the adjunct faculty of most of the Florida law schools. So many titles, so little humility.

O'Connell began his argument. "Your Honor, we're before the court today on Defendant's Motion to Dismiss Plaintiff's claims for failure to state a cause of action against us. Plaintiff just doesn't have any evidence that my client has done anything wrong in this case."

Worthington went on for twenty minutes, explaining why Grover had been unable to satisfy the pleading requirements of the Federal Courts to keep his case alive. With every word, Grover was turning redder in the face until he was sputtering. He kept popping up and down, bursting to interrupt. He didn't dare. I run a tight courtroom and I don't allow the lawyers to berate one another or talk between themselves during argument. Grover is well aware of my rules. He didn't say anything out loud during Worthington's argument, but he certainly let me know, along with the few remaining people in the courtroom, that he would sure like to.

After several minutes of long-winded argument, Worthington was finally winding up. "And for those reasons, Your Honor, which have been more fully outlined in our papers, we request that the Court dismiss this claim against my client."

Grover slowly stood up to his full six feet, three inches, buttoned his double-breasted jacket, pulled down on the French cuffs of his shirt, smoothed his hair and moved to the podium, poised to begin what I'm sure he planned to be a speech worthy of the congressional record. I held up my hand.

"Mr. Grover, just a moment. Let me talk to Mr. Worthington. Mr. Worthington, you've made an eloquent argument. I'd like to grant your motion. I happen to agree with many of the things you've said." Grover was like a six-year-old who needed to go to the bathroom. He could hardly contain himself. I continued to hold up my hand, preventing him from talking at all. "However, we've thoroughly researched the issues and the cases you've relied upon are not sufficient to allow me to grant summary judgment to your client under Florida law. I'm denying the motion at this time, without prejudice to your right to bring it again. I'll prepare the order. Thank you gentlemen."

I stood up and left the bench while the bailiff was still saying "all rise." When my law clerks were back in the office, I could hear them laughing.

"Did you see the look on Christian Grover's face? I don't think anyone has refused to let him talk in fifteen years."

"You got that right," the other clerk replied. "I've never seen anybody shut him up before!" At least that would give them something to talk about over dinner this evening and Worthington could go back to his office and profess his victory over Grover, even though he lost his motion.

By some miracle, my afternoon calendar was clear. I tried to work, but I just couldn't concentrate. If I didn't get to the bottom of this thing with Carly, I knew I'd never get any work done. Weary of waiting for the problem to solve itself and not getting the answers I needed, I grabbed my purse and headed for the judge's garage. If I dropped in unannounced, Carly would have to see me.

I drove to MedPro, which was across the Gandy Bridge on Roosevelt Boulevard in St. Petersburg. In the parking lot, I pulled into the only empty spot marked "visitors." I'd never been to MedPro before and I was impressed with the aesthetics of the building. There was a small pond out back with a long dock running from the building to a large gazebo. The building itself was pristine white with "MedPro, Inc." in large blue letters over the door. The lobby was similarly clean and decorated in a contemporary style. It continued the azure blue and bright white color scheme.

The receptionist smiled brightly at me as I approached her. Do you need great teeth to be a receptionist? "Good morning. My name is Wilhelmina Carson. I'm here to see Ms. Carly Austin." When she asked me if I had an appointment, I lied.

I heard the receptionist call Carly's office. The receptionist continued to smile at me, but I could tell that what she heard from the other end of the phone was not what she wanted to hear. Her smile faded. Unexpected visitors were apparently not the norm at MedPro, Inc.

When she hung up the phone, the receptionist told me nicely, but with a shade less warmth, that Ms. Austin's secretary would be right down. The secretary arrived less than three minutes later, introduced herself, gave me a visitor's badge to attach to my jacket and asked me to follow her.

It was a long walk back to Carly's office through several

corridors. Each time we came to a door, the secretary held up a security card to an electronic reader and the door automatically unlocked. I noticed that the card readers were located on both sides of the doorway, so that it was impossible to travel throughout the various departments without security access, both in and out.

"Ms. Austin is in a meeting at the moment," the secretary said. "She asked me to make you comfortable in her office and to tell you she'd be with you as soon as she can. Would you like coffee or soda?"

I assured her I would be fine waiting for Ms. Austin until she arrived. She left me alone in Carly's office, which faced the small pond I'd seen from the parking lot. It was really quite a lovely view, complete with wildlife, including a couple of gators sunning themselves on the bank.

Carly's office was pretty nice for a junior counsel. It was about twelve by sixteen feet with a reasonably sized desk and credenza as well as a small conference table, a bookcase and two client chairs facing the desk. The windows covered one entire wall, opposite the door. The office had no personal effects in it: no pictures, no artwork, no desk accessories. Carly had worked here almost three years and if she left tomorrow, new counsel could move into this office without so much as rearranging the furniture. Comforting thought to a young lawyer—you're an interchangeable chair.

Carly's secretary didn't close the door and neither did I. I stood with my back to it, looking out the windows for what seemed like half an hour, but was probably closer to ten minutes. Then I sat down in one of Carly's client chairs and noticed a copy of MedPro's Annual Report on the table. I picked it up and read the biographical section on the company's history.

MedPro was formed in 1980 by three doctors, one of whom was, to my surprise, Dr. Michael Morgan. The other two founders were Dr. Carolyn Young and Dr. Alan Zimmer. Morgan, Young and Zimmer were all faculty members and research scientists at CFU Medical School in the early seventies when they discovered new applications for silicone technology on a grant funded by one of the major silicone manufacturers.

The report said that, at the time, the manufacturer was looking for a more "responsive" gel for its breast implants, something that would more closely approximate the feel of human tissue. A silicone breast implant is much like Jello in a baggie. The research challenge was to come up with a gel that would be firm enough to resist leaking through the outer envelope and hold up well inside the breast tissue and yet soft enough to approximate the feel of human breast tissue.

At the time, radical mastectomy was the surgical method of choice for the treatment of breast cancer. The procedure was physically and psychologically devastating to the patient and everyone was racing to find an implant that could be used in reconstruction at the same time as the initial surgery.

Study after study had shown that waking up after mastectomy, either bilateral or unilateral, and observing her scarred and flat chest, was more emotionally devastating to the patient than the initial cancer diagnosis. If the reconstruction could be done at the same time as the mastectomy, then the initial shock of the surgery was significantly blunted.

The problem was that the implants available were hard and conical. If both breasts were removed, replacing both with implants would result in a symmetrical appearance. If only one breast was removed, an implant would be obvious.

Even in a double mastectomy case, the harder implants were

often undesirable because they were so obviously not a part of the more mature body of a woman likely to have breast cancer. Most breast cancer patients are over fifty and have borne children. Their breasts didn't look like an 18-year-old's before surgery, and implants that made the breast look like an 18-year-old's after surgery weren't acceptable to many patients. The patients wanted to look and feel just like they had before the surgery, no better and no worse.

Dr. Young became interested in the project after her mother had a mastectomy and was required to wear a prosthesis. Dr. Young, already interested in silicone chemistry, sold her concept to a group of manufacturers at the American Society of Testing and Materials. Three of the manufacturers took her up on the proposal and issued a multi-million dollar grant to her and her two colleagues.

This was a complete paradigm shift for me. I had no idea of the history behind the development of breast implants. It was hard for me to reconcile the chauvinistic product to the altruistic picture painted by the annual report.

After three years, the report continued, Drs. Morgan, Young and Zimmer did discover a suitable responsive gel and all three manufacturers began to make implants using the formula the doctors had created. The new implants were an instant success and immediate reconstruction became the standard of care following unilateral or bilateral mastectomy.

Dr. Young's mother was one of the first patients. A long testimonial letter from her was reprinted in its entirety. A footnote to the report indicated that Mrs. Young had died less than a year after receiving her implant and had granted permission for an autopsy to further her daughter's research. No results of the autopsy were included.

Later, after observing the success made of their discovery and wanting to get in on the money, Drs. Morgan, Young and Zimmer formed MedPro, Inc. They mortgaged everything they owned to get the company started. At first, they manufactured breast implants using their responsive gel. Later, they developed other breast implant products to deal with issues such as hardening of the breasts and rupture of the implants that would sometimes occur a few months to a few years after implantation. After the initial lean years of start up costs, MedPro grew so quickly it went public in 1985.

From my discussions with George about initial public offerings, I knew Drs. Morgan, Young and Zimmer must have become immediate millionaires on paper based on the value of their stock when they went public. What must that kind of money have meant to research scientists used to eating potted meat on a regular basis?

The infusion of capital from the stock sale enabled the company to branch out into the manufacture of other medical devices. They acquired a patent and marketed kinetic therapy products to prevent bedsores in bed-ridden patients. They produced lifesaving silicone catheters and hydrocephalic shunts. By late 1991, their sales exceeded five hundred million dollars. In 1992, MedPro was listed as one of the top ten publicly-traded companies in Florida.

That was as far as I got when I heard Carly come in. I slipped the Annual Report into my purse for further reading at another time. It was a public document. I wasn't stealing anything.

CHAPTER ELEVEN

Tampa, Florida
Friday 12:45 p.m.
January 8, 1999

"WILHELMINA, I'M SURPRISED TO see you here. Please sit down," she said as she closed the door.

I looked at her closely. She looked in worse shape than she had been Wednesday evening. She was pale, drawn and gaunt. There was an air of desperation about her and I thought she was silently entreating me not to mention our previous conversation. Until I could figure it out, I'd play along.

"It's been so long since George and I have seen you. I was driving by MedPro and, since I've never been to your office, I thought I'd stop in for a short visit. Would you be interested in giving me a tour or your facility?"

Carly seemed relieved that I'd understood her signals. She flashed a brilliant smile and offered me the tour.

We left her office and turned right, in the opposite direction from the lobby. Carly began a walking monologue, explaining the offices, the plant, the manufacturing practices and the products made here at MedPro. She repeated much of what was contained in the Annual Report, and I got the impression that this was the public story, reproduced in every medium.

In truth, the tour was fascinating. MedPro, Carly told me, was a small manufacturer of silicone-based and other medical products. While going through the manufacturing portion of the plant, we were required to dress in sterile gowns, masks, caps, gloves and booties. During the entire tour, Carly pointed out the precautions taken to follow sterile procedures, packaging, labeling and other FDA related requirements.

When we arrived at the research and development lab, Carly told me about MedPro's latest venture.

"The Company is currently experimenting with natural implants. The process uses a woman's own cells to generate natural tissue inside her breasts. Other researchers are experimenting with vegetable oil and fat-filled implants, but our process is different. Within three to five years, if it works, we'll be able to remove tissue samples from somewhere on the body and grow additional cells in a lab. The cells would then be implanted into the breast where they would become real breast tissue."

"Are you saying you're experimenting with cloning humans?"

"Not exactly, but kind of like that. Here's the theory: a tissue sample with cells similar to those in breasts—"

"You mean pure fat?" I joked. I was relieved to see Carly smile, too.

"Not pure fat, but high in fat, yes. Anyway, those cells would be removed from the patient's thigh or abdomen."

"Those other gorgeous anatomic areas." I was trying to

lighten the mood, and Carly seemed to appreciate the effort.

"It's surprising Hugh Hefner and Bob Guccione have been able to make so much glamour out of so much blubber, isn't it?"

By this time, we were both smiling, as Carly continued to explain the new process. When she'd finished, I asked her, "How close is this to becoming a reality?"

"Well, there are still a few things to work out. Three to five years away, at least."

"It's an expensive project. What if it doesn't work?"

"We try not to think about that around here. 'Negative thinking never solved anything' is the researcher's motto."

Carly continued this charade all the way back to her office where she told me how pleased she was that I had come and asked me if I could join her for lunch. I told her I'd be delighted and we went out to my car.

Once we were out of the building and in my car, Carly slumped against the seat and closed her eyes. The charade had drained her.

I drove the few miles from the plant into downtown St. Petersburg and parked my car at the Vinoy, a large art deco hotel right on the water. We went in and were seated in the teak paneled dining room. After I ordered iced tea for both of us, I looked at Carly directly.

"At some point, you're going to have to tell me what is going on. Why did we go through that charade back at the plant?"

Carly seemed no more willing to talk and no less ill at ease than when she'd first come to the house. Since she wasn't willing to begin, I said, "You need to know that George and I told the police who the body was." Her eyes widened, she pushed herself away from the table and started to rise from her seat. I put my hand on her arm to keep her from leaving or making a scene in a place where both of us were well known.

"We made an anonymous call from a pay phone. All we said was that the body could be Dr. Morgan. Nothing more." She sat back down, slowly, and relaxed a little.

Then, more sternly, I said, "It's time for you to fill in some of the details you left out, or I'm going to have to go to the State's Attorney. This is serious business for me, Carly. I can't have any appearance of impropriety around me or my office over a murder. I want to help you, but you're not making it easy."

"I saw you reading our Annual Report," she said.

"So?"

"What it doesn't say in there, and what you'd know if you read the local papers closely, is that the breast implant controversy came to a complete head and nearly destroyed the company when the FDA ordered a moratorium on the sale of silicone breast implants."

"The report said the company had diversified its product by that time. How much of MedPro's business was breast implants when the moratorium was declared?"

"Over fifty percent. We had to close one of our plants and lay off a lot of our sales and manufacturing people, and we beefed up our other products."

"That just sounds like prudent business, not the end of the world. People get laid off and plants close every day."

"Yes, but the loss was devastating to a young company like MedPro. Dr. Morgan and the other two founders went from being multimillionaires to being in threat of bankruptcy overnight."

"I don't mean to sound heartless, but sometimes wealth

easily gained is easily lost. And it's not like any of those doctors are going to starve."

"You're right. And they were weathering the storm pretty well, under the circumstances. Dr. Young's husband had just died, so she was an emotional basket case anyway. Zimmer went to our creditors and restructured our debt. We thought we were going to come out ok.

"But then the lawsuits and the publicity started. The public revilement of everyone associated with the implants was devastating, personally and financially."

"A cynic would say it's the price of fame," I told her.

"You have no idea what it was like. We were under siege. Every day for months, the company was picketed by the Silicone Sufferers support group. We had to hire extra receptionists just to handle the calls. We got two feet of faxes and six feet of mail every day, most of it nasty. Our employees were constantly harassed. A lot of them quit because they were afraid to come to work. Every night for a month, we were the lead story on the six o'clock news." Carly's voice was becoming louder with each sentence. Other diners were looking at us.

"You mean, until a former NFL running back was arrested for killing his wife and the media had something new to report?"

She smiled weakly and calmed down a little. "I know it sounds like a nine-day wonder now, but it wasn't then. None of us handled the pressure well. There were frayed tempers, shouting matches and shoving contests somewhere in the plant every day, and not only on the production floor. More than one thousand complaints were filed against MedPro and our insurance was canceled. I became a litigation manager. Just answering complaints and discovery requests was more than a full time job. The shunts, catheters and kinetic products were not enough to keep us going. It didn't look like we were going to get out alive."

"So how did it all work out?"

"It hasn't yet. We started preparing our bankruptcy petition, and were close to filing it when the bankruptcy of the largest defendant temporarily halted the litigation and gave us some breathing room."

Carly stopped talking as the waiter brought our lunch and made a major production of arranging it on the table. By the time the bread waiter brought the rolls and the beverage waiter brought refills on our iced tea, a family of four could have ordered, received and consumed a fast food meal, at less than half the cost of our salads. I made a mental note to remind George that not every meal needs to be a dining experience.

Once we were alone, I asked, "What does all this have to do with Dr. Morgan? Are you saying he committed suicide over the business reversal, by shooting himself in the head, then bound and gagged himself, and jumped into the Bay?"

"Of course not. But Dr. Morgan had been calling me every day or two for about three months before he died."

"Did he say what for?"

"Oh sure. Over and over, in fact. He wanted to make a presentation to our scientists at MedPro."

"What kind of a presentation?"

"He wouldn't say. He would only say that it was a presentation that had to be made to sophisticated scientists because lawyers wouldn't understand it.

"He said he knew why women with breast implants were ill and he wanted to explain his theory. He was writing a book about it but, for old times sake, he wanted to give MedPro a preview. He didn't mention what a successful defense would do to the price of his stock, but he didn't have to."

"But that's a fabulous scientific breakthrough!" I said. Her face let me know how wrong that was. "If there's a scientific explanation for women with breast implants becoming ill, then isn't that something everyone would want to know?" I asked her.

"No. I mean, I guess it depends on what the explanation is. If the explanation is related to the product, then the answer is, MedPro doesn't want to know. We can't know. That will put our company out of business."

I was beginning to see the problem. If the women's illnesses were related to the product itself, then MedPro would be at fault.

"Did you set up the meeting he requested?"

"I took it to my superiors. They weren't interested."

"Why not?"

"What they told me, through the proper channels, was that Dr. Morgan is a crackpot. He's a defendant himself in several hundred cases. They believed anything he might have to say would be an attempt to save his own skin, and the value of his stock. They didn't want to be associated with him any more than they already were. It seems everything MedPro does these days ends up on the front page of the papers and on the evening news. If it became known that we were working with Dr. Morgan, we would be the laughing stock of the medical community and he would be forever associated with us in the litigation. They couldn't believe that he had anything to offer that the best minds at the big, well-funded institutions weren't able to discover. They just didn't want to get involved with him."

"But if he was an owner and founder of the company, why did he need you to set up a meeting?" I asked her.

"Dr. Morgan had been removed by the board and only

owned his stock. Which, at that point, wasn't worth much."

"Why?"

She looked at me, trying to decide whether to answer. Finally, she shrugged. "This is very hush hush, Willa. If this gets out, MedPro would be in a lot more trouble than it is now, if that's possible."

"Keeping secrets is a lawyer's stock in trade."

"I know, but some lawyers are better at it than others." She eyed me pointedly. I had, after all, made George call the police once already.

"True. All right. As long as I'm not required to disclose what you tell me, I'll keep it quiet."

"Dr. Morgan got into trouble with drugs a few years ago. He went to jail for selling cocaine and he lost his license to practice."

"That makes him a man who's paid his debt to society, not an ignorant incompetent without an intelligent idea."

"Yes, but during the prosecution of his case, it was discovered that he'd been having sex with his patients while they were anesthetized."

"You're kidding! How did they ever prove that?"

"He videotaped the surgeries, and he kept the tapes. The police found them in a routine search of his beach house."

The things you don't know about your own friends and neighbors are amazing. "Then why did he think MedPro would be interested in his presentation after he'd been fired by the other two founders when he went to jail?"

"Because he said his discovery would prove MedPro's innocence and the safety and efficacy of the implants. It was his way of trying to make it up to Young and Zimmer."

"And saving his own ass in the bargain," I said.

"That, too. Since Morgan lost his license, no medical insurer would touch him and no one else wants to be involved. He was begging me to schedule the meeting and, because he seemed so contrite and pathetic, I couldn't turn him down cold. I did tell him that, unfortunately, my management wasn't interested. The last time I talked to him, he told me someone was blackmailing him. He'd run out of money, and the blackmailer had threatened to kill him if he didn't pay. He sounded really desperate. I told him I thought he was exaggerating and he got angry with me and hung up."

"You never heard from him again?"

She hesitated before answering me, took a bite of her salad and washed it down. "No. He'd never given me a number where he could be reached. He always called me at prearranged times to talk. I've tried tracking him down through the Yellow Pages and directory assistance. I even hired a private investigator to look for him. No luck. When I heard they'd found a body in the Bay and about how long they thought it had been there, I just got this weird intuition that it was Dr. Morgan."

"Then why did you call me? Why didn't you just go to the police?"

Carly looked away for the first time in our conversation. Softly, she said, "Who would have believed me?"

"What do you mean? You could have told anyone. Why wouldn't they believe you? You're a lawyer, an officer of the court."

She was impatient again. "I really don't want to get into it. Let's just say that I knew for sure there was no one I could go to with the information. I'm glad you notified the police. With your tip, at least they'll check to see whether it's Dr. Morgan or not. I really want to stay out of it from this point forward. I need this job, Willa, and I like it. There's no one else to take care of me. I don't have a wealthy husband, I don't live on my own island and I don't have a lifetime appointment to the federal bench. Please," she leaned forward, pleading, "don't screw this up for me."

Like the little boy who killed his parents and then complained because he was an orphan, Carly seemed to have no understanding of how much more serious she was making this situation than it already was. She acted like she'd just failed to appear for a court date, when what she had involved us both in was so much worse. Maybe tough love was what she needed now, I thought.

"I have no intention of screwing anything up for you, Carly. You seem to be able to do that all by yourself. Do you know what will happen if it turns out this body is Dr. Morgan and people learn you knew or had reason to believe it was him for over a month and didn't tell? Your career as a lawyer will be ended. If you're lucky, you won't be arrested for obstructing justice, or murder." My harsh words seemed to shake her.

"What do you mean? I certainly had no reason to kill Dr. Morgan. I don't even know for sure if it's him, for God sake." She was genuinely shocked.

"Well you were concerned enough about it to come to my house and ask me a hypothetical question. You're concerned enough about it that you wouldn't allow me to talk to you in your office. What do you think, your office is bugged?"

"I know it is," she said.

"How can you know such a thing?" I could hear myself getting shrill and insistent with her, but this was getting to be too much.

She explained with exaggerated patience. "The entire plant is under constant surveillance. Every phone call, in and out is recorded. All of the offices have video camera surveillance. The making of medical products is a highly competitive business these days. The company guards its secrets. Any breach of security and you're out. No second chances."

"Well if Dr. Morgan really had a solution to the breast implant health mystery, why would anyone want to kill him for it?"

She looked at me as if I had just revealed my own insanity. "Have you no idea what you're saying? Do you realize how large a business this breast implant litigation has become? Fred Johnson, for one, is in this thing for millions of dollars. If there's a logical explanation for this, do you really think the plaintiff's bar is going to let go of all that money? And, if there really is a health hazard, do you think MedPro wants that to become public knowledge? The only peaceful coexistence lies in not knowing. As soon as we know, one side or the other loses."

"But what about the women? Aren't they the ones with the most at stake? Don't they have a right to know whether they're going to get sick or not from these leaking implants?" I asked her.

She shook her head. "I never thought of you as naive. Don't you understand the big business of litigation? Believe me, the number of people who would kill to keep such information quiet is limited only by your imagination."

I refused to believe Carly's words, but I would keep her confidence. At least for now. In turn, she promised to let me know if she heard from Dr. Morgan or if she heard any other information about his disappearance. We finished our lunch and I dropped her off at MedPro before heading back to my office, but only after she promised to return my calls and check in with me regularly. I thought then that I could trust her, but I was wrong.

CHAPTER TWELVE

Tampa, Florida
Friday 3:00 p.m.
January 8, 1999

I INTENDED TO GO back to the office, but couldn't muster the enthusiasm. Nothing on my calendar until Monday morning. A good time to play hooky. I pulled over to the side of the road and put Greta's top down.

Driving over the bridges, the water on either side, the wind blowing through the car and the top down rejuvenated my spirit, if not my hairstyle.

On the way home, I couldn't help thinking about Carly and what kind of child she had been before she learned *the big secret*. Kate had two sons when Mom and I came to live with her. Later, Carly was born. Since I was ten years older, I learned about the birds and the bees a lot sooner, and I knew Kate had been widowed far too long to have another baby. The boys must have at least suspected, too, but Kate was so happy about the pregnancy and kept referring to the baby as "your brother or sister," that none of us was willing to challenge her on it.

When Carly was born, and as she grew up, it just ceased to be important to all of us who Carly's father was. To us, she was our sister, so it didn't matter. And Carly never questioned it. Until the year she was ten. That year, her science class studied the gestation time for dogs, cats and human babies. She began to ask questions about why her appearance was so different from the dark hair and eyes her brothers had, and finally, the exact date of their father's death.

From that point on, Carly began hounding Kate about the identity of her father. And the boys, being boys, wanted to know with whom their mother had had an affair. Kate refused to say, at least to her children. I don't know what she told my mother at the time. Kate would only say that all her children were hers and they were brothers and sister.

For Carly, it was as if she had lost all perspective. I'm not sure ten-year-olds are supposed to have perspective, but Carly did. At least, until she decided finding out her father's identity was to be her sole mission in life. She pestered all of us endlessly about it. She made a list of all the men she knew, and relentlessly questioned my mother, Kate and the rest of us about them. When did Kate meet each one? How? How well did they know each other? She kept completed questionnaires on all of them, and meticulously correlated their relationships with Kate to her birth date and what she calculated as her date of conception. She'd interview them in circumspect ways, always trying to find out if he'd been around at the right time, if he was the right age. Each time she ruled out someone she considered desirable, she'd go into a deep depression and refuse to talk to any of us for days. By the time I was in college, Carly had filled several loose-leaf notebooks of father contenders, viable and rejected.

It was hard to tell whether the serious rift between Kate and Carly resulted from a secret kept too long, or the natural animosity of a teenage girl toward her mother. In either case, Carly was never the same toward any of us. She went away to college at the University of Colorado and rarely came home after that. None of us knew her, really, since we hadn't talked to her seriously since she was a child. Mark was the closest to her, and she was the most jealous and distant from me. Carly has always seen me as some kind of competition for her place in her family. She knew I wasn't really a blood relative, and she felt she wasn't a full blood relative either. The self-imposed competition made her brittle, even a little flaky.

When Carly secretly moved to Tampa, after her mother and I moved here, we didn't even know it for a long time. I think she did it partly because she was jealous of my relationship with Kate, and partly because she was beginning to grow up. She entered Stetson Law School and became a lawyer like her two brothers and, not coincidentally, me. It's hard to beat the competition if you're not in the same game. Carly wanted a real contest.

Once she moved here, she still saw her mother rarely, but in a typical Carly move, signed up for my class. Even now, she's a bundle of contradictions; independent and rebellious, brilliant but immature. I couldn't really fathom how it must feel not to know who your father was, to feel that rejection and deception. Carly certainly seemed to be struggling with it still, and I wasn't sure she'd ever get over it.

Comparing my childhood to Carly's wasn't really possible. Kate says that I was a dreamer as a child. I spent all of my time either reading or daydreaming, making up a world far different from the one I lived in. In school, I was always planning the next event, looking forward to activities next month or next year.

After Mom died when I was sixteen and Dad left me with Kate and her family, I became even more out of touch with what was going on around me, but I held onto Kate and her family as if I were drowning in abandonment and only familial affection would save me. For her part, Kate took the role of my mother in the same way she mothered her own children. She went to parent-teacher conferences, threw birthday parties, and had her picture taken at my graduations, just as she did with her other kids. She even played the part of mother-of-the-bride when George and I married. Kate is my mother, for all practical purposes, and has been for longer than I knew my real mom. If it wasn't that I'd feel so disloyal, I'd call her "mother." She's suggested it. It's a step I'm not ready to take.

So maybe Carly is right to be jealous of me. Maybe I said or did something those last few years when I lived with Kate's family to justify it. But even if I did, I can't relate to how she treats her mother. Because if my mother were still alive, no matter what she'd done, I'd never treat her the way Carly treats Kate.

Mom died of cancer. While she was ill, we spent so much time together and I wanted to savor every moment of it. She wanted me to go to school and the truant officers insisted that I go at least half a day. But the last few months of her life, they let me stay home when I promised to test out of the tenth grade after she died.

That was such a glorious time. She taught me how to make bread, arrange flowers, put on a dinner party. She told me all of the secrets a mother imparts to a daughter about dating and dealing with men. Some of what she said scared me. "Never let a boy put his hand on your knee. If you do, he'll want to put it under your skirt." I wasn't sure exactly what she meant by that, but it was advice I followed until I met George years later.

Mom and I had our own little world then. Dad was traveling, as he always had, even at what was clearly the end of his wife's life. On some level, I never forgave him for that. But on another level I was glad for the time it gave mother and me to be together. Maybe that was his present to both of us.

It was while Mom was sick that she told me she'd wanted to be a lawyer instead of a nurse. And I promised her that I would do what she had not done. Eventually, Mom died and her husband, the man I'd called my dad since she married him when I was five, never came home. I went to live with Kate and, as I promised, I tested out of the tenth grade. I graduated from high school at seventeen and then went directly to the University of Michigan.

What doesn't kill you makes you stronger. I know now that I was lucky to have loved my mother for sixteen years, and to have had her unconditional love while she lived. She sent me off into the world with that, the love, desire and support necessary to make something of my life. Every time I think of her, I think, "I could be better," not just as a lawyer, or a woman, but as a person. She believed that what's important is how you live your life, how you treat others. She taught me always to do my best and to help those who need it. It was a hard lesson to learn at sixteen, but I learned it, and it sustains me. It also gets me into trouble. Mighty Mouse does save the day, but it's not easy.

Carly was still dealing with Kate from anger and abandonment. I doubt Kate had ever sat her down and asked her to consider the alternative—being born to Kate's family or not at all. But Carly is the closest thing to a sister I'll ever have. She may be flaky and irresponsible and irritatingly self centered, but there's no way I could let her get seriously hurt. Kate would never get over it and I'm not sure I would either. I didn't want to lose anyone else in my life.

About twenty minutes after I left Carly, I was turning onto Plant Key Bridge. I forced my mind back to the present and filled my senses with the approach. Florida is so flat, and Plant Key so far below sea level, that from the bridge, I could only see the top of Minaret. And a spectacular top it is, too.

The house is named after its most prominent architectural feature, a large minaret on the top of the third floor roof. The story goes that Henry Plant had visited Turkey and became enamored of the bulbous onion domes he saw there. He put several on the top of his hotel and one on the top of his home. Ours is shiny steel and the sun glints off of it most of the day, making it shine bright blue with reflected skylight, orange with the sunrise or grey with the clouds. The rest of the house isn't in any way reflective of Middle Eastern architecture, so the minaret itself is somewhat out of place on top of the southern style home. It's sort of like Jimmy Durante's big nose, something you come to appreciate over time.

As I left the bridge, I drove down Plant Key's version of the Avenue of Palms. Ours are not so old or so tall as the ones at the entrance to Palm Beach, but they stretch for about a half a mile and give one the impression of grandeur an entrance onto Plant Key should have. To show the proper respect to the original, our avenue is unnamed. It opens out to the front lot entrance to Minaret, which is red brick, paved and circular.

Plant copied the entrance from the Breakers Hotel, built

about the same time by Plant's great friend Henry Flagler. If you've been to the Breakers, the Ritz in Naples, or seen pictures, you've seen our front entrance, except ours is red brick and not yellow. We have a round fountain in front of the *porte cochère*, and a drive that runs through. In those days, Florida storms were as fierce as they are now, and the ladies and gentlemen needed a shelter from which to leave their carriages. Now, it makes a great valet parking entrance to Minaret, particularly if you're arriving in the summer between four and seven o'clock in the afternoon when we get our afternoon storms.

Puttered across the bridge, onto the island, and toward the house. I asked the valet to put the top up on the car and went inside, intending to change into running shorts and a T-shirt and take the dogs out.

But when I walked into the lobby, I saw Kate sitting in the dining room with Victoria Warwick and Cilla Worthington.

Tried to sneak around to the winding staircase that goes from the main entrance to the house up to the second floor, but Kate saw me and waved me over. Shook my head furiously, signaling her that I didn't want to come in, but Victoria spied me, too.

Trapped.

Failed to appear gracious as I walked into the dining room and approached their table.

CHAPTER THIRTEEN

Tampa, Florida
Friday 4:45 p.m.
January 8, 1999

"WILHELMINA, PLEASE JOIN US," Victoria said, her speech slurred just enough to let me know how many Bloody Marys she'd already consumed in addition to the one in front of her on the table. Kate and Cilla both insisted that I sit down and I couldn't graciously refuse.

Kate and Cilla looked like what they were: middle-aged matrons at lunch. But again today, Victoria had on a bright pink dress suitable for a much younger woman, tight in the bodice with another low-cut neckline. She wasn't wearing a bra. Sunlight illuminates everything: she was no longer twenty-five years old, or even fifty-five. But she was blessed with a long neck and her bosom did look fantastic. She laughed loudly, put her hands on the sides of her breasts to push them up almost out of the top of her dress. She said, "It's impolite to stare, my dear, but aren't they fantastic?"

Embarrassed to be caught looking, I blushed but had to agree.

"I had them done in New York about six months ago. I'll tell you it wasn't easy to find a doctor who would do them, even though I offered to pay twice the normal cost. I tried to get Mike Morgan to do them for old time's sake, but he wouldn't return my calls. Men are such assholes, especially the ones you've slept with. They think it gives them the right to be an asshole for some reason."

Cilla's nostrils flared, whether at the crude language or the mention of Victoria's well-known philandering, I couldn't tell. "It's bad enough that you've slept with every man in town, Victoria. Is it necessary to broadcast it, too? It's not like you're the only woman in Tampa to have had an affair with Mike Morgan. Take a number." She was impatient, and snappier than usual. And she sounded too bitter.

More to distract them from Morgan than anything, I said, "I've never known any doctor to refuse to do elective surgery. There's so much profit in plastic surgery. If you agreed to pay twice the cost, why would they possibly refuse?"

Victoria was remarkably coherent, and much more voluble than she likely would have been if she hadn't been drunk. "Well, there's been an FDA moratorium on breast implant surgery for several years. The only way to get silicone breast implants now is to become a part of a controlled study. And, of course, for the controlled studies they want younger, more vigorous women or cancer reconstruction patients. You wouldn't believe all the releases I had to sign and the strings I made the senator pull to get them to do it. But they did, obviously." She giggled, looking down her chest. No kidding.

"But aren't you afraid of the health risks? Tory, really, this is a fairly stupid thing you've done to your body." Cilla was out of patience. She may be a grand dame, but she doesn't suffer fools.

Victoria looked at all of us with open hostility. "I think it's fairly obvious that my body is no temple. It takes years for the ill health effects from implants to develop, according to the doomsday theories. I'm sure I won't live that long, if my darling husband's wishes have anything to do with it. A widower is so much more electable than a man with an adulterous wife, you know. Everyone wants to know *why* she cheats."

None of us had a response to that. Kate changed the subject to some recent charitable activities they were involved in and that gave me my excuse to leave. As I walked out of the dining room, they were still discussing the budget for the next homeless shelter benefit, and I was trying to figure out why discussing Tory Warwick's affair with Dr. Morgan would make Cilla so angry and Kate so quiet.

CHAPTER FOURTEEN

Tampa, Florida
Friday 5:15 p.m.
January 8, 1999

UPSTAIRS, BOTH HARRY AND BESS were guarding the door waiting for anyone who happened to come in so that they could immediately lick intruders to death. Both bounded toward me whining to jump on my suit for ear scratching. I waved them down and changed into running clothes. Then gave in, got down on the floor and rolled around with both of them for awhile. Together, they out-weigh me by thirty pounds.

Bess is black and Harry is yellow. Like their namesakes, they're fiercely independent, no-nonsense dogs, thoroughly devoted to one another. We got them originally for protection as guard dogs because so many strangers come into what is, after all, our home.

Pricilla Worthington told me once, after Harry slobbered all over her Dior dress, "If you had a gun, and knew how to use it like everyone else in Tampa, you wouldn't need these noxious creatures."

But I'm from Detroit. Nothing as sissy as handguns for protection for us.

Of course, anyone who spends five seconds with Harry and Bess realizes what useless guard dogs they are. They do have big barks and that counts for something, at least to strangers. We still pay the alarm company every month, just in case.

After I put on my running shoes, we went down the back stairs, avoiding everyone else who might be in the restaurant, to the beach. I threw sticks and toys into the water for them to chase for a while before we began our run. After fifteen minutes of having wet sticks returned by two ninety-pound dogs, I was as wet as they were. I threw the last two sticks and took off in the opposite direction, counter clockwise around the island. If I don't play with them some beforehand, there's no way I can keep up.

By the time they got the sticks out of the water and came after me it took them, maybe, fifteen seconds to pass me up. It's a little contest I have with myself. I've made it as far as twenty seconds ahead of them, but I have to throw the sticks pretty far out first.

When I'm in good form, I do an entire lap around Plant Key, or maybe two. Other days, I just do half a lap and take a golf cart back. Because I was feeling guilty about leaving the office early and I had plenty of time before sundown; today would be a complete lap day.

A lot of people run just for exercise, hating every minute of it. For me, though, it's a spiritual experience. I love the sand, the water, the sunshine and the companionship I get from Harry and Bess. After years of running, I'm able to get to the runner's high in about three minutes and it carries me the remainder of the run. Sometimes, I have to consciously make myself stop. Otherwise, I might be like the tiger chasing Sambo and run around so long and so fast that I melt into butter. During the summer I feel like I'm melting.

Today I considered what I'd learned on my visit to MedPro and at lunch from Carly. Something about her explanation just didn't fit with the facts. It was nagging me and the more I tried to focus on it, the more elusive it became. I attacked it another way. Why would Dr. Morgan call Carly with his discovery when he could have called Zimmer or Young directly? He knew them better and they had a history together. Why would he pick a young, gullible and inexperienced employee to disclose such allegedly valuable information? It just didn't make sense, unless he planned to use that inexperience for his own ends. Or, and this was more likely, Carly wasn't telling me everything. I worked out a plan for finding out the rest.

As I came up the back stairs after my run, our private phone rang and George answered it.

"Its Marilee Aymes, for you," he said as he handed me the cordless. I wondered how she got the number. Like my office number, it's unlisted and only given out to the family.

"Dr. Aymes. So nice to hear from you again." Another lie. To the best of my knowledge, information and belief, as we lawyers say, Marilee Aymes had never called me before.

"Wilhelmina," she said, imperious as usual. "We have a foursome for next Sunday and we've lost one of our group. The handicapper said you're a ten, which would place you at the high end of the group, but he suggested we ask you to fill in. Are you free?"

Kate would say when you want a thing, it happens. I had been trying to figure out a way to talk to Marilee Aymes, and she just called. There are no coincidences in life. I accepted.

GEORGE AND I HAD a wedding to go to that night.

We went, we ate, we came home.

I always make Friday night an early one. It's a pleasant end to a long week, and besides, I play golf every Saturday at 6:00 a.m. with my former partner, Mitchell Crosby, out at Great Oaks.

We've tried playing other courses, just to keep our skills up, but there's something about the familiarity of the holes, the fairways and the greens that challenges us to beat our best games. We play best here, on our home turf, but that's not the reason we keep coming out to the same 18 holes every weekend.

I'm not an early riser and I can't make it to the office before 9:00, at the earliest. But on Saturday, I jump up before sunrise, slip on a golf shirt and Bermudas in some wild combination of colors, and sneak out of the house so as not to wake Harry and Bess. For a while there they were on to me, and they'd sleep right next to the bed so I couldn't get away from them. If they wake up, they have to be fed and run before anything else. They know they're the center of our universe and the world revolves around them, not George, although he likes to think he's the Master Cylinder.

So, if I don't get out without waking them up, we can't tee off until 7:00, which doesn't sound like much of a problem unless you're a golfer in Florida in July. If you are, you know what I mean. If you're not, you don't want to hear about it anyway.

On this particular Saturday in January, it was dark at 5:30 when I woke up, and a little too cool. George had opened the windows sometime during the night and the warmth of our Egyptian cotton sheets and down comforter almost sucked me back in for another couple of hours. But I knew Mitch would be on the first tee in thirty minutes. He lost five dollars last week, and whenever he was down in our weekly wagers, he couldn't rest until he won it back. If I skip a day like that, he declares himself the winner and will not back down. Mitch is more than a little obsessive, overbearing and stubborn. Some would say we're perfectly matched.

Once I was washed and dressed, I ran out to the car. Dew on the St. Augustine grass and impatiens gave everything a crystalline shimmer. As I drove out the circle, the sun was lightening the sky over the Port of Tampa and Harbour Island. By the time I crossed the Plant Key Bridge, the sun glinted on Hillsborough Bay and two dolphins swimming side by side raced Greta and me the length of the bridge. They won. It was glorious. I've always loved morning. It's just that I usually sleep through it.

It's a short drive to Great Oaks. As I approached the large, plantation-style clubhouse, I realized, as I always do, how amazing it is that such a beautiful 36-hole golf course is nestled right in the center of South Tampa. I parked the car and walked to the pro shop. Since I play every Saturday, the caddies had my cart set up with my clubs. I went into the women's locker room and put on my golf shoes before meeting Mitch at the cart. Of course, he was ready to go, already behind the wheel. On the golf course, as on the road, men do the driving if the women don't get there first.

At the first tee, Mitch hit a drive 200 yards with his Big Bertha driver and was feeling pretty smug, thinking, I'm sure, that he'd be getting his $5 back today. By the end of the first nine, though, I was two strokes under and he was becoming surly. I remembered my mother telling me that I needed to let the boys win; otherwise they wouldn't play with me anymore. She obviously hadn't known Mitch. It's when he's winning that he wants to stop.

We always eat lunch in the clubhouse. Today, Mitch wasn't quite as interested in gloating over his winnings as usual.

"What's up?" I asked.

"Actually, I was feeling sorry for Mrs. Junior. I've always liked her, even if she is rather homely." He said, referring to the CJ's daughter-in-law, his only son's wife, using the nickname we've privately, and derisively, given her husband.

"Why?" I asked, "She has everything in the world. Aside from having to live with Junior, I'd say there are only about fifty million women in the country who would gladly trade places with her."

"Not today. Junior made a complete fool of himself a few years ago and his wife, too. He resigned from our firm yesterday because the scandal broke."

"No kidding! Junior, heir apparent, the anointed one, one day to become the second great and powerful Oz himself? What on earth possessed him to do that?" This was truly juicy news, if only because it would cause the CJ so much consternation. Junior was detested by every partner in my old firm lower on the ladder than he was, and by some who were a little higher up. It's not that Junior was really such a bad guy, it was just that he got his privileges the old-fashioned way—Daddy bought them for him.

To be fair, he probably would have done well enough on his own if he'd been a little more pleasant. But he was one of those guys who always had sand kicked in his face as a kid. He was scrawny, wore glasses, and had a sour personality. In truth, he was one of the reasons I sought a judicial appointment after he came over to the firm a few years ago. Practicing another twenty years with Junior running the show was more than I could bear. Maybe I had to work with his father as the Chief Judge now, but the CJ had no real power over me. Working with Junior as my managing partner was unacceptable. Now, then, and always.

"You have to give me all the details. And don't you dare leave anything out." We ordered burgers and beer, our standard Saturday lunch. The beer came in tall, frosty mugs while we waited for the well-done burgers cooked the Jimmy Buffet way: cheese, lettuce, pickles, tomato and onion. Fries, too, of course.

"Well, you know Junior was the rising star in our downtown office." Mitch is like James Michener; he always begins at the very beginning of time.

"Sure, as the saying goes, he came from money, married money, and made a lot of money. All the makings of a successful lawyer, even if he is a twit."

"Willa, that's not very becoming of you," Mitch scolded as he grinned. He doesn't like Junior any more than I do.

"It seems an attractive, sexy, female lawyer was hired in the prosecutor's office when he was over there. And for reasons that can only be attributed to a mental handicap or extreme nearsightedness, she apparently found Junior attractive. Maybe it's the power that turned her on or the promise of future power. I could never understand Lyle Lovett and Julia Roberts, either."

"I'm with you." When the waitress came around with our burgers, we ordered another beer. In addition to the $5 bet, I had to buy lunch and he was making the most of it.

"Anyway, she appears to be attracted to him and he, who never had a date in his life that didn't have to wear a bag over her head, is besotted. Everyone notices. Rumors fly. She's bright and capable and could make it on her own merits, but the favoritism he shows her makes her the target of vicious gossip."

"Imagine that." The drinks arrived, and I settled in for the rest of the story.

"Such sarcasm. Anyway, you know Junior's granddaddy was the President of the First Federal Bank of Tampa, and when Junior's daddy took the Federal Bench, Uncle Bishop got the bank job. The largest bank in town, and not coincidentally, one of the firm's major clients, is controlled by Uncle Bish. The CJ and Uncle Bish were afraid Junior had gotten totally out of hand. The scandal would shake his place in society. Uncle Bish, a powerful man himself, can't have that, even if it would otherwise have been okay with Oz, senior."

"This is delicious. What did Bishop do?" I licked the juice off my fingers and dipped a French fry in mustard. Mitch frowned at my poor table manners. He handed me a napkin.

"Uncle Bish called our State's Attorney in to lunch, and, friend to friend, asked him to squash the whole situation by firing the young associate and putting Junior on a big project that would take him out of town for a couple of months."

"A few months away from hearth and home and the floozy and he should start thinking with his big head again, instead of his little head. I can see the logic of it." I smiled, a mouthful of beef, cheese and mustard dribbling down my chin. I picked up the extra napkin so as not to interrupt the story again.

"Right. But the truth is, Uncle Bish is more than a little proud of Oz's sprout. Junior has never before exhibited any traits of real manliness, you see. He's always been sort of a bookworm weeny. Now, at least we know he's capable of manliness. But that doesn't mean Oz wants Junior destroying his dynasty. Junior has four children, after all, and a very respectable wife." Mitch was chewing his burger with gusto. He was really getting into this now.

"How sweet." I said. "A little meaningless dalliance. Well, that's a time-honored privilege of the privileged, but throw away the future the family has planned for Junior on a pair of long legs, even very attractive and smart long legs? No."

"Is this my story or yours?"

"Sorry. It's just so predictable."

"No problem, but watch it." He gave me a mock slap on the wrist. "So, the State's Attorney agrees to the plan because what choice does he have? Besides, he's been totally oblivious to the gossip and didn't even realize what was going on in his own office."

"It's really true that the farther up the ladder you get, the less people talk to you." I waved for some extra napkins again and the waitress brought them over. Mitch took a couple this time, too.

"Right. Besides that, you know the State's Attorney is one of those true blue types. He's been married since he was twenty-five and he's never even looked at another woman."

"He's never really looked at his wife, either." I couldn't resist. I figured if I was going to be a gossip, I might as well go all the way.

"True, but sex has not been his aphrodisiac. He can't understand how otherwise intelligent men let their dicks do the thinking."

"Amen." I signaled for another round, trying to decide if I should switch to something lighter. I did have to drive home, and I wasn't interested in explaining a drunk driving ticket to the CJ. I could just see it. "Oh, Oz. Junior's story was just sooooo interesting. I couldn't help myself." I'd stick with the beer for now. What the hell.

"So, the State's Attorney himself calls Junior into his office and gives him the ultimatum," Mitch continued.

"Let me guess. 'This is unseemly. It's embarrassing. It's affecting your future'," I said, covering my sarcasm well, I think.

"In the tradition of the way these things have been handled from time immemorial, he tells Junior to put a stop to 'this relationship' at once, or the young assistant will be fired."

"That's outrageous!" I nearly spit out my beer. "Why didn't they fire him? What he's doing was immoral and illegal. The State Attorney could find himself on the wrong end of a sexual harassment suit over this."

"Don't I know it. Labor law is my *forté*, remember? But does anyone ask me? No." Mitch sounds more than a little put out by this. Everyone's got his own ox to gore, every time. Count on it.

"Junior must have been incensed. He is next in line to the throne, after all. Not only the family throne, but Uncle Bishop's throne as well."

"Make that 'was.' The way I heard the story, that was exactly his thinking. So Junior calls Dad and lays it on thick about the lame-brained behavior by the dotty old State's Attorney. But, shock of shocks, Dad agrees with Uncle Bish."

"Junior must have been having a cow! I wish I could have seen it!"

"And you'd have had to stand in line. Anyway, Junior told his cronies later that Dad said 'a piece of ass is nice, Junior, but it's not worth your credibility, your family, and your job.' He wouldn't support him on this one."

"What did Junior do?"

"Junior thinks about it for two hours. He decides to put an

end to the affair. He calls her into his office and tries to explain it to her. She cries. She pleads. She sits on his lap."

"So, Junior's little head snaps to attention and he throws caution to the wind." The sarcasm was so thick you'd have to cut it with a chain saw.

"Right. He called the guy I heard this from, really hot. They're not going to railroad him. He'll show them who's boss. And so forth. His pal tries to get him to calm down. No dice. He calls a guy who's been courting him to come over and join our firm for months. He agrees to come if he can bring her with him." The finish was kind of a letdown, although the story had been a good one.

"You have got to be putting me on. It's interesting to finally learn how he got to the firm, but why would all this ancient history cause him to resign now?" This was real news. If I ever leave the bench, it actually gives me a place to go back to.

"Because everybody found out about it this week. Uncle Bish had managed to keep the whole thing quiet, but lately there's been some rumblings in our associate ranks that Junior's up to his old tricks. Someone reported him to our managing partner, who called Junior in for a little talk. Junior told him to take this job and shove it."

I don't know if it was the story or the beer, but the whole situation seemed so funny. We were laughing so hard that other patrons in the clubhouse were staring at us.

"I would have paid, paid you understand, to see the look on your managing partner's face when Junior quit. This is precious."

When he could talk again, Mitch said, "Yeah, but the managing partner is really sweating. Now he's really pissed off Oz, Senior, and Uncle Bish, and he knows it. He doesn't know what to do. What will he say? Everyone was planning on Junior to be managing partner when his time came."

"Well, I can't believe many of your comrades are too upset about it. I'm thrilled, although if you repeat that I'll deny it." We signed the check and went out to our cars. Certainly one of the more entertaining golf dates we've had lately, even if it did cost me fifty dollars. I had a nice little buzz going. We said our goodbyes and were about to leave the course for the day, when one more question occurred to me.

"Mitch, just out of curiosity, where did Junior's floozy go, anyway? Did she come with him to your firm?"

"No. She left Junior at the same time she left the State Attorney's office and took an in house counsel job for some medical device company in St. Pete." Buzz kill. Fifty bucks wasted, but that solved one mystery, at least. How had Carly thought she'd ever keep such a secret? And no wonder she thought she had no credibility with our local authorities.

CHAPTER FIFTEEN

Tampa, Florida
Tuesday 9:00 a.m.
January 12, 1999

BY TUESDAY, MY PATIENCE was exhausted and my
annoyance level off the charts. I'd spent the weekend alternately
in front of the television or the newspapers and trying to reach
Carly. The news was all about the upcoming Gasparilla
festivities, Tampa's version of Mardi Gras. Carly was nowhere
to be found.

Jones v. General Medics started promptly at 9:00 Tuesday
morning, as the judge promised, and I was in no mood for
nonsense. The case was scheduled for three weeks on my docket,
but the way jury selection was going, I was sure it would take
three months. Just great. Three whole months of Christian
Grover. I couldn't wait. *Voir dire* dragged on through 12:30, and
we broke for lunch.

When I came back to my chambers for the lunch recess,
there was a message from Carly. The message read *don't worry*

I'll be back soon. No number. I asked Margaret, my secretary, whether she had talked with Carly and how she sounded. Margaret said someone else had taken the message and I asked her to find out who. She looked at me quizzically, but knew better than to argue. She said she'd let me know.

As Margaret was leaving my office, she said, "By the way, the CJ called. He wants to see you this afternoon when you recess for the day." Interesting. He's staying late to talk to me. This can't be good, I thought. More than that, it promised to be a pain in the ass. Maybe I'd recess early and get out before he came by.

I also had a message from Mark, Carly's brother. Thinking he might have heard from Carly, I called him back. He was out and I left another message. In private practice, I used to bill for telephone tag. Now, it just takes up my time and makes me irritable.

Just before we reconvened after lunch, my secretary came to tell me that she'd asked around and no one remembered taking the message from Carly. She seemed puzzled and promised to keep trying.

Before bringing the venire back into the courtroom, I strongly admonished both lawyers, on the record. "Gentlemen, I've had enough fooling around in this case already. So there hasn't been a breast implant case in the country that's been tried in under four weeks. This one will be the first. When we get started, I will finish *voir dire* myself. When we have the jury, Mr. Grover, you may give your opening statement. You have twenty minutes. And" ...I looked at Grover steadily, "there will be none of your infamous shenanigans or I'll mistry this case so fast you won't know what hit you."

I turned to O'Connell. "Mr. Worthington," I said, just as

sternly, "you'll have twenty minutes for your opening and we *will* get our first witness on today."

I addressed my bailiff before either man could say a word and instructed him to bring in the jurors. Once the panel was seated, I apologized for keeping them waiting and told them that we would finish the case in three weeks. I asked the few relevant *voir dire* questions I thought had been missed, gave the lawyers their preemptories and finished the selection in ten minutes flat. I instructed the jury, asked them to give the matter their undivided attention and we got down to work. Appealable error be damned.

Grover has a reputation for outrageous behavior in the courtroom, and he doesn't care whether his verdicts get overturned on appeal. I was surprised when he delivered a colorful, but proper, opening in nineteen minutes. As O'Connell concluded his opening remarks, I could see Grover's mind and attention were elsewhere. I couldn't fault him for that; my mind wasn't on the trial either.

I asked Grover to call his first witness. The trial proceeded quickly through the afternoon hours and we recessed at 4:30. I admonished everyone to be back in the courtroom promptly at 8:30 the next morning and left the bench. I couldn't remember a thing that had been said by either side, and I hoped the jury was paying closer attention.

Because I needed the distraction, I had called Pricilla Worthington during the three o'clock break and asked her if I could come by for a cup of tea and bring over the bill for food service for the AIDS benefit. Cilla is the only woman I know who still has a full tea service in the afternoon. She hesitated just a little too long over the request and I thought for a minute she might actually refuse. But then, gracious as always, she said of course I could come.

I arrived at their Bayshore mansion about five minutes early, and I parked under the *porte cochère*. It was a gloriously sunny day, about seventy degrees, and no wind. The sailors would be unhappy, but for the rest of us, it was the kind of day Floridians live for.

I walked up and rang the bell and Mrs. Smith, the Worthington's ancient black housekeeper, finally got to the door about ten minutes later. She hugged me, and escorted me into the parlor, where Cilla was waiting, her silver tea service set out on the coffee table.

"Willa, dear, do come in. The tea's just ready. You're right on time." I sat down on the antique camelback sofa across from Cilla, and admired the room, as I have countless times. I don't think there had been a new piece of furniture placed in that room in more than fifty years. Cilla told me once the house had belonged to her parents, and she and O'Connell had moved into it just as it stood when her father finally died in '64. It was old, but it was clean, and all the pieces were in excellent repair. The rugs alone were worth a fortune. I wondered just how big the Worthington estate would be when their children inherited. And now I was also wondering why her brother, the CJ, didn't live in the house.

Cilla and I spent some time discussing the fundraiser, how successful it was, and how much the Junior League had Senator Warwick to thank for that. I gave her the bill, ostensibly my reason for coming. She took it as if it were a piece of junk mail, and set it on the side table. I was sure George would eventually get paid, but it's a mark of extreme wealth that Cilla believed it wouldn't matter exactly when the League settled up.

Finally, I was able to bring the conversation around to the real reason for my visit. "Cilla," I said, as if it was, oh, just a little curiosity, "do you remember the other day when we were at Minaret with Kate and Tory Warwick?"

"Of course I remember, Willa. I'm old, but I'm not senile." Just a little edgy. Uncharacteristic of her. Maybe O'Connell or the grandchildren were misbehaving lately and it was on her mind.

"I wasn't suggesting anything of the kind. It's just that I forget things sometimes, and I thought maybe you did, too." I tried to placate her. I resolved not to get old. Old people are so inflexible.

"No, I remember the day perfectly well. What did you want to ask me about it?" To the point, as always.

"Well," I set down my teacup and leaned forward, suggesting I'd keep the conversation confidential without saying so. "Tory said something about having an affair with Michael Morgan years ago and you seemed to know about it. I thought maybe you'd tell me what happened."

"You surprise me, Willa. I didn't take you for a gossipmonger." She sat straighter in her chair, and cloaked herself in her grand dame persona. I could imagine many an intimidated child had been on the receiving end of the steely look down that long, patrician nose she was giving me now.

"It's not gossip I'm interested in, Cilla, but facts. You know Dr. Morgan is a witness in a number of cases on my docket. I'm concerned about letting him testify because of his background and I thought you might be able to help me." It was a white lie, and the wife of a lawyer should know a judge doesn't investigate a case. But maybe O'Connell doesn't talk shop at home, because she answered my question, after a fashion.

"Why would you think that?"

"You've been around Tampa as long as anyone. I've heard

some wild stories about Dr. Morgan. I thought you might be able to separate fact from fiction."

She considered the question and the explanation. She was wavering. I just kept looking earnest. Appealing to vanity usually works. On that score, Mrs. O'Connell Worthington was no different from anyone else.

Finally, she said "Just because Tory had an affair with Mike Morgan doesn't mean anything. That was a long time ago. There have been a lot of women in this town who've succumbed to his charms. And, I would bet, a lot of women in many other towns. If you want to talk to all the women he's slept with, you'll have to take a leave of absence to interview them all." She poured herself another cup of tea, offered me a cookie and took three for her plate. I could only imagine the number of calories it took to support her size.

"I don't think I'm interested in all of them, just Victoria Warwick." The cookie melted in my mouth as I mentally calculated how long I'd have to run to compensate.

"Well, I suppose she'd tell you herself if you asked her. Everyone knows about it anyway. It was about ten years ago. She and Shel were having problems again. The way she deals with it is to find someone else to distract her. Mike was the distraction of the moment."

"So it wasn't serious?" What the hell. I reached for another lady finger. Damn, those things are good. But why? Nothing to them, really.

"I don't think Tory Warwick has ever been serious about anything, except Sheldon. She's always been seriously in love with him. He just doesn't notice, or doesn't care."

"Well, what happened to their affair? Tory and Morgan, I mean?"

"She got tired of him, just a couple of minutes before he got tired of her. And it was over. As far as I know, it didn't last long, and it wasn't repeated. They both went on to other things."

"Other lovers?"

She looked at me again, with disapproval and a serious frown in her broad forehead, both of her caterpillar eyebrows coming together over her nose. "Perhaps so."

Pushed my luck. "Does that mean yes?"

She'd had enough. "It means Michael Morgan is a vile man who has no scruples and no character. I don't know him well enough to know all he's done in his life but enough of my friends have suffered at his hands that I know he's always done whatever it took to get what he wanted."

It could have been just her southern lady disdain for his distasteful affairs, but it didn't strike me that way when she said it. I noticed she spoke of him as if he was still alive. I asked her softly, "What did he do to your friends?"

"You'll have to ask them, and they'll tell you if they want to. The only thing I'm going to say about it is that Michael Morgan has always lived a lot higher on the hog than any other Tampa doctor I know."

It was all she would say. She had some inside information, but she wasn't sharing. And I knew her well enough to know she wouldn't tell what she didn't want to tell.

Through Friday, the trial continued. Every day, I listened to the morning news and both editions of the evening news. I read both local papers cover to cover while waiting for the monotonous scientific evidence to be introduced. Nowhere did I see or hear a report identifying Dr. Morgan as the body in the Bay. By Saturday morning, I was convinced that George's anonymous tip had never been passed on.

Mark called twice during the week, but I missed his calls and we continued to play tag. I was tempted to ask Mitchell what was going on, but I was afraid it would be a breach of Mark's confidence, so I didn't. Neither did I hear from Carly, although I kept trying to reach her. Some days, I would get messages that she'd called, but every time Margaret denied talking to her and couldn't find anyone else in the office who had. By the end of the week, I was exhausted and I fell into bed at 8:30 Friday night. George said if he'd known what being married to a judge was going to do to his sex life, he wouldn't have encouraged me to take the job.

CHAPTER SIXTEEN

Tampa, Florida
Saturday 7:00 a.m.
January 16, 1999

SINCE I WAS PLAYING golf Sunday with Dr. Aymes, I had canceled my Saturday game with Mitchell. I got up and snuck out while George was sleeping to take the dogs for their run.

I tried to work through what I knew about Morgan and Carly. If it was Michael Morgan in the water, who killed him? And why? And why hadn't the body been identified? I was hoping, with my fingers crossed almost the entire time, that it wasn't him. Maybe it really was the lost tourist they had first believed. And if it was Morgan, I knew that both my ethical obligations as a judge and lawyer, and my concern for Carly and her family would keep me involved in this until it was resolved.

I tried to think of all the angles, the reasons someone would want Morgan dead. Who had a motive? Opportunity? My legs started to tire because I was too focused. So I just let my mind soar free. Before I knew it, I had done the entire ten miles and was back at the house.

I went out to the water and jumped in. Harry and Bess were already there. This is the part of our run they like the best because they get to submerge me and each other in the water ten or twenty times before I'm completely exhausted and give up. Then we got out, rinsed off outdoors and I put them in their screened sun porch to dry off while I ran up the back stairs.

I was in the shower, letting the warm water cover my face, inhaling the soothing vanilla fragrance of the bath gel and trying again to think of a way to disclose Dr. Morgan's identity that would actually make someone take notice, when George came into my bathroom.

"Willa," he said as gently as he could and still be heard over the running water, "Carly's here. My God, she looks like she hasn't slept in days. She has dark circles under her eyes, and she looks both exhausted and, at the same time, in a high state of anxiety. I gave her some hot tea and showed her to the bathroom where she could take a comforting soak. By the time she finished, she was yawning and standing in the kitchen with her eyes closed. So I put her in the guest room for a nap. She hasn't regained consciousness."

I turned off the shower with trepidation. I'd wanted her to surface and she had. Maybe I should have been more careful what I wished for. Now what? "Let me get dressed, and we'll see if we can wake her and find out what this is all about." When I came into our small galley kitchen, George was finishing two cups of breve, one of my many indulgences. He carried them out to the veranda along with the Saturday *Times*, talking over his shoulder.

"Come out and have a coffee before you wake her. I think we both need some fortification first."

In the end, we decided not to wake her and Carly slept for hours. I worked for a while in my study and waited. When I walked into the kitchen just after four o'clock, she, too, was making coffee and Cuban toast, wearing an old Key West T-shirt and nothing else.

"Well you look a lot better. I hope you feel better," I told her.

She smiled, albeit slightly, more like a slice of acknowledgment. She didn't act like the weight of the world was off her shoulders. "Do you have any idea what it's like not to be perfect?"

The way she said it, perfection was certainly not an admirable trait. She was snide, almost nasty about it, like being "perfect" was worse than being a child molester. Carly's never been subtle. What you see is what you get.

"Oh, I know you have that little gap between your front teeth and those red highlights in your hair have to be touched up every few weeks. I'll bet it was just really trying to be six feet tall in seventh grade. And George's constant devotion is probably just smothering." She carried her toast to the small table and added skim milk to her coffee making it that sickly shade of green I imagine all waifs must admire. Otherwise, how can they drink the stuff?

"You know, Carly, if I didn't know better I might confuse you with one of my political enemies, not a guest to whom I've been extremely hospitable." I said it lightly, but I was surprised how much her derision of what she viewed as my "perfect" self annoyed me, and I filed away for the moment the serious introspection I should be doing to find out why. I'd been worried to death about her and all she could do was chastise me for not having my life in as big a mess as hers was. Besides, whether one lives a beautiful and privileged life is often in the eye of the beholder, no?

"Look, Willa, all I'm saying is that you don't know what it's like to be less than beautiful in American society. We grew up playing with Barbie dolls and thinking that our lives would be fabulous if we had perfect measurements, the right nose, and long blond hair. If we had all that, then we'd get Ken, the perfect mate. Most women I know still wear high heels, for God's sake. Is it any wonder that the breast implant industry is booming and has been for almost forty years? Women have put all kinds of things in their bodies to get that 'perfect' look. Who are the real victims in all this, anyway?" She was working herself up into a fine snit, waving her arms around and pacing back and forth in the small kitchen.

Enough. "Although I'm beginning to understand the point, I'm not getting the connection between this enlightened social commentary and your behavior of the last few weeks," I told her.

"Don't act like a judge with me, Wilhelmina. Despite Gloria Steinem, who by the way is very attractive herself, most women in America just don't feel very pretty. They're constantly bombarded with images of women who are taller, sexier, thinner, more attractive and 'built'," she gestured the "hourglass" figure.

"This is hardly a new or astounding social insight. What does it have to do with you turning up on my doorstep looking like you have neither eaten nor slept since I saw you a week ago?" In my head, I heard my mother admonishing "grace under pressure, Wilhelmina," so I tried to smile at her as I said it, but it took some effort.

She'd run out of steam, just as suddenly as she'd started. She bowed her head and cupped her coffee in both hands. I sat down across from her. After a long while, without looking up, she said, quietly, "Dr. Morgan is dead. If it wasn't for this screwed up insistence on physical perfection, he'd be alive today."

"Tell me exactly how you know that," I said as calmly as I could and in my best judicial voice. She was frayed around the edges, about to fall apart. I needed the information before she cracked completely. I hoped her courtroom training would keep her together until she got it out. She spoke so quietly, and her voice trembled so much, that I could barely hear her over the quiet humming noise of the rotating ceiling fan. She had her head buried in her arms so I couldn't see her face.

"On Friday, after you left me, I went to his house. He wasn't there. He hadn't been there for well over a month. The newspapers were stacked up on the porch and the cat's litter box was overflowing. The cat looked starved. I took him to a vet."

I skipped the lie she'd told about not knowing where Dr. Morgan lived, but it confirmed my suspicions about how many other lies she'd told me. "How do you know the litter box was full and the cat hadn't been fed?"

"I went in, of course. I looked around. The place had been trashed." She looked right at me, turned her lips up at the corners in a rueful smile; her hands were shaking, sloshing the sickly green coffee over the sides of the cup. "I don't think the cat did it. Drawers were pulled out, papers scattered all over. Just like on television. Someone slashed all of the sofa pillows and the mattresses. There was no computer in the apartment at all and all the books were on the floor. I don't know what they were looking for, but I don't think they found it."

She set the cup down in the spreading puddle of green coffee, continuing to hold the cup. She lowered her head again. I didn't know if I should wait to hear more or ask a question. After a long time, she looked up and there were tears streaming down her cheeks. Her lip was quivering, her nose red and running.

"I found b-blood and b-brains all over the k-kitchen." She broke down completely. She was hysterical, sobbing uncontrollably, keening as if Dr. Morgan was here in the kitchen with us and she'd just seen him. I went around to her and held her, but she was sobbing hard enough to shake both of us. George came to the doorway, arched one eyebrow at me and I nodded him in.

"Help me get her into the bedroom please, and bring me a Valium from the medicine cabinet." Calmly. Trying not to let her know I'd like to be falling apart, too. She had been such a bubbly child. How did she get like this?

George went to get the Valium and water. I gave it to Carly and we helped her back to bed. She'd calmed down some and I sat with her while she either passed out or went to sleep, I'm not sure which. I closed the door to her room and went out on the veranda, where George was waiting. It was early for drinking, but he'd poured both of us a Sapphire and tonic. I took mine with a twist of lemon and without a twinge of remorse. Three gulps later, I got up for a refill.

"Now, Willa, suppose you tell me exactly what's going on here," George said, "And I'm not kidding around."

It was perfectly okay with me. I'd never seen a murder scene and I was pretty sure Carly never had either. Just hearing Carly describe it shook me up. I have a very vivid imagination. I see movies in my head when I think and just her description was enough. Besides that, now she'd have to go to the police and I wasn't sure exactly how to convince her to do it. If she wouldn't, I'd have to do it myself and then there'd be all kinds of hell to pay, with Kate and the CJ for starters. Before, I only suspected a crime had been committed. Now I knew for sure. I'd taken an oath to uphold the law, and I had to do it or face the consequences. I hoped George would have some insight.

We talked for a long time, about Carly and her predicament, and about mine. We poked and prodded the problem, looked at it from all the angles. There was just no way around it in the end. One of us would have to go to Chief Hathaway. I didn't want it to be me, and Carly obviously didn't want it to be her. I knew what my reasons were, but I wasn't clear on hers. If we'd had a different relationship, I might have told the CJ. As it was, I was hoping he'd never find out I was involved. It would be just one more thing for him to ride me about. George and I agreed the only thing we could do was to try to persuade Carly to call Chief Hathaway when she woke up. If she wouldn't, then I had some tough choices to make.

After we finished our third gin, it seemed important to get more facts from another source before pressuring Carly, as I fully intended to do. She'd lied to me at least once that I knew of, and I couldn't trust the rest of her story. There was no way I was going to get any deeper into this; I was afraid of walking right into the middle of something worse that neither Carly nor I could control.

It could be that Michael Morgan's death, if he was dead, had nothing to do with this breast implant business, but the chances of that were really slim. When the largest breast implant manufacturer went into bankruptcy a couple of years ago, I remembered reading in the *Tampa Today Business Journal* that several of the law firms in town had financed the costs of breast implant litigation. One of them was my former firm, some of my former partners having gone over to the "other side" representing women with implants.

I called Mitchell and asked him to meet me for a drink here at Minaret this afternoon. Although he said he was surprised to hear from me since I had canceled our weekly golf game, he agreed to come. If you're a lawyer in a small town, it's not wise to ignore the summons of a judge, even though it may be a purely social call. Knowing this, I try not to use the advantage too often. This was one of those times when it was necessary.

I was waiting for Mitch in the Sunset Bar and when he arrived, I suggested that we take our drinks to a secluded table. The bar was deserted, so I didn't expect any interruptions. The last thing I needed was to be overheard discussing the very cases I'm supposed to be presiding over. I had recused myself from all of my former firm's cases, so it wasn't technically a breach of ethics to talk to Mitch about it generally. Nevertheless, I didn't want to have to explain myself to anyone on the issue, particularly the CJ, who is always looking for something to complain about where I'm concerned. Anyway, if I didn't get this worked out, I was going to have a lot more to explain. Private conversations on privileged matters would be the least of my worries.

"Mitch, didn't I read that your firm is very involved in representing plaintiffs in breast implant cases?"

"Why, Judge, do you want to file a claim?" He eyed my chest speculatively, but with a smile, hoping I wouldn't be offended. He was wrong. I would never look at some man's crotch and suggest anything about the size of the bulge, at least not to him.

"Fortunately, no. I am looking for some information, though, and I was hoping you'd just give it to me voluntarily."

"Well, it's not a secret. Of course, we don't have as many cases as Christian Grover. But he advertised on a billboard and in *The*

Tribune for months, so he got a lot more calls than we did. Besides that, his partner Fred Johnson, seems to have some inside track on the Morgan cases. Morgan was the hardest working plastic surgeon in town where breast implants were concerned. I've heard estimates as high as forty-five thousand surgeries he did. He claims to have made $35,000 a day doing implants in the eighties. We only took what we could get that we thought were sure winners."

"How many cases does Grover have?"

"There's no real way of knowing that. He brags at bar meetings that he's got three-thousand-five-hundred plaintiffs, not including Johnson's cases."

"Really? I had no idea Grover represented so many women."

"Oh, sure. We have about two-hundred clients, all referred by other lawyers. Grover got most of his cases directly through advertising, but he got a lot of referrals, too."

"Why would one plaintiffs' attorney want to refer cases to another?"

"Well, the thinking is that a particular plaintiff's attorney will learn the science and make it his business to become experienced in handling the cases so that he can maximize the value of each claim. The referring attorney then gets a percentage of the final fee. It's done all the time."

"Doesn't it get expensive to advance costs for all of those claims?" I imagined piles of dollars looking like the ransom money for one of the Rockefellers.

"Yes, in the beginning it was less expensive because the manufacturers were paying to remove the implants. Now, most of them refuse and the insurance carriers won't pay, either. So, if your client wants to be explanted, which improves her case, you have to make a decision about advancing the costs. It can be as much as $5,000 a case."

"Do you mean to say that Grover and Johnson can have as much as $1.5 million in costs in these cases?" I was incredulous. Tampa isn't Los Angeles. A million dollars is still a rare commodity here.

"Actually, they could have more. That would just be the price of the removal surgery for each woman. There's the cost of experts, getting documents and all the other trial preparation stuff. My firm alone has over $300,000 invested in these cases, and we're a relatively small player. I've heard stories that some of the Texas lawyers are putting out over a million dollars a month."

"How can they afford that?"

He smiled. "Everything's bigger in Texas." Since I didn't return his smile, he said, "I can't speak for anyone else, but frankly, we can't afford it. We took out lines of credit and loans with the local banks when we thought the cases would only last a year or so. Now, it's been going on for years and the interest payments alone are staggering." He drained his glass and I offered him another. He got up to get a beer from the bar for himself and Perrier for me. When he came back with the drinks, I'd had time to consider what he'd said. The mathematics were easy, but it was a hell of a way to gamble.

"What will you do?"

"Fortunately, our firm is well-funded. We've had our big successes over the years and we only accepted a limited number of cases. It's not a real problem for us." Sounded like wishful thinking to me, and I was not surprised when he continued a little more subdued. "Although we've all been taking home smaller incomes the past couple of years."

He said this as if it were an afterthought. I was embarrassed for him. He was obviously trying to put the best face on it, but money must have been tight. Another thing I hadn't noticed. Maybe Kate is right and I do spend too much time wrapped up in my own world, oblivious to others.

After a few moments of silence, he said, "I hear, though, that Grover is really having a problem. He not only borrowed enough money to fund his cases, but he also has been living off the anticipated settlements, which have just not happened as quickly as we all thought. They may not happen at all."

"He always seems to be fine to me."

He nodded and lifted one shoulder briefly. "The funny thing is that Johnson seems to be flush with cash all the time. I don't know what their financial arrangements are, but it's odd that one partner would be doing fine and the other struggling, when they're both handling the same files."

I thought about it, sipping my Perrier around the lemon wedge. Something was tickling my brain, elusive, but present. I let it go, and it boomeranged back.

"What do you mean, the settlement may not happen at all?"

"Well, in the beginning, when these cases were first filed, the science was unclear and it appeared that the plaintiffs had the better end of the argument because of the common sense approach, you know, 'where there's smoke there's fire'." George had said almost the identical words a few days earlier. Maybe he reads things other than the financial pages, after all.

"And now?" I asked him.

"Well, now scientific study after scientific study is coming out on the side of the safety of the implants. Just like the manufacturers said all along. Even though we can prove they didn't properly test the product, it's becoming more and more difficult to prove that these implants cause any adverse health effects."

"This makes no sense. The last time I looked, causation was an essential part of any plaintiff's case. If you can't prove causation, why haven't all of the cases been dismissed?"

He grinned again, kind of lopsided this time and lifted his glass. "It's the American way. There's still enough evidence to get the cases to the jury. As long as there's no definitive proof that the illnesses these women are suffering are caused by something other than their implants, then the cases still go to the jury and the juries are still sympathetic enough to award damages to the victims in the most severe cases."

Mitch's face changed. He set his drink aside and crossed his hands on the table between us. How sincere he can look when he wants to, I thought. No wonder juries have been so sympathetic to him, giving his clients whatever he asks for.

Mitch said earnestly, "What I'm curious about is why you asked me over here on a Saturday afternoon to talk about this when we could have discussed it any Saturday morning. What I'm telling you is public knowledge, and I'm sure you're going to get most of it from that *Jones* case you're trying right now. Why the rush?"

A legitimate question I'd been waiting for but didn't intend to answer. "It doesn't have anything to do with the *Jones* case, Mitch, but that's all I can say. I do appreciate your coming over on such short notice and filling me in, though. How's Annie and the kids?" Such an obvious change of subject; he got the point.

Mitch graciously let the matter drop, and we talked about his family awhile before he said he needed to get home for dinner. I thanked him for his advice and wished him luck with his financing.

When I went back upstairs to talk to Carly, she was nowhere to be found. I searched the remainder of the house, the restaurant and the grounds. Her clothes were gone and when I got outside, her car was gone. She had to have left while I was talking with Mitch. Déjà vu, dammit. This is just great. Now what? People think I have no patience, but really, I'm just patient for such a long time that when I finally lose it, they're surprised. I mean, really, wasn't more than twenty years of patience with Carly enough already?

I didn't bother running as I went down the stairs out into the parking lot. I asked the valet if he had seen Carly. He said she had run out to her car and sped off across the bridge about fifteen minutes earlier. Again, I had no idea where she'd gone or how to find her. I went back upstairs and tried the cellular phone in her car, her office, and her house, all with no luck.

These disappearing acts were really beginning to make me angry. Besides that, I hadn't had a chance to persuade her to go to the police. Now what was I supposed to do? It would serve her right if I just called Hathaway and turned it all over to him.

Old habits die hard. So I let it sit through the weekend, and give Carly one more last chance to come back, go to the police, or do something to report what she'd seen. If she didn't do it, I would have to. I picked up some distractions, a glass of iced tea, the Friday *Times* I hadn't had the energy to read yesterday afternoon, and Saturday's *Tribune*, and took them out onto the veranda to try my mind control theory: think about something else. It worked briefly until page three of the *Times*, below the fold, the mention of Morgan's name caught my eye.

Dr. Michael Morgan's friends and colleagues have been cooperating with Tampa Police in an effort to locate Dr. Morgan, missing for over a month. Yesterday, one of the neighbors reported sighting a woman entering Dr. Morgan's house by the side door. When he was unable to locate the woman, Chief Ben Hathaway obtained a search warrant for Dr. Morgan's home today. Although details of the search have not been released, Chief Hathaway said that he now suspects foul play.

I dropped the rest of the *Times* and picked up Saturday's *Tribune*, searching all the pages in the first section until I found another small item.

Limited details of the disappearance of Dr. Michael Morgan were released to the press today in a news conference by Chief Ben Hathaway. Chief Hathaway said in a prepared statement: "We are trying to identify a dark four door sedan, possibly a Lincoln Town Car or a Cadillac, seen by a neighbor outside Dr. Morgan's home three weeks ago. We are now treating Dr. Morgan's disappearance as a homicide. We believe Dr. Morgan's body was in the car. We identified tire tracks on the grass near the side door of Dr. Morgan's house."

An eyewitness came forward yesterday. Chief Benjamin Hathaway told reporters that the witness saw the car, saw its lights go on and saw it drive away. Chief Hathaway told reporters that Dr. Morgan's home contained evidence relating his disappearance to homicide.

"We found evidence of a struggle, blood soaked tile and other physical evidence consistent with homicide."

It was getting more and more difficult to protect Carly, not to mention me. George and I struggled with the issues most of the night. We didn't get to bed until 3:00 a.m., and we were no closer to a decision on what to do. I wondered what other careers I might like all through the sleepless night, but I could only see the down sides to all of them.

CHAPTER SEVENTEEN

Tampa, Florida
Sunday 5:30 a.m.
January 17, 1999

IT WASN'T HARD TO get up for my golf game with Dr. Aymes Sunday morning since I never went to sleep. I was in no mood to play, but it was way too late to cancel. George was more fortunate; he was snoring softly when I crept out of the bedroom. I snatched the Sunday papers off the front porch and searched for further news of Dr. Morgan. I didn't have to look far. While the disappearance of a once prominent surgeon may not command front page coverage, his death did, although still below the fold.

No closer to solving the mysterious disappearance of Dr. Michael Morgan, Police Chief Ben Hathaway released further details of the investigation Saturday. He said police found Dr. Morgan's scheduling notebook inside his home and are in the process of interviewing everyone with whom Dr. Morgan had contact in the weeks before his disappearance. Because there are

no signs of forced entry or burglary, police believe Dr. Morgan
may have been killed by someone he knew.

And maybe someone we all know, I thought. The rest of the
article repeated the information printed in the earlier stories.
Incredibly, there was no link, and no speculation, connecting
Morgan's disappearance with the unidentified body. How could
they be so dense? Wasn't it obvious to everyone? The timing, the
disappearance, the homicide? It just didn't make sense to me and
I couldn't figure it out. But George wasn't up yet so I could
discuss it with him, and the dogs are good listeners but
somewhat short on analytical ability. I couldn't wait any longer.
I left the paper propped by the coffee pot and dashed out to Great
Oaks.

You know you're playing with serious golfers when they
have a 6:30 tee time on Sunday. Only a serious player gets on the
course at prime time. I was paired with Dr. Aymes. The other
two golfers were Grover's partner, Fred Johnson, and another
doctor I didn't know. We walked up to the first tee promptly at
6:30 and the men were 240 yards down the first fairway four
minutes later.

I thought Dr. Aymes was just being snide when she said my
ten handicap was high for the group. She wasn't. These golfers
were going to end up waiting for me, and it put me at an
immediate disadvantage. It wasn't until later that I figured out
she had deliberately invited me knowing I wouldn't be able to
compete, even if I'd had a clear head for the game. In my
present state, I was about to get killed. On the golf course, that
is.

Marilee hit her first drive from the blue tee about 220 yards.
I held my head high, hit from the red tee, and landed just about
thirty yards behind her. We got into the cart and she drove.

"Nice shot, Willa. But if you want to play with the better golfers, you've got to shoot from the blue tees."

"Not today," I said.

"No guts, no glory."

"Maybe, but with this group, I'll be lucky if I can keep my head above water." My temples were starting to throb, a dull pounding resembling the beat of a Johnny Mathis tune. I put my sunglasses on as well as my visor. The dim pre dawn light was too much. I was just thrilled with the idea of bright, glaring sunshine in half an hour.

"Just hit 'em straight, and you'll beat these two. I always put them together because they end up in the woods and it saves time." I couldn't tell if she was being sarcastic or just being Marilee.

She zipped the cart over to my ball and we were off. I finished the hole with a double bogey and felt grateful. Marilee missed a par by a five foot putt.

By the third hole, Marilee had me laughing with her outrageous commentary, and I'd decided her sharp wit wasn't meant to be malicious. My headache was a slow Bob Seeger tune by this time, but rock 'n roll suits me better anyway. "Who's your usual partner, Marilee?"

"Michael Morgan. But he hasn't played in a month."

"Why not?"

"He's out of town or something. I haven't heard from him. And his substitute is Carolyn Young, but she couldn't make it today."

"Why not?" I felt like a parrot.

"I don't know. When I called her, she just said she couldn't play."

This was an opportunity too convenient to pass up, and I was glad I hadn't just called and canceled. I asked her, feigning nonchalance, how she knew Dr. Morgan and Dr. Young.

"We were all at various stages of our practice at UCF about fifteen years ago. We had a foursome including Dr. Zimmer going on then."

"I had no idea you all knew each other so well." Even in my weakened state, I silently blessed the concept of synchronicity. Maybe I'd become a believer yet. Somewhat like Dorothy on her return trip from Oz, I began to repeat to myself, "There are no coincidences in life, there are no..."

"We were all close until Carolyn stole my project. Then, I stopped talking to them for ten years. Mike wormed his way into this foursome and then Carolyn started coming. When she plays, I play with Johnson. I certainly couldn't spend two hours in a golf cart with her."

"What did she steal from you?"

"The whole thing. Everything they used to start MedPro. The idea, the grant prospect. All of it."

She tried to act like this was ancient history, but I could tell she was still bitter about it. "We were close once, Carolyn and I. We shared an apartment and we both worked in the research department at UCF. She was younger than I, and she always seemed so vulnerable, somehow. I tried to take care of her, I guess. It was my idea to concentrate on a more responsive gel. I had a grant prospect I thought I could sell to UCF and I was putting together a proposal. It's up to a tenured professor to find enough money to pay at least sixty percent of her salary, so it was an important prospect to me. It would have covered my salary for three years. I was excited, so I told her about it and she stole it. As simple as that."

We were on the fifth hole by this time. It's a long hole, but it dog legs to the right, and I was trying to figure out which club to hit off the tee for the best position on my second shot.

"Try your three wood," Marilee said. "Your driver will put you past the turn."

I pulled out my three, hit the ball way off to the left and cursed under my breath. "It works better if you hit it straight," she smirked.

"Thanks for the tip." I said, with as much sarcasm as I dared, as she walked up to the tee.

"Carolyn Young never had an original thought in her life." The venom in her words might not have sent the ball that extra twenty yards, but if the ball had been Carolyn Young's head, she'd be in the next county. If it had been my head, at least this damn pounding wouldn't be connected to my body any more.

Marilee must have read my thoughts. "That's how I improved my game. Every time I stepped up to the tee, I imagined Young, Morgan or Zimmer's head instead of the ball. Improved my drives two-hundred percent."

On the way back to the cart, I asked her, "How did Carolyn Young steal your project?"

"She told Morgan and Zimmer that she had done the work. She batted her eyes, swished her hips." Marilee jiggled her behind back and forth exaggeratedly as she walked. "Then she screwed Zimmer, so they believed her. He was the leader of our little foursome then because he was the oldest. She didn't care that he was married and had five kids." She waited for me to get my ball out of the rough before driving us over to hers, lying right in the fairway, a straight 250 yards from the green. She hit a three iron and the ball fell about seventy-five yards short.

"Carolyn convinced Zimmer, and Morgan followed along.

She gave them all my written work, which she stole off my desk one night when I was out at the lab."

"Why didn't you just tell them it was yours?"

"I did. They thought I was just jealous. They knew she was brilliant and her mother had been diagnosed with breast cancer. Her mother needed an implant. They believed Carolyn had extra motivation. That she'd worked on the idea night and day. Hah!" She hit her ball within two feet of the cup, then walked back to where I was standing and waited for me to make it to the green.

She seemed to want to talk about it, so she just kept pouring out the story. "Later on, I actually started to play with them so I would win every week. We bet. High stakes. I always win," she said as she sank the putt easily for an eagle making her five under par for the first five holes.

"What about Johnson? When did he come into the picture?" I set up for my putt, squatting down to visualize the line perpendicular to the hole.

"Zimmer had a heart attack last year. Scared him and Matildy. I guess he stared mortality in the face and decided an old grudge match was not the way he wanted to end his days. So he quit. Morgan brought Johnson into the group."

"Was that okay with you?" I tapped the ball lightly, but the green was fast and I over played the hole. Another two putt. At this rate, I'd be lucky to finish last even if the headache didn't finish me first.

"It's a good news/bad news story. The good thing about Johnson is he loses as gracefully as the rest of them do. The bad thing is he's a lousy golfer, although he's better than you." She just couldn't resist. "And he's a less pleasant s.o.b. to be around. He's especially offensive to Morgan. I don't know why Morgan doesn't tell him to kiss off. I've considered it a couple of times myself."

We finished the game in record time. I don't think I've ever played with such a competitive group. My score wasn't worth mentioning when they all settled up at the nineteenth hole. The day's entertainment would have cost me two-thousand dollars, but they made it a gift since I hadn't known the rules in advance. The shock killed my headache and I went home, wiser in every respect.

George wasn't at home when I got there, so instead of just brooding about Carly and Dr. Morgan, I did something a little more productive. I went upstairs into the den and sat down at the desk where Aunt Minnie had done her household accounts as a young bride. It was a partner's desk; one person could sit at either side and both could work in the middle.

I took out the ubiquitous yellow legal pad and wrote down everything Carly had told me, and everything else I had surmised or discovered about Dr. Morgan's death in the past few days. I put each separate fact on a separate sheet of paper. For each fact, I listed everything I'd like to know about it to determine if it had any significance. I had acquired quite a bit of information, most of it useless. I noticed that I was now calling it Dr. Morgan's death, even though I still didn't know for sure that he was dead. I told you I was no scientist.

I had a lot more questions than answers, but I found some glaring discrepancies, too. Not the least of which was that I knew Carly hadn't told me everything and I didn't know why. She was worried about something, and emotionally keyed up over the whole thing to a much greater degree than I would have expected.

I was still writing, considering and analyzing when George came in with Harry and Bess. They let me know they were feeling neglected, so I put aside my work and we all went for a long walk and then a little afternoon delight, you should pardon the pun.

After that, I turned it all over to my subconscious, fell into a deep and blissfully untroubled sleep until early evening.

George and I were going to the Florida Orchestra with Bill and Betty Sheffield, meeting them just before the baton was raised at 7:30 at the Performing Arts Center. I still had to hustle to get showered and changed, but George was already dressed and ready to go.

I apologized for missing the cocktail hour, and told him I might have time for a quick glass of wine in the car, but George wanted to drive instead of getting a driver, so I left him to drink alone while I finished getting dressed. I quickly did my makeup and was just slipping on my jade silk jumpsuit when George called to me that it was 7:00 and we needed to get moving.

I selected my pearls and black satin sandals to complete the look. Bright red lipstick seemed too flashy somehow, so I selected a deeper wine color, threw a few things into my evening bag and dashed downstairs. George drove the Bentley and we arrived just in time to use the valet and find our seats before the program began. Bill and Betty were already seated. We whispered hello and then fell silent for the program.

At intermission, Betty went toward the ladies' room and the rest of us headed outside so Bill could have a cigarette. As we walked out, Bill asked George how his investments were coming and they began to discuss the risks and benefits of technology stocks during the current bull market. I practiced the art of appearing to listen, and allowed my mind to wander until the mention of MedPro brought my attention sharply back to the conversation. When I tuned in, Bill was still attempting to convince George of the merits of investing in emerging medical products manufacturing companies.

"Which companies do you think are the best buys?" I asked, surprising both men by my sudden interest.

"Well, pacemakers are and will likely continue to be a successful medical product. But the problems they've had with lead failures make investing in those companies risky. I think you need to consider companies that blend medical technology with geriatric science. The graying of America is big business and will continue to be for the next several decades. If you can find a company that makes products used in the health care of elderly patients, and by elderly I mean fifty-five and over, assuming the company is well managed and not under-capitalized, it should be a sure winner." Like all investment types, Bill talked like the opinion column of the paper's financial section. If you zoned out a second, you'd be hopelessly lost.

"I'm interested primarily in the local economy, Bill," I said. "Are there any companies that make geriatric medical products here?"

Bill looked at me quizzically, too polite to suggest that this was the subject of the conversation I had not been listening to, even though I had pretended I was.

"Well, as I was telling George, I think there are three or four companies like that around here. I've invested a lot of money for our depositors in both Nations' Health Corp. and MedPro in the last six months. The stock has been rising steadily and I've even been able to take profits a few times. Those would be my choices but there are others." He'd finished his first cigarette and lit another off the smoldering butt before he flicked it out into the street.

"Well, George is the trader in our family, but I might be interested in some information on that." Carly hadn't mentioned that MedPro's stock was rising.

"Well, sure. What about if I have my secretary drop the information in the mail to you tomorrow?" I assured him that would be fine, then we heard the chimes indicating the orchestra was about to begin the remainder of the program. We walked back inside and George gave me his "what are you up to" look; puzzled but not concerned. I was hoping he'd stay that way. I was beginning to get an idea about MedPro and Dr. Morgan and I didn't want to have to explain it just yet. It needed time to germinate.

As we were walking back to our seats, Victoria Warwick walked up behind me. "Willa, darling," she said, in a mock whisper, "I hear you've been asking Pricilla Worthington about my personal life. The next time you want to know something, just ask me. A woman with as many secrets as Cilla shouldn't be speculating on the lives of others."

I must have looked mystified that Tory knew about that conversation; I was sure Cilla wouldn't have told her. "Servants, darling. They know everything. Don't ever get any." And she walked on past us closer to the front of the theater.

When we got home, George went down to check on the restaurant and we spent the rest of the evening quietly, upstairs. I told him what Tory Warwick had said to me at intermission.

"Maybe you should go talk to Tory and find out just what some of those secrets are, Willa. It could be important. Tory might be erratic, but she's well informed."

What an understatement that turned out to be.

CHAPTER EIGHTEEN

Tampa, Florida
Monday 9:45 a.m.
January 18, 1999

THE MORNING DELIVERED ONE of those gloriously convenient federal holidays providing us government workers a Monday off: Martin Luther King Day. I spent the morning puttering around the house trying to put the whole Morgan mess out of my mind to give my subconscious a chance to sort it through. But no matter what I tried to concentrate on instead, I couldn't get it off my mind. Of course, this line of thinking brought me right back to the Carly problem.

Not knowing what else to do, I felt I had no choice but to follow what George and I had decided was the only available Plan B, particularly now that Morgan's disappearance was being treated as homicide. It was what I should have done when she first told me about finding the body—I called the chief of police.

Chief Hathaway's secretary put me right through to him.

"Ben, Willa Carson here."

"Right."

"Any chance I can see you today?"

"I can come over to Minaret. You can buy me a coffee. Or you can come to the station and I'll buy you one."

"See you soon," I said. Lucky for me Tampa PD operates twenty-four-seven.

Called downstairs looking for George. Not so lucky this time. For a panicky moment I thought he might have gone looking for Carly. But George was much too level-headed to do that. Hopefully.

Should I call Kate before I caused bigger problems for Carly? Or leave Kate out of the loop? Plausible deniability was a good thing. I couldn't decide what was best.

My internal monologue on the issue resembled a child's seesaw. Procrastination is a wonderful thing. Chief Hathaway arrived before I'd made the decision.

I invited him into the living room. If I hadn't wanted to be seen talking with a breast implant plaintiff's attorney, I certainly didn't want it getting around that I was having quiet conversation with the Chief of Police.

Hathaway was a big man, not just tall but heavy. Yet, he had the agility of a ballerina, Jackie Gleason like. He looked around for a seat sturdy enough to accommodate his heavy frame. He finally chose the straight back Louis XVI chair directly across from the couch.

Offered him coffee, he accepted, and we exchanged pleasantries. I just couldn't seem to get started.

He must have had a lot of experience with reluctant informants because finally he said, "You know, I think this is the first time you've ever called on me professionally. I'm assuming there must be some very urgent reason for that."

For a moment, I worried I might be making a mistake.

Then I remembered Carly's description of Dr. Morgan's house and realized the police had already been there, after she was. They had her fingerprints already. Like all practicing lawyers, her prints were on file. If we came clean now, she might seem less guilty somehow.

Besides, in Carly's account there might be something the police had overlooked. The evidence might already be too old to be useful. Although some coroner could probably have figured it out, I wasn't too sure about our local talent. I told Ben everything Carly had told me. When I finished, he looked at me thoughtfully. After a time, he asked me a question I cursed myself for not expecting before I called him.

"How well do you know this woman?"

I said, "I've known her all her life. Why?"

"Well, let's be professional about this, shall we? She seems to have a lot of information about a murder. How reliable is she? Should we consider her a suspect?"

I don't know what came over me. My response was as cold as winter in Alaska and just as outrageous. "Ben Hathaway, there is no possibility that Carly murdered this man. I want you to put that thought out of your mind right now. If you persist in pursuing her as a suspect, I will personally issue a restraining order against you."

He flinched. But his response was controlled. "If you did that, Judge Carson, it would be a gross abuse of your judicial authority. There's a limit to your power."

I waited.

More reasonably, he said, "Interfering with the investigation of a crime was enough to bring down Richard Nixon. It's not something you want to get involved with."

"Maybe so," I replied, unable to back off. "But, I'll do it nevertheless."

We stared each other down for a few minutes. Whether he concluded I would be true to my word and tie him up in red tape for a month, or simply recognized we wouldn't get anywhere tonight by testing me, I don't know.

He adopted a much more conciliatory tone. "Okay, let's abandon that line of thinking for now. But consider this: If she's not involved now, she soon may be."

"What do you mean?"

"You said she'd been talking to Dr. Morgan regularly before he disappeared. Then, you told me that when she went to his home, someone had searched it. If they found what they were looking for, and then killed him, you better hope what they found didn't implicate your little rabbit. As near as I can tell, just about every woman 'of a certain age' in Tampa would have a motive to kill him, not to mention their husbands. And that doesn't even count the business enemies." He ticked off the possibilities like reading a grocery list. No one was above suspicion as far as he was concerned.

"Well obviously, that makes it that much more important that you find Carly, and that you find out immediately if Dr. Morgan is the body in the water and, if he's not, where he is and who is after him."

"I don't need you to tell me how to do my job," Hathaway snapped at me. "I've been doing this a lot longer than you've been a judge. If you'll just keep your nose out of it, I'll take care of my end. If you think of anything else that might be helpful, call me and talk only to me. Here's my private line." He threw his business card down on the coffee table between us. "And then you better spend some time finding your friend a good criminal lawyer. She's going to need it. If she doesn't end up dead first."

He walked out. I refused to go after him, and I was more than a little annoyed at the arrogant way he treated me. But I was scared, too. He was right to be pissed off that I had knowledge of a potential crime and, as far as he knew, hadn't advised the police. On the other hand, Carly certainly did not kill Dr. Morgan and, if he focused his energies on making her the murderer, he wouldn't be finding Morgan's real killer. If Morgan was dead. I kept hoping he wasn't.

Come to that, how many missing persons reports would he have to consider when he was looking for the identity of a dead body, anyway? There can't be that many people disappearing from the city of Tampa without a trace.

I had one of those "ah ha" moments Kate's always talking about: I realized there was no information on Morgan's identity in the press before Carly went to the house because Hathaway knew who the body was. Morgan didn't have any relatives to notify, so they felt comfortable keeping it quiet, waiting for someone to do just what I did. Identify him.

Hathaway must have believed that the killer would be more likely to make mistakes the longer it looked like the police hadn't identified the body. Now, I had given them Carly and confessed that I'd known about Morgan for two weeks. Carly and I might not need a lawyer, but we needed advice from someone who was thinking a lot clearer than George and I were. I decided to talk to a criminal lawyer tomorrow. In the meantime, I picked up the phone and called Kate. It was time to come clean with her. She wasn't home and I got her machine. Shit! Doesn't anybody ever answer their telephone anymore?

I had to find Carly before Hathaway did and persuade her to

tell the rest of what she knew. One thing I agreed with Hathaway about; she hadn't come clean with me on her conversations with Morgan and what they had been working on together. Whatever it was, it was enough to get Morgan killed and Carly might be next. Carly's real motivation for keeping her conversations with Morgan secret should have occurred to me, but it didn't. Not for a while, anyway.

I put on my running shoes and got my car keys. I went down the stairs two at a time, racing (decorously, of course) toward my car. I knew where the spare key to Carly's apartment was and I would start there. She lives in a gated community and I wasn't sure I'd be able to get in without her consent. A year or so ago I was listed on her limited access list, and I hoped she hadn't changed it. I needed to get to her apartment before Hathaway got there. I knew he would dispatch officers immediately, as soon as he figured out where she lived. He'd left in such a rage he hadn't asked me, and the way he had behaved, I wasn't sure I would have told him.

I drove my car about twenty-five miles an hour over the speed limit all the way from Minaret to Carly's apartment complex in St. Pete Beach. It's a 25-minute drive under normal conditions, and I made it in fifteen. Because St. Petersburg is outside Hathaway's jurisdiction, I was hoping that it would take more than fifteen minutes to get a police car dispatched to Carly's home, even if he could immediately locate the address.

As I pulled up into the guard station at the entrance to her complex, there were four cars in line ahead of me in the one lane driveway. I watched as the security guard talked to the driver of the first car. They were having a friendly chat about the weather, or the last Devil Rays baseball game at the Tropicana Dome or something. What seemed like an hour, and was probably no more than three minutes, passed while the security guard wrote out a visitor's pass for the car and allowed it through the gate.

All of us inched up one car length. The routine was repeated with the second car, and then the third. By this time, I'd waited in line longer than it took me to drive there. Finally, finally, finally, the security guard approached my car. "Good afternoon, ma'am," he said. "How are you today?"

I swallowed my impatience. Everyone else seemed to be on island time, so I tried to fit in by appearing laid back. I don't think he could see my toes tapping, but I'm not sure. "Fine, thank you. I'm here to see Carly Austin. I think I'm on her access list. Please don't call up. It's her birthday and I want to surprise her." I smiled my brightest smile, flirting with him a little. How old was I when I figured out that older men are easily manipulated by a woman who flirts?

"And what's your name, miss? I'll just look it up quickly and then I can let you in," he said with a big, conspiratorial smile. I gave him my name as I looked in my rear view mirror.

I could see no police cars, or at least no marked police cars, either behind me in line or coming up the driveway. There was a satisfyingly long line developing, and I was pretty sure that a police car would have the same difficulty getting through the gate I'd had. Once the cars had lined up at the guard shack, there was nowhere for them to go but through the gate into the complex. The cops would have to wait their turn like everybody else.

Eventually, the guard returned from the shack with my visitor's pass and a smile. He opened the gate and waived me through. He said, "Say happy birthday to Ms. Austin for me. I thought she was out of town. She's one of our most pleasant residents and I haven't seen her much lately."

"Thank you," I sang, smiling and wiggling my fingers at him as I went through the gate, watching the orange and white arm of the gate fall down behind my car.

I drove into the complex, looking all the while for a police car or uniformed police officers from Pinellas County or the City of St. Petersburg. I didn't see any.

When I got to Carly's apartment, I picked up the fake rock out of the planter next to the door. It was easy to find because the flowers hadn't been watered in so long they were all dead. I opened the hidden slide on the fake rock, pulled out what I hoped was the real key and let myself in. Carly's apartment complex was on a small peninsula that's particularly vulnerable to hurricanes. Because of the building codes, the garage was on the first floor and the apartment was one floor up. It's a town house style, and the stairway opens into a great room combination of living room, kitchen and dining room. In other words, once you got to the top of the stairs, there was no place to hide except the bedrooms and the closets. I started calling out to Carly as I walked up. I heard nothing. As I came up the stairs and looked into the great room, I could see that the guard was right. Although Carly hadn't been there for quite some time, someone else had been; it was impossible to tell how long ago.

Things were strewn everywhere. The furniture was upended and the fabric bottoms of the chairs and couch were sliced open. The throw cushions were thrown, all right, but they were sliced, too. I looked into the guest room, and the shambles was the same. Just the way Carly had described the search at Dr. Morgan's house. I opened the door to the master bedroom, still calling Carly's name. As soon as I walked in the door, I felt a bowling ball fall on my head. I hit the floor, just like a bowling pin. Strike. They all fall down.

When I woke up, it was dark outside. I tried to raise myself off the floor but the second I lifted my head, it began pounding the way Spielberg showed the footfalls of an approaching T-Rex and I felt nauseated. I lay back down, slowly, slowly, and the room stopped spinning. In fact, it felt so good to lie there, I took another nap.

The next time I woke up, faint daylight showed through the mini blinds. I knew I'd been there way too long. I was thinking well enough to understand that George would be worried sick about me and for some reason, no police officers had ever appeared. For that matter, neither had Carly.

I tried once again to get up by raising the top half of my body. No sudden moves this time. Nice and easy. I thought I was talking to myself, but I realized I didn't hear my voice. The thudding in my head sounded like Indian war drums and, while I still felt queasy, I thought I might be able to sit up. I tried it, gingerly, and had to wait a few minutes for the room to stop spinning. But I didn't throw up and I took that as a good sign.

I tried to stand and the magnitude of it nearly knocked me down again. I lay back down. I'd wait a few minutes, take it easy, look around. No hurry. After a while, I figured out that I wasn't too far from the bedside phone. I sort of scooched over there on my stomach so I didn't have to actually sit up. After three or four hours, I made it to the telephone. I lay back against the bed, exhausted. Maybe I'd just take another nap, then I'd have enough strength to move forward. That's not such a bad idea, right? No, better call George instead. He'll be worried. Just take several deep breaths and try to stop your hands from shaking so you can dial the phone, and then you can take a nap.

After a while, I was able to reach up and grab the phone. Thankfully, it was a model with the buttons in the receiver. I dialed Minaret first. Evie, the hostess, answered the phone with the voice she uses for callers making reservations. It must have been dusk, and not dawn. How wonderful. I had to clear my throat three times before I could speak.

"Evie." The first time it came out so softly. I didn't recognize my voice and I was sure Evie wouldn't either, even if she could hear me. I cleared my throat and tried again. "Evie."

I could hear her saying "Hello? Is anyone there?" over and over. I tried the third time.

"Evie." I shouted. My head started to vibrate again. My eyes were impersonating Niagra Falls. My voice must have been a mere whisper, but enough for Evie to catch it. I'm going to recommend to George that she get a raise, I thought.

"Evie, it's Willa. Get George. Now." I tried to put as much authority into my voice as I could, but I knew it didn't sound like me. To her credit, Evie didn't ask any more questions, she just asked me to hold on while she got George. A big raise.

After a few minutes, George came on the line. "Wil? Willa, is that you?" I heard him. I was so relieved. I acknowledged the tears leaking out of my eyes from the sheer effort of trying to avoid them. When I heard George, I began to cry harder. It was several moments before I could answer him. In the meantime, his voice was getting more frantic and he just kept repeating the same thing over and over. "Willa, is that you? Willa, is that you?" Finally, I managed to pull myself together enough to whisper/shout into the phone. "George, I'm at Carly's. Come get me. And call Ben Hathaway."

George kept trying to soothe me over the phone and find out if I'd been hurt. I just didn't have the strength to talk any more so I hung up. Then I lay down on the floor and went back to sleep.

The next time I woke up, George and two Tampa police officers were in the room. Ben Hathaway was there too. George was holding me, helping me to sit up, treating me like a china doll even though my body was behaving like a rag doll. I'm lucky to have George, I remember thinking. George always takes care of me.

Ben Hathaway wasn't interested in how I felt. "Why didn't you tell me where you were going? Why didn't you tell me where Carly lived? We've been trying to track down her home address ever since I left you yesterday!" Hathaway was truly angry. His yelling caused my head to pound harder and louder.

"Compound question," I said weakly as I laid my head on George's chest and closed my eyes. I don't know if they heard me or not. I couldn't say anything else. I heard George ask for an ambulance. When it came, we left.

The ambulance took me to General Hospital (really) where there were no obvious doctor/nurse affairs going on, but our good friend and family physician met us. They did a CT scan of my head and decided there was nothing wrong with it that two weeks rest and ten years of psychotherapy wouldn't help.

At my insistence, they released me into George's custody and we went home. By the time we got back to Minaret, it occurred to me that I had, for the first time in my short career as a judge, and my entire career as a lawyer, missed a scheduled day of trial. I was just too tired and too hurt to care. I didn't call the office or make any excuses. When we got back to Minaret, I fell into bed. George woke me every four hours to make sure I wasn't dead. I might as well have been; I didn't wake up again until the next day.

CHAPTER NINETEEN

Tampa, Florida
Wednesday 2:00 p.m.
January 20, 1999

BY THE NEXT AFTERNOON, I was thinking that in two more weeks I'd begin to feel like a human being. Never again would I believe those movies where the hero gets bopped on the head and jumps right back up for another round. They hadn't found whatever it was I'd been hit with in Carly's apartment, so I was still insisting on the bowling ball theory. If it wasn't a bowling ball, I don't ever want to be hit on the head with anything again.

George brought a tray to the bedroom with some fabulous consommé and fresh bread. Then, looking a little like a new colt with wobbly legs, I walked into the den and sat down. George seemed relieved I was up and about and eating. He made me hot tea and told me that he had called my office, told Margaret that I was ill and asked her to cancel the trial for the remainder of the week. The lawyers and their clients were angry but couldn't very well argue with the explanation. George called the CJ and explained that I had a bad fall and was being treated at home for a concussion. The CJ, true to form, was solicitous of my health. Although we have our little test of wills going, he would never admit to anyone that he wasn't able to control his own team.

Once George figured out that I was going to survive, he released his vivid anger. He went on for quite awhile, but I only tuned in to the last part. "Wilhelmina, what in the hell is wrong with you? Did it not occur to you that someone could go with you to Carly's apartment? Why didn't you tell me where you were going? I would have gone along."

"No, you wouldn't. You would have tried to talk me out of it, and you know it. You would have said, let Ben Hathaway handle it." I tried talking calmly the way I've seen television cops calm raving lunatics. It didn't seem to be working.

"So what if I had? That certainly would have been the more reasonable thing to do, anyway. If you'd done that, then whoever hit you might be in police custody now as opposed to you sitting there in that chair just barely able to move around." I can't remember a time when George had ever been so angry with me. In the seventeen years we've been married, we've had relatively few fights. The ones we have had were almost always over my personal safety. I knew his reaction stemmed from concern for me, but it made me bristle nonetheless.

"George Carson, you can just stop trying to boss me around. I don't do what you want me to do or what you say I should, and you know it. I make my own decisions."

"And a fine one this was." He stomped out of the room, leaving me and my pride to deal with my pounding head, which had returned with the shouting. I sank back on the pillows and closed my eyes.

After he left me with my dignity intact, I had to admit to

myself that he might have been right. Unless it was Carly who hit me, which I couldn't believe. And then I realized that I'd heard nothing about Carly or where she was and I didn't know if anyone else had heard from her. I still wasn't strong enough to get up and walk after George, but I could reach the phone.

I called Hathaway. This time, when I asked to be connected, his secretary said he was out of the office. I told her Judge Carson was calling and asked him to call me back. She said she'd give him the message. I had the impression that he'd left standing orders with her that he wasn't to be bothered by Judge Carson. Ben can be so pouty.

I tried reaching Carly at home and at the office, and I tried again to call her car phone. As before, no answer, no answer and no answer. Then, it occurred to me to check my voice mail. When I did, there was a message from Carly. Technology is so wonderful.

She'd left the message on Monday morning. Her voice sounded normal, which made me think she'd called from work where she believed her activities were constantly monitored. "Willa, I wanted to let you know that I'll be going to Minneapolis for a few days and not to worry about me. I'll be checking my voice mail, so leave me a message if you need to reach me."

I replayed it three times because I couldn't believe she hadn't said anything more, and then I saved it so I could hear it again later if I needed to. I hung up the phone softly and tried to think logically about why Carly would be traveling to Minneapolis and when she would be back.

I saw that George had saved the newspapers the last two days and I picked them up to look through them. In this morning's paper, on the front page of the Florida Metro section, was a small article with a headline that read *Body Identified as Local Plastic Surgeon.*

Two columns, about four inches long, and after a few minutes I was able to focus my eyes well enough to read it.

The body discovered in Tampa Bay near the Sunshine Skyway Bridge two weeks ago was, in life, Dr. Michael Morgan, a local plastic surgeon.

The body, following autopsy, contained abnormally high levels of alcohol. Although it appeared Dr. Morgan was a victim of foul play, it also appeared that he was intoxicated at the time of death. He had been plagued in recent years by debts. His estate was valued at less than $10,000. He left several ex-wives, and no children.

Grover was interviewed. He was quoted as saying that he'd had no contact with Dr. Morgan since settling a 1990 malpractice case against Morgan, and he assumed Morgan was living a quiet life.

Chief Ben Hathaway was quoted as saying that the investigation into Dr. Morgan's death was ongoing and his department was pursuing several suspects.

A similar article appeared in the *Times.* In the *Times* obituary, many of Dr. Morgan's past accomplishments were listed. He had graduated from medical school at the age of twenty-five and then served his internship, residency and specialty residency all at the Mayo Clinic. He opened his practice in Tampa in 1970. He had been the plastic surgeon to Tampa's stars for several years until he succumbed to drug abuse. A series of malpractice claims followed, culminating in the case that caused him to surrender his license. Dr. Morgan was brilliant. He wrote several major articles and two textbooks. One of the textbooks, on immunology, had made him a millionaire. It was rumored that his will left the continuing royalties from his books to local lawyer Carly Austin. Certain specific bequests and the remainder of his assets went to charity. Ms. Austin had not been available for comment.

I shook my head and blinked several times to clear my blurred vision. That couldn't be right. He left royalties from his books, potentially millions of dollars, to Carly? I read it through twice more. I couldn't believe Carly knew she'd inherited from Morgan, but I knew someone would quickly misconnect the dots and draw a jail cell around Carly's body. I was getting in deeper and deeper. Even a good swimmer can drown if she's too far out in the Gulf.

Morgan's funeral was to be held the next day. Since the autopsy was completed and no family to notify, there was no reason to wait. A closed casket, obviously. We got there just before the service started.

Even though it was such short notice, and held in the middle of the week, the church was full. Nothing like the funeral of a locally notorious man murdered in his own home to bring out the curious and the faithful. Then there were the real mourners. Those were the ones I was interested in and why I had convinced George we should go even though I was far from back to normal.

"Michael Morgan may have been a good man at some time in his life, but by the time somebody killed him, he deserved it," Dr. Marilee Aymes said as she sat down in the pew beside me. George frowned his best at her, signifying his desire that she be quiet in church, but she was unfazed.

"He was a thief, and someone stole his life from him. Poetic justice," she said.

The curious couple seated in front of us apparently didn't have George's sense of respect for the dead. They turned around to see just who was making such vivid pronouncements. When they did, I saw she had perfect breasts.

I looked around the church more carefully. Almost every woman in the room was over fifty-five, long past the age for low necklines or see though tight-bodiced frocks. But there they were. Only Dr. Aymes and I and a few others didn't fit the profile, as it were.

"Look at all those perfect Morgans." Her voice, still loud, startled me.

"What?"

"Just look around. Have you ever seen so many perfect tits in one room? 'A pair of Morgans' we used to call them. We could always tell."

CHAPTER TWENTY

Tampa, Florida
Wednesday 3:15 p.m.
January 20, 1999

GEORGE GLARED HER INTO silence just as Dr. Carolyn Young walked by us. She was dressed head to toe in black and had a veil over her face. She walked up to the closed casket and knelt in front of it. From the back I could see her shoulders shaking. She stayed there so long one of the ushers went up to her and helped her to a seat in the front pew—the one usually reserved for family—which was empty.

It seemed all of Tampa society filled Sacred Heart Church for the occasion. Cilla and O'Connell Worthington were there, Fred Johnson, Christian Grover, Sheldon and Victoria Warwick, even Kate. Probably the first time that many Tampa WASPs had gathered in a Catholic Church since the mayor remarried ten years ago.

The priest who delivered the glowing eulogy was a young man who obviously hadn't known Dr. Morgan. If he knew anything about Morgan's less illustrious accomplishments, he refrained from mentioning them.

After the service, I watched a small group gathered outside around Carolyn Young at the bottom of the steps. "You'd think she was the only woman he ever screwed," Dr. Aymes said with disgust, "instead of just the last one."

"Carolyn Young and Michael Morgan were having an affair when he died?" I felt like the dim-witted straight man in a comedy team. Things everyone else took for granted kept coming as revelations to me. I took solace in the rumor that Tommy Smothers was the smart one.

"Willa, you've got to get out more. Carolyn Young was in love with him for years. Their affair was current, but her lust wasn't. In the old days, you had to stand in line to screw Michael Morgan. I'll bet he slept with every woman in that church." Dr. Aymes turned to look first straight at Kate and then pointedly toward Cilla Worthington.

Cilla hadn't heard the comment, and Kate returned Dr. Aymes' stare, although she blushed deep crimson. Then Kate looked away while Aymes was still staring at her.

"You're just trying to make me jealous, Marilee," George, ever the gentleman, said as he took first Kate's arm and then mine. He started down the steps, pulling us along. "But it's much too pretty a day to dwell on it." We dropped Kate off at home and then went back to Minaret.

Later in the day, I was in the den when I heard voices. I recognized George and I thought I recognized Chief Hathaway with him. I folded up the newspapers and turned on the television.

George and Ben came into the room and Ben seemed less angry with me than the last time I'd seen him. After asking me how I was feeling, Ben sat down in the same chair he'd taken last time and George offered to get us both some fresh coffee, leaving the two of us alone in the living room. Now, wasn't that convenient?

"I'll come right to the point. Someone trashed both Dr. Morgan's and Carly Austin's apartment, in the same way, obviously looking for the same thing. I don't think they found it. Dr. Morgan is dead, but Carly Austin isn't, which is not to say she won't be if I don't find her before the killer does. If you have any idea where she is, you need to let me know that so that I can keep her from getting killed." He spoke calmly, rationally, but not convincingly.

I looked at Hathaway closely. He's probably been a cop too long to betray his true intentions, and I wasn't at all sure whether I believed he was trying to help Carly or arrest her. I knew he was waiting for my analysis to conclude that even if he arrested her, she'd be better off than if her pursuer found her first. The wheels in my head were still turning, albeit slowly. Maybe I would live after all.

"She left a voice mail on my machine saying that she was going to Minnesota and she'd call me when she got back." I could see that this news caused him some serious agitation, but he was trying to control his temper. I didn't tell him I thought the message was another of Carly's lies.

"Look," I said, "Don't shoot the messenger. You asked me if I'd heard from her, I told you what I know. Don't you think I understand she's better off in jail than she is dead?"

I was really running out of patience with this guy. I didn't get to be a federal court judge at the age of thirty-six because I'm stupid. We might be out of each other's jurisdiction, but he certainly wasn't winning any points with me, either.

178 | DIANE CAPRI

"All right," he ran his hand over his head, through his thick, dark hair in obvious frustration. His hair looked like it was used to this treatment. It was wavy and constantly messed up. "What would she be going to Minnesota for? What's in Minnesota? Does she have family there, or did Dr. Morgan have family there? You know her. What's she doing?"

I thought I heard preaching in his voice. I hate it when people try to manipulate me. "Don't you think I've been asking myself that same question ever since I got the message? It might help if we knew what she and Dr. Morgan were talking to one another about. Have you been able to shed any light on that?"

Let's just put the burden back where it belongs, I thought. He didn't like it. He was having difficulty conducting a civil conversation. At that point, George walked back in and tried to diffuse the situation.

"Ben," George said, "I think she might have gone to the Mayo Clinic. I read in Dr. Morgan's obituary that he trained there. Carly doesn't have any connection with the Mayo Clinic and she didn't go for business, did she?"

"I checked with her boss. He said she hadn't been in to work in three days and it was most unlike her. He didn't know where she was, or at least he said he didn't. Your Mayo Clinic theory makes as much sense as anything else, George. I'll check it out." Hathaway got up to leave.

"Wait a minute," I said. "What about my question? Have you found out what she and Morgan were working on or why they were communicating with each other?"

He studied me for a long time. "Okay," he finally said. "The only thing that makes sense to me is that they were working on some aspect of this breast implant litigation. Her company, MedPro, derived about fifty percent of its revenue in the 1980s from the sale of breast implants. They've been selling them in Britain and France following the FDA moratorium here in this country. The lawsuits were threatening to put the company under. I think Dr. Morgan and Carly Austin were working on a strategy to defend the claims."

I let out a long breath of air I didn't realize I'd been holding. "Let's just suppose that's true, why would that have gotten him killed?"

Hathaway looked at me as if the rumors of my intelligence had been greatly exaggerated. "The first rule of police work, Wilhelmina—follow the money," he said as he walked out. I was beginning to hope that he found Carly soon because that would mean I could stop talking to him all together. Maybe forever. I made a mental note to take him off our guest list.

George apologized for getting angry earlier and I promised not to take any more chances with what he called facetiously, my "pretty little head." I had to laugh at that, and the laughter made my head hurt. George is the farthest thing from a chauvinist I've ever met.

After we had the coffee, I turned in for the night. Since he'd already canceled my trial for tomorrow, I'd take advantage of the break.

I skipped my run the next morning. I was beginning to feel closer to normal, but not up to pounding of any kind. I dressed in a denim shirt, chinos and my black Cole Haan flats and, after breakfast, drove myself to the office. Some federal district court judges have law clerks who act as chauffeurs, but I really enjoy driving Greta. I've been told she's too flashy for me to drive now that I'm on the bench. If you're from Detroit, cars are the essence of life itself. How could I give up Greta just for a job?

As I went over the bridge off Plant Key away from Minaret,

I turned right onto Bayshore heading toward downtown. I was impressed, as I always am, with the view. Hillsborough Bay, particularly along the Bayshore, is truly beautiful. Not many years ago, the Hillsborough River, the Bay and Tampa Bay were completely dead. After a massive cleanup campaign, fish, dolphins, rays and manatee are regularly spotted in all three waters. In fact, the Tampa Downtown Partnership sponsors an annual fishing tournament, giving prizes to the largest fish caught in the downtown area. Thankfully, there are fish to catch. You can eat them, too, if you're brave enough.

The drive down Bayshore, over the Platt Street Bridge, toward the Convention Center is one of my daily pleasures. I could feel my mood lightening and I actually felt better physically. Downtown Tampa, once a ghost town, is making a comeback. There is the one new office building at Jackson Street, Landmark Tower, where O'Connell Worthington has his offices. A series of storefronts and Sacred Heart Church makes up the four-block stretch to the Federal Building housing the federal courthouse. But on the other side of Platt Street, the Lightning play hockey in their new arena. A convention hotel is planned, Garrison Sea Port houses cruise ships and the Tampa Aquarium's glass dome lights the sky.

The Federal Building itself is circa 1920. In 1920, the Middle District of Florida was a much smaller place than it is now that what we Floridians affectionately call "the Black Rat" has moved into Orlando. The building is old, decrepit and much too small for the district's current needs. A new Federal Building is under construction, but for a while yet, we have to make do with small courtrooms and crowded conditions.

As the most junior judge on the bench, in terms of seniority, age and the CJ's affection, I have the least desirable location. It's the RHIP rule; I have no rank and no privilege. My courtroom and chambers are on the third floor, in the back. Getting there from the parking garage helps me keep my schoolgirl figure.

I pulled into my reserved spot and parked Greta illegally across two parking places. Building security got the meter maid to write me a ticket the first time they found my car parked like this, and I smiled remembering that I personally vacated it. I may have no rank with the CJ, but I certainly rank higher than a meter maid. This parking garage was built with the very minimum allowable tolerances. There is just no way I'm going to park Greta where she can be hit by other car doors. If the building loses revenue, they should have thought of that when they were marking off the spaces. If all the spaces were large enough to hold a Greyhound bus, we'd all have enough room, wouldn't we?

When I got to my office, there was still no word from Carly. I did some paperwork, and rescheduled the *Jones v. General Medics* case to start again tomorrow. Then I went home and went straight to bed.

The next morning, the hours dragged on interminably. My mind was definitely not on the trial and I kept thinking about where Carly could possibly be, when she would return, and whether she'd be dead or alive.

By the time I recessed the trial at 4:30, the inactivity was driving me crazy. Off the record, but in open court, I said "Mr. Grover, I want to see you in my chambers. Mr. Worthington, I represent to you that I don't want to discuss anything related to the case with him and I will not hear anything related to the case from him. If you want me to declare a mistrial and you can appeal this ex parte communication, all you have to do is ask."

I could see O'Connell's astonished face as I hurried off

the bench, while he shouted toward my back, "Judge, this is most irregular!" And Grover was simultaneously exclaiming, "Judge, you'll create reversible error in my trial." I ignored them both.

When Grover came into my chambers, I had removed my robe and was sitting behind my desk. He came in somewhat gingerly, not knowing what to expect. When he sat down in the ugly olive green client chair across from me, I studied him a long moment before saying anything.

Grover looked worse than I had ever seen him. His sartorial excellence is legendary. He usually dresses like Armani is his personal tailor. He usually looked every inch the successful lawyer and I could see why other attorneys would refer their big cases to him. He was well known, successful and a formidable adversary. I didn't care about any of that.

"Christian, I've known you a long time. We've never seen eye to eye on cases or politics and I don't care. I know you're deep into this breast implant business and you have several suits pending against MedPro. Do you have any idea where Carly Austin is?"

I watched him closely. I didn't expect him to tell me the truth, but I was hoping that I would be able to tell whether he was lying. He was a good poker player. He appeared astonished at the question, with just the right touch of puzzlement. All trial lawyers are actors on some level and Grover was in the top ten percent of the local performers.

"Judge, I don't even know *who* Carly Austin is."

"What you don't know, Christian, is that I know Carly very well. So I know that she clerked in your firm when she was in law school. You definitely know *who* she is. What I want to know is whether you know *where* she is. And now that you've lied to me once, I'm not sure I'll believe you no matter what you say. But answer the question anyway."

"I'm not clear just exactly what right you have to ask me this question, Judge Carson. Carly Austin, and any relationship I may or may not have with her, has nothing to do with you. I know she's a friend of yours, but that doesn't give you any right to pry into her personal life." His indignation may have been genuine, but it's hard to say.

"Are you saying that you and Carly have a personal relationship of some kind?" I was incredulous. The possibility not only of Carly having a relationship with Grover, but that she would have a relationship with him and not tell me, was very disturbing. How far was she going to take this rebellious teenager stuff, anyway?

"What I am telling you, Judge Carson, is that it's none of your business. If you have some professional reason for asking me, which I can't imagine in the light of the fact that you told Mr. Worthington you would not be asking me ex parte questions about this case, then tell me what it is. If you're asking me on a personal basis, I don't have the kind of personal relationship with you that would make me answer that. I don't intend to discuss my personal relationships with you. If Carly wants to tell you, she will. Why don't you ask her?" He was belligerent now, feeling he was on firmer ground.

"I would if I knew where she was." I snapped.

"Just as I thought," he snorted. "You're not as close to her as you'd like to believe. If you don't have anything else related to the case, Judge, I do have to prepare for my next witness." We sat there staring across the desk, measuring each other for a few moments until he got up and left. Without my permission.

If I hadn't heard the Junior story, I'd have said it wasn't

possible that Carly could be involved in a personal relationship with Christian Grover. Apparently, Carly's taste in men runs from the unsuitable to the unthinkable. As the corporate counsel of a defendant in the breast implant cases, Carly's relationship with a notorious plaintiff's attorney bringing cases against her company would have been enough to get her fired if not disbarred. But then, maybe that's why she hadn't told me about it. Being sexually disgraced in a town where everyone knows everything about you might have snuck up on her the first time. She wouldn't allow that to happen again. She didn't tell anyone about it. And maybe that's why she was so reluctant to pass on Dr. Morgan's theories to her superiors at MedPro. Maybe she didn't want Dr. Morgan to be right.

Poor kid, what a dilemma. If she chose her job, she lost her lover and if she chose her lover, she lost her job. For Carly, who apparently believed she had nothing else, either choice would be an impossible one. I could feel my Mighty Mouse tendencies creeping up again.

If I gave this information to Ben Hathaway, he would believe he was right, that Carly did kill Dr. Morgan. It wouldn't be the first time love prevailed over ethics. His view would be cast in concrete. He'd likely arrest Carly on sight. If she'd killed Morgan either for love or money, her motive wouldn't matter to Chief Hathaway.

And what about Grover? If he knew where Carly was, that would explain his lack of concern over my questions. Of course, that would be true whether she was dead or alive.

I turned it over and over in my head, and I could think of no reasonable alternative but to tell Hathaway. But if I did that, Carly would be arrested and charged with Dr. Morgan's murder. I had to concede, at least to myself, that Carly might be involved in a sexual relationship with Grover. He could be wickedly charming and certainly had enough conquests to prove it. Carly had so little experience that the attention of a rich and powerful lawyer like Grover would certainly have impressed her.

But I knew Carly wasn't capable of murder and the way she reacted when she described the murder scene to me convinced me that she hadn't killed Dr. Morgan. I thought she knew, or at least she believed she knew who had killed him. But what I didn't know was why. Did Carly believe Christian Grover killed Michael Morgan? It was a plausible reason for her behavior. She believed Grover did it and she wanted to protect him. But did he kill Morgan? And, if he did, why? Wasn't Morgan worth more to Grover alive?

This is the point where Mighty Mouse is stuffed into the box and thrown into the ocean. Until I could figure it out, I wasn't turning over this piece of information to Chief Hathaway or anyone else. He already had enough incriminating evidence anyway. If withholding this piece, which I only suspected and couldn't confirm until I found Carly, put the final nail in my impeachment coffin, I'd just see how well I could adjust to unemployment.

I recessed the case for the day. The best way to keep my job, help Carly, and confirm or disprove that her lover was a killer, was to do some investigation into the business of breast implant litigation.

CHAPTER TWENTY-ONE

Tampa, Florida
Thursday 5:20 p.m.
January 21, 1999

FOLLOW THE MONEY, HATHAWAY had said. I asked my law clerk to bring me a list of all of the breast implant cases I had currently pending on my docket together with the names of the attorneys and law firms representing both parties. She ran the request through the computer and had it for me in thirty minutes.

I was surprised at how many cases I actually had. The computer list was ten pages long. I asked her to sort the cases by lawyer and defendant. The list I got back reflected the majority of the plaintiffs' cases were being handled by Grover and his partner, Fred Johnson. Only one or two other plaintiffs' firms were represented and then they only handled one or two cases.

On the defense side, there were about five firms listed. The majority of the cases appeared to be against two corporate defendants and one individual, Dr. Michael Morgan. Each of those defendants was represented by E. O'Connell Worthington.

The remaining third of the cases against various defendants were represented by as many defense firms.

Most of the cases had been filed more than two years, and involved a husband and wife as plaintiffs. One case was noteworthy, however, because it was a class action, listing the individual names of more than three-hundred-fifty plaintiffs and the defendants were each of the named manufacturers. In the three-hundred-fifty-plaintiff case, all of the manufacturers were represented by one defense counsel, E. O'Connell Worthington. Plaintiffs' counsel was Grover.

I then looked at the trial calendar. Because ninety-five percent of all civil cases settle, I schedule about twenty trials a week during my jury term and twenty-five trials a week during non-jury term. There were ten to fifteen breast implant trials scheduled every jury term for the next twelve months.

The class action case was scheduled for trial six months hence. As many cases as were still on my docket, more than twice that many had been transferred to Federal Court in Georgia to the multi-district litigation being handled by my good friend, Judge Franklin. I had no idea what was happening with Judge Franklin's cases, so I called him. Miraculously, he was available to speak to me.

After the pleasantries were exchanged, I asked, "Steve, what is the status of the breast implant litigation you're handling these days?"

"We've got a global settlement almost completely negotiated. It's been approved by the plaintiffs and the defendants. I have a couple of motions by insurance companies and Medicare and Medicaid to decide and then I'll make a decision on final approval."

"What will happen to the settlement if it's not approved?"

"I haven't let myself think about that." He laughed. "But, if that should happen, then I guess we'll start having trials on all four-hundred-forty-thousand claims. I figure I'll get done about the time I am scheduled to depart the earth, or this will kill me prematurely!"

I laughed politely in commiseration. Judges don't get paid overtime. "And what will happen after the settlement is approved, if it is?"

"After approval, the only step left is for the individual plaintiffs to submit the medical proof necessary to establish their entitlement to payments under the terms of the settlement grid."

"Settlement grid?" I felt like I was learning a foreign language.

"We've worked out a system where women with different types of diseases will be paid different sums of money. The least amount a woman will be paid is five-thousand and the most is one million."

I whistled. "That's a hell of a lot of money, especially to the lawyers. How will the legal fees be paid?"

"Well on the plaintiffs' side, I want to limit transaction costs to twenty-five percent of the total settlement amount. Of course, the plaintiffs are squealing like stuck pigs over that because they're used to forty percent fees, exclusive of costs, and the defendants are objecting that it's too high because they're the ones that get to pay it."

The figures he quoted were staggering. Following the money seemed to be the first rule for lawyers as well as murder investigators. "And what about defense attorney fees?"

"Defense attorneys will be paid by the defendants through whatever arrangements the defendants have made for paying them. I haven't gotten into that because the defendants haven't asked me to. I don't see how I could resolve that anyway."

"There seems to be some new urgency in my courtroom by the plaintiffs to get these cases on for trial. I noticed today that I've got ten trials set every jury term for the next twelve months. Do you have any idea why?"

"I think that's happening all over the country, partly because it pressures the defendants to settle and partly because in the last several months the scientific studies that have come out have all been supporting the defense side. The plaintiffs feel they're playing beat the clock. If they don't get their judgments soon, they're worried the defendants will start trying the causation issues and winning. The defendants are pushing the cases to trial because they think they can win or at least they can make the plaintiffs work and then the plaintiffs' will get more reasonable. If I don't get this settlement put to bed pretty soon, I'm afraid the whole thing will fall apart."

I thanked Steve for his help, and went back to studying my list. I noticed that Grover had all of his cases set for trial, but none of Johnson's were scheduled. Worthington's cases were all set, but they ran into the next three years, pretty evenly spaced out. The remaining attorneys seemed to be either behind the curve in requesting trial dates or, perhaps, not prepared for trial.

I did some quick multiplication in my head. If each of the plaintiffs Grover represented would settle, it looked to me like just the cases on my docket would net him attorneys' fees of $270 million under Florida's forty-percent fee rule. Of course, he could have made arrangements to accept lower fees based on the volume of business, and he probably owed referral fees to a number of lawyers who had sent him their cases to handle as well. Still, he stood to gain a tremendous sum of money if these cases were all tried and won. Not as much as the tobacco lawyers would get, but certainly enough to keep him and his four ex-wives off food stamps.

More realistically, setting the cases for trial would force settlements and Grover would get the money more quickly. He'd have to discount the value of the claims to settle them now, but he probably wouldn't have to discount them much, considering the costs of defense. It was curious that Grover's partner, Johnson, hadn't done the same math.

And I couldn't see the advantage to the defendants in pushing the cases to trial. Agreeing to prompt trial dates would put a significant amount of pressure on most of the defense law firms. They just didn't have the manpower to do the work required to defend multiple, four-week trials. And even if they did have enough lawyers to put on the trials, their other work would suffer. A defense firm that puts all its eggs in one client basket makes big money while it lasts, but can't withstand the business loss when the cases are over. And why did only two of the plaintiffs' lawyers want to take their cases to trial now? Why not the rest of them? Both Grover and Worthington were in a game of high stakes poker and I wasn't at all sure which one was holding the better hand.

I began looking at the individual plaintiffs' names. I was shocked to find so many I recognized as my friends, neighbors and colleagues. I found myself smiling involuntarily every time I recognized the name of a woman whose cosmetic enhancement had not been obvious to me.

From the defense side, Worthington's two major clients surfaced repeatedly, but there were also quite a few cases against Carly's company, MedPro, and other defendants, both local and national. I recognized some as George's investments. Others were common corporate America household names.

I continued looking at the list and trying to discern patterns within it. I wasn't sure what I was looking for, but I thought something might jump out at me if I just kept looking. It didn't.

When I looked at my watch, it was 8:00 p.m. and I needed to get home. I put the list out of sight, but not out of mind.

The other thing I couldn't put off any longer was an extended conversation with Kate. She deserved to know what was going on with Carly, and with me. I stopped by her house on the way home.

I saw Kate standing at her kitchen window when I pulled up in the driveway of her South Tampa home. Kate lives two doors off the Bayshore on Oregon, in an old bungalow type house. It was charming, but it was on a corner lot and the kitchen looked out over a busy side street. Both George and I were worried about just anyone being able to drive up and see her standing in the kitchen, but she said we watch too much television. She wouldn't even put blinds on the windows. She said she had moved to Florida for sunlight.

I sat in the car and watched Kate work for awhile before she noticed I was there. She was a beautiful woman still. She hadn't changed that much from the first time I saw her, when I was three. I loved her sparkling blue eyes, and her wide, generous smile. She wore her hair in the same French twist she'd always worn, and if there was a little more grey in with the brown, it looked beautiful none the less.

Kate should be married, I thought, for the hundredth time. She's such a nurturing person. She raised three children of her own, and me since Mom died, without any help from anyone. She'd be a great wife, and a great mother if Carly would just let her be.

Kate eventually looked up from her cooking and saw me

sitting in the car in the driveway. She waved me inside. I walked up to the back door and she came to let me in. At least we'd been able to talk her into locking the door when she was home alone.

"Willa! What a nice surprise," she said as she hugged me with one arm while the other held her paring knife. "Will you stay for dinner? Nothing as fancy as you could have at Minaret, but I still make a pretty good veal loaf." I was following her into the kitchen, and she just kept talking without waiting for my reply. I don't remember her doing that when we all used to be around. Maybe living alone was getting to her. I decided to speak my thoughts when I finally had a chance to get a word in.

"Kate, what really happened to your husband?" I hid my face in the refrigerator, ostensibly looking for a bottle of beer, avoiding her gaze. We'd never talked about this, and I wasn't sure she'd think it was any of my business. But she didn't seem to mind.

"He just left one day and never came back. He didn't even have enough originality to come up with a good story. He said he was going out for cigarettes." She had pulled out three potatoes to peel after she put the veal loaf in the oven.

"When he didn't come back from the store, you must have been frantic." I took up the green beans, washing them at the sink and cutting off the ends so they could be steamed.

"Oh, sure. Crime in our neighborhood was as bad as anywhere for 1975. I called all the hospitals, the police department. No one had seen him."

"How do you know he wasn't injured or killed or something?" I put the beans in the saucepan with a little water, salt and the steamer.

"Here, let me season those. I put rosemary in them. Gives them a nice flavor." She took the pot out of my hand and emptied the water in the sink. She refilled the pot, added rosemary instead of salt, and put the beans back in the steamer. She turned the burner on under it, and moved back to the potatoes.

"He wrote to me, about ten years after he left. He'd found another woman he wanted to marry, and he asked for a divorce, which I gave him, of course. He never asked about the boys." She was putting the potatoes on to boil, adding whole garlic cloves to the water, and then moved to the refrigerator to get out salad greens.

"That must have been enough to sour you on men for a while," I said, sitting down at the table. It was apparent she didn't want any help, so I moved out of the way.

She nodded. "For a long time, I didn't understand it. I thought there was something wrong with me. Since I never told the boys I'd divorced their father, I couldn't very well tell them I planned to date. And for a long time, I just wasn't interested."

"Well, at some point, that must have changed."

"Because of Carly, you mean? Yes, but that was years later, and quite unexpected, really. Would you open that red wine, Dear, I think I'll have a glass with you while you have your beer." I opened the bottle as she got a wine glass out of the cupboard for each of us and began to set the table for two, even though I'd never said I would stay. She lit tall green candles in pewter candlesticks that I knew, from long familiarity, she'd inherited from her mother. I went to call George and tell him I wouldn't be home for dinner.

When I came back into the kitchen, the potatoes were done and Kate was mashing them, drinking her wine and adding large dollops of butter. Tomorrow, headache or no, back to my running or I'd soon weigh as much as Pricilla Worthington.

When the veal loaf was done, and Kate had made the Burgundy gravy to go with the garlic potatoes, green beans and salad, we sat down to eat with another full glass of wine each. The intimacy, and the wine, gave me the courage to take up our conversation again.

"How did you meet Carly's father, anyway?" I tried to make it sound casual, as if I knew, but had just forgotten. Nothing could be further from the truth. Kate had never told any of us anything about him. In fact, this was the first time I'd ever had the nerve to suggest we all knew Carly's father was not the same man who had fathered the boys. With Kate, somehow, we'd known the topic was taboo.

I'm not sure if Kate was more surprised that I'd asked, or that she answered, but eventually she said, "Your mother was responsible for that, actually. She had a party and she invited him. We met. We danced. I let myself go. I woke up in his hotel room. We had a lovely breakfast, and I never saw him again. Except for every time I look in Carly's eyes."

She was trying to keep it light, but her voice became very soft and I could tell that, whatever she thought now, she had loved him then. I sensed she wanted to talk about it, finally, this thing that had made her so happy, but had caused her daughter so much pain.

"Carly looks just like him, you know. His hair was curly and red like hers. And her flashing, deep blue eyes. People think she got those from me, but she didn't." She paused, remembering.

"When I found out I was pregnant with Carly, my first reaction was pure fright. Single mothers were not accepted anything like the way they are today. And it may have taken Carly ten years to do the math, but my family and my neighbors figured it out right away." She was recalling bitter words, now, I was sure.

"But what could I do? I had two sons at home and I was divorced and pregnant. That was the reality of it. There was no choice. I could be pregnant and unhappy or pregnant and make the best of it. Your mom was great. She'd wanted another child after she married your dad, but she just couldn't get pregnant. She was so happy she'd be Carly's godmother. Your mom really helped me through those days." She emptied the Merlot bottle into our glasses and we sat quietly while she remembered that far away time and tried to decide how much to share with me.

"And then something curious happened. I started to be really happy. I was smiling all the time, looking forward to the baby coming. I don't think I'd ever been quite as happy before that time, and I'm not sure I've ever been that happy since." Her face lit up now with the memory.

"Just the pregnancy hormones, you think?" I was staring at the flickering candle flame, almost hypnotized.

"It was partly that, but something else, too. You see, Wilhelmina, I believe in the affluence of the universe. I believe you make your own life. You decide what it is that you want, and then the universe gives it to you. It's not that you don't have to work for it, but the law of least effort applies more often than not. If it's too much trouble, it's usually not worth it. Happiness is first, seeking happiness is the most important quest, and achieving it is life's best goal." Philosophy often comes in a bottle of wine, I've found, and it was no different with Kate.

"I don't mean happiness from a pill or a syringe. I mean real happiness that comes from obtaining your life's desires. It's hard to achieve happiness because real happiness is so often confused with things. You look for a new house or a new job or a new relationship, because you think those things will make you happy. Really, the opposite is true. If you're happy, you'll enjoy your job or your house or your relationship, and all good things will flow to you." She took a deep breath. I waited, afraid to break the spell.

"And when I was pregnant with Carly, I finally accepted that I had wanted another baby, and I had gone to that party looking for just such an available man as I met, and I got what I wanted. For all Carly's angst over her paternity, she was the most wanted baby ever conceived and certainly one of the most loved."

I went over and gave Kate a big hug. I blinked my tears away, but Kate wasn't crying. To her, this was an old story and she remembered it with obvious, almost ethereal joy.

We were having such a wonderful evening that I didn't want to spoil it by telling her what I'd come to say. But I couldn't let her hear about it from one of the town wags, either. Fortunately, Kate never read the newspapers or watched television news. She said they only reported bad news, and she wasn't interested. So, after we put the dishes in the dishwasher and sat down with our coffee, I gave her a very abbreviated version of Carly's situation. I omitted my own troubles. I felt I had gone into this deal with my eyes open. No point in blaming it on Carly or putting the burden of my decision on Kate.

She didn't seem at all dismayed, and I couldn't quite understand why. After everything she'd told me tonight, I knew she loved Carly as her chosen child, maybe even more than the rest of us (although before tonight, I'd always thought that particular honor belonged to Jason, her first born).

"Kate, you don't seem very worried. Carly is in serious trouble. You understand that, don't you?" I was beginning to think she'd had more wine than she could handle, but I'd underestimated her again.

"Willa, there's no chance that Carly killed Michael Morgan,

or anyone else for that matter. As to where she is at the moment, I'm sure she'll turn up with some reasonable explanation. There's nothing I can do for her until she comes to me with the same questions you've asked tonight. Carly has to get over being angry with me for keeping her father from her, and start being grateful she's had such a wonderful family. Until then, there's nothing I can do for her except love her, and trust that she'll be all right. The same thing I do for all of you."

So, in the end, I gave her a hug, told her I loved her and left, uneasy in the knowledge that I'd underestimated her again.

CHAPTER TWENTY-TWO

Tampa, Florida
Thursday 10:00 p.m.
January 21, 1999

MY CONVERSATION WITH KATE left me with a lot to think about. Finding Carly before she got hurt and solving the relationship problems she had with Kate shouldn't have been my mission.

But somehow it was.

The connection between Carly, Dr. Morgan's murder, Grover and Johnson had to be related to the breast implant cases; nothing else made sense.

Hathaway had said to follow the money, so I tried piecing the puzzle together with the money in mind.

Carly said Dr. Morgan had been conducting research and believed he'd found the scientific explanation for the occurrence of symptoms in some women with breast implants. Something like that would have to be worth a lot of money on the legitimate market, not just to the interested parties to the litigation.

The most obvious place to start looking for Dr. Morgan's theories were the two places that had already been searched, his home and Carly's, but only if you knew the two of them had been talking about it.

Who knew that besides Carly?

Grover? Probably. Who else?

No names popped into my head. Changed course.

Those failed searches had been excessive. Whatever the guy hoped to find must be either a paper document or computer data. Otherwise, each search was way too through.

And whatever he was searching for hadn't been found.

He'd kill Carly, but not until he found what he wanted. I hoped.

I needed a fresh approach. Which is why I'd gone from Kate's directly back to my office and spent the evening poring over the court file in the *Jones v. General Medics* case. Complaint, answer and other papers yielded nothing. Expert deposition transcripts were dry as flour.

One surprise: Dr. Morgan was listed as a witness for Grover's side.

Scoured the file, but Dr. Morgan's deposition transcript wasn't there. We don't lose things once they're placed in our court files. So where was it?

There were several notices scheduling his testimony, but no proof that the deposition had taken place or the transcript filed. Odd.

Dr. Morgan had been named as an expert early in the case. The notices for his deposition were repeatedly filed as the case continued plodding forward on the docket. Decidedly odd. Too much paper for too little result.

The last notice scheduled his deposition two days before he died. Odder still.

"Okay, Willa," I said aloud. "Think this through."

My grandmother taught me that talking to oneself was not a sign of insanity, as long as we don't answer. So I guess I'm insane.

I replied, "Only two choices, right? Either Morgan testified two days before he died and explained his theories, in which case why kill him? Or, he was never deposed. And, in that case, how did Grover explain the failure to produce him? Why didn't O'Connell file a motion to strike his name from the list if he couldn't be produced for deposition?"

This time, I had no answers. Just questions. As well as a sore back and tired eyes.

I stood and stretched like Harry and Bess do every time they get up. Tried the downward dog, which I've never been as good at as they are, but it gets the kinks out. They do a whole-body-shake afterward, but there I draw the line.

Needed to move.

Trotted to the courthouse library to get the kinks out of my legs.

Using the online computer services so kindly supported by our tax dollars, I pulled up all of the newspaper articles relating to breast implants in the past five years. The computer listed 1,765 articles. Too many to read quickly.

Narrowed the date range. Articles published after the largest manufacturer's bankruptcy and before Dr. Morgan died. 432. Still, too many to read closely.

Excluded articles about the bankruptcy. Risky. Produced 142 articles. Better.

Reprinted in the local papers were stories from *The New York Times*, *The Wall Street Journal*, *The Washington Post* and the major wire services. Printed the list.

After eliminating the duplicates, sixty-eight recent newspaper articles remained.

Sent all of them to the printer, leaned back, propped my feet on the desk, and read each one as they rolled slow and hot off the laser.

Some articles simply weren't helpful. They covered individual cases or ongoing medical studies. I scanned them quickly and moved them to one side.

None dealt with MedPro. Somewhat surprising since it was a small but significant player in the local and national market.

Only a few concerned Dr. Morgan and his death. Three were obituaries.

I rubbed the back of my neck and looked at my watch. It was 11:30. No wonder I was exhausted. I signed off the computer, gathered my research, returned to chambers and called my husband.

"Yes, I'm sure I haven't been abducted by aliens," I responded to his testy question. He disconnected. "Unfortunately," I whispered into the empty air.

Less than fifteen minutes later, home, dogs greeted, husband placated.

George handed me a Sapphire and tonic with a twist. He brought a small Glen Fiddich and joined me in the den.

I sprawled out, feet up, held the frosty glass against my forehead while I relayed the day's events. George paced. Harry and Bess were unconcerned.

He didn't approve of my plan.

Nor had I expected he would.

We argued awhile.

George thought it was Ben Hathaway's job to catch killers, not mine.

Ordinarily, I agreed. I'm liberal enough to believe that *some* innocent people are wrongfully convicted, although the odds are overwhelmingly against it.

This was Carly, though. I had to be certain Hathaway caught the right killer.

George said Hathaway could handle it; I wasn't willing to take the risk.

Minds were not changed by increasing the argument's heat.

"I give up," George said, throwing both hands in the air for emphasis. Harry and Bess followed him into the bedroom. Before he closed the door, he said, "Don't stay up all night."

"Love you," I replied, but I doubt he heard.

Mixed another drink; pulled the newspaper articles out again and set to work.

By 3:00 a.m., I had sorted, diagramed, and thoroughly digested each. Made pages of notes on a fresh yellow pad. Compared them to my other facts.

So what?

Gin, effort, exhaustion, and the late hour pulled my eyelids toward closure. I pinched both eyes open and held them open by thumb and forefinger above and below. Eyeballs dry. Gritty.

Ran the facts through my head while staring at my tiny notes. Tried to find connections. Failed. Again. Again. Again.

"The hell with it," I said. Time to give up. I was getting nowhere. Again.

Trudged wearily to bed. Tossed and turned and thought about what I'd read. Bedside clock glowed brilliantly; 5:30 a.m. before my brain simply shut down.

CHAPTER TWENTY-THREE

Tampa, Florida
Friday 7:00 a.m.
January 22, 1999

WHEN THE ALARM WENT off at 7:00, I cursed my promise
to keep Grover's case moving quickly. Promise in haste, repent
at leisure, I guess.

We began trial again promptly at 9:00.

Grover looked like he had spent a later night than I had.
O'Connell and his associate didn't look well-rested either.

I remembered too well the years I'd spent preparing long
into the night for trials, and attributed the defense team's
weariness to that preparation.

Grover's ego would never have allowed all-night grunt
work. What was his excuse?

Throughout the morning, I found myself studying him,
seeking evidence of stress or mental strain caused by anticipation
of his arrest for murder. Saw none, unfortunately.

The afternoon session was filled with video depositions,

always a boring part of any trial. Rulings were made in advance to avoid interruptions. Lights lowered, courtroom quiet, testimony long and complicated. Always a lethal combination if the goal was to keep the jury awake.

Plaintiffs' national experts; doctors making a killing by testifying around the country in breast implant cases. It was rumored that some of them charged as much as $25,000 just to review a patient's medical records, $10,000 for a deposition and $50,000 to testify in court, which they would rarely consent to do.

One of last night's articles said that many experts made a more prosperous living as professional witnesses than they'd ever earned practicing medicine. The legitimate medical community was appalled, of course, but the experts were doing nothing illegal, or even novel. As Sheldon Warwick had said at George's party, product liability lawsuits were a growth business.

This afternoon's witnesses were experts on the surgical techniques for implanting and explanting the breast prostheses. Their testimony consisted of diagrams and charts and videos of actual surgeries, which left most of us squeamish.

I nodded off a couple of times. Maybe no one noticed. I'm fairly sure I didn't snore. But I sat up straighter in my chair and tried to pay attention. It wasn't easy.

Grover's final video of the day was the deposition testimony of an expert immunologist, a doctor specializing in the human immune system.

Grover questioned him for almost an hour before he reached the finish line. "Implants cause the immune system of an implanted woman to turn on itself and destroy her own cells? Is that what happens?"

The doctor said, "It's like AIDS. Debilitating. Progressive. Degenerative."

Grover said, "And like AIDS, doctor, breast implants kill?"

The doctor said, "Absolutely."

Worthington glowered at the testimony in the dark because we already knew his cross-examination didn't dent the doctor's confidence.

The videos finally ended. The jury seemed more sleepy and bewildered than impressed.

I dismissed the jury and then the parties and returned to my chambers at 4:35, hoping to sneak out before the CJ arrived for the meeting he'd insisted my secretary put on the calendar.

Like a high school principal, he had been the victim of this dodge before; he'd arrived early and waited. I pretended to be pleasantly surprised to see him; he feigned joy at the prospect; he entered my chambers.

Before I joined him, I raised my voice and said, "Hold my calls, Margaret," which was our code for "come in and rescue me in ten minutes."

CJ said, "Wilhelmina, you know I think the world of you and your husband."

He knew, and I knew, he thought no such thing and, even if he did, what was the point? I smiled and nodded and waited for the punch line.

"Wilhelmina, I'm concerned about you. You were absent last week after you were, as I understand it, attacked by a mugger. Today, you look exhausted. You have some control over your schedule. You need to pace yourself." He sounded genuine, but that tic at the corner of his left eye proved the effort stressed him out some.

Nice backhanded way to say I looked like hell.

Quite sure we hadn't gotten to the point of his visit yet, I said, "I appreciate your concern, Oz."

CJ cleared his throat and finally spit it out, like a wad of phlegm.

"I've been asked to tell you that your conduct is being perceived, by some, as well, not what we'd hoped for." Another throat clearing thing. "It's true you have a lifetime appointment, but you can be, uh, impeached."

My temperature shot up ten degrees. Nostrils flared.

He noticed. Rushed on. "It doesn't happen often, but it has happened before."

Hard words. "I see."

CJ's voice squeaked, like the wad of phlegm had settled against his vocal cords and pressed his wind. "I suggest you leave the homicide investigations to Ben Hathaway, particularly when the deceased is someone as disreputable as Michael Morgan."

He could barely eke out the name. Swallowed. Sweat dotted his forehead.

Now, he had my full attention. My ears burned like hotspots. Eyes narrowed. Brows dipped toward my nose. Fists clinched under the desk where CJ couldn't see them; where I couldn't use them to throttle the little shit.

He stood as if about to bolt. "I doubt there's a person worth knowing in Tampa who's sorry to see Morgan dead. You want to be careful who you make your enemies, Willa. People in this town have long memories."

My breaths slammed full and hurt my chest. Fists opened, closed; again, harder. I might actually do something here I'd regret later. *Grace under pressure, Wilhelmina.* Mom's voice played in my head, but it didn't lower my temperature.

Ever since I'd mistakenly taken his parking place my first day on the job, the revered first spot next to the door reserved for the Big Guy, the CJ, Oz himself, he'd been on my case. His reaction was more than a little bit strange for such a minor infraction. He gave me the worst case assignments, the smallest chambers, the most meager courtroom redecorating budget possible. At meetings, he ignored my suggestions and just generally made it known, without saying so, that I was far from his favorite. Okay. I'd come to actually treasure all of that because it meant he left me alone.

But this was the first time he'd ever said anything overtly threatening to me. It was so out of character, so inappropriate and so unjudicial, that I wasn't totally sure I'd heard him correctly. I *was* tired. I *was* stressed. My visceral response seemed extreme. Could I have misunderstood?

"Are you threatening me, CJ? And if you are, are *you* threatening me or is this a message from someone else?" I asked him coldly.

He'd reached the door. Had his hand on the knob. But he watched me like a sniper. "Don't take that tone with me, Wilhelmina. I'm trying to give you some good advice. If you don't want to take it, the risk is yours."

He slammed the door on his way out. Hard enough to knock one of the ancient framed photographs off the wall. It hit the floor, landed on a weak corner, and burst apart, sending glass shards everywhere.

Too bad it wasn't the little dweeb's head that shattered.

Margret rushed in. The alarm on her face was almost comical. "What happened?"

"Old glass, I guess. Do we have a broom? I'll take care of it," I said.

She replied, "That's ridiculous. Go get coffee. Leave it to me."

When I returned, all traces of the broken glass were gone. The spot where the old photo once hung showed the most god-awful green blank spot. The thing was almost as big as CJ. If it had landed on his head, he might literally have shattered, just as I'd wished.

The silly thought cheered me up. Along with the Cuban Coffee, good cheer cleared my head. But the situation was as murky as ever.

"Why did CJ give me that warning?" I asked myself aloud.

Heeding Grandma's warning about answers, I skipped speculation and went right ahead with questions.

"Does he think I've disgraced his precious court? Does he hold me somehow responsible for Junior's recent loss of face? Did someone who once contributed heavily to his reelection campaigns ask him for the favor?"

He has aspirations to higher office. Maybe it's a black mark against him if he can't keep his junior justices in line, and he won't be considered for the Court of Appeals?

If so, that would be most unfortunate.

The only chance I had of getting rid of him was the Peter Principle: get him kicked upstairs.

It was quite a while before I figured out the real reason for his warning, and it was I who had to be hit over the head with it even then.

CHAPTER TWENTY-FOUR

Tampa, Florida
Friday 5:30 p.m.
January 22, 1999

A FINE SNIT IS a terrible thing to waste.

I picked up the telephone and called Ben Hathaway.

He was as cool to me as I was to him. I asked him what news he had of Carly and he told me that an ongoing police investigation was none of my business.

"If you want me to keep out of it, you'll tell me what you found, if you found anything," I snapped back.

"You'll keep out of it if I tell you to keep out of it, federal judge or not!" and he slammed down the phone.

I slammed down my receiver immediately afterwards. What a shame he couldn't hear it.

Now what?

"Go home, Willa. You're exhausted. You're fighting with everyone. That's not like you. Go home."

My face frowned quickly of its own accord. Grandma never

said whether it was insane to answer questions never asked aloud. Yet the truth was obvious not only to CJ. As much as it pained me to agree with him on anything, I was exhausted.

On the way home, I concluded Hathaway must have nothing to report. If he'd found Carly or knew where she was, he would have been only too happy to tell me.

In fact, she'd be in custody if he'd found her.

Small comfort. I'd grown weary of not knowing what the hell was going on.

I wasn't conscious of it, but somehow, Greta decided it would be a good idea to drive by Michael Morgan's house instead of going immediately home. I found myself driving west on Kennedy to Westshore, turning south and into the Beach Park subdivision, scouting the address imprinted on my memory.

The house itself was old and fairly small, a typical Florida ranch perched on an ordinary South Tampa lot. A Beach Park address, but not one of the more glamorous homes in the neighborhood. When it turned over, the house would likely be a tear-down.

Like me, Morgan's killer must have been cursing his luck; like so many homes in Florida, Morgan's had no attached garage. The west side of the house was exposed and visible.

Anyone could have seen a black car in the driveway, just as the witness told the police.

Greta pulled up the length of the driveway to the back of the carport. No matter. Exposed and visible.

Tried the side entry door; discovered it unlocked.

It took me about two seconds to decide.

Greta is distinctive, and someone would notice. But I was already here and Morgan was already dead and I was already obstructing justice as well as in trouble with the CJ.

What more could I risk?

So I went in through the side door.

Opened directly into the kitchen. I ducked under the crime lab's yellow plastic tape to enter.

Morgan's kitchen held an oak drop-leaf table set parallel to the door, maybe forty-two inches round when the leaves were up, and two matching oak chairs. Splattered blood and grey matter marred the wall behind the chair facing the door. The chair was snugged against the wall now and from the mess, seemed to have been in that position at the time of death.

The opposite chair, closest to the door, was tucked close to the table. Unoccupied at the time of the murder? Or replaced afterward?

Had the killer stood right inside this side door and pulled the trigger?

Or had they been seated across from each other at the table when he did it?

No doubt blood spatter experts would determine the answer. But my experience said it could have gone either way.

The door-jamb didn't appear tampered or damaged. Nor did the door. Locks not forced either open or closed, I'd say. Black fingerprinting dust all over the knob now, but not before the murder. No obvious finger prints lifted. The killer wore gloves? Suggested premeditation. Or maybe wiped in cleanup if the murder had been more spontaneous?

The dining room stood north of the kitchen and contained formal furniture. Chair seats had been slashed, but the china cabinet seemed undamaged. Doors open, but dishes remained in place. Had the room and its contents been dusted for prints? Had the evidence vacuum been run over the floors? Nothing seemed particularly clean. Hell, I wasn't even sure if the Tampa police had an evidence vacuum.

The living room visible through the dining room's open archway. A total shambles. Seat cushions and seat backs were ripped to shreds. The chairs and the love seat turned over, and the bottoms slashed, too. Books strewn everywhere, bindings cracked and open.

Quickly walked through the rest of the house. Every room was similarly destroyed. Whatever the searcher sought, there was no reason to believe he'd found it. Otherwise, why destroy the remaining hiding places?

I'd been inside five full minutes. How much more time would I have?

I went outside and looked around the grounds. Impossible to tell if Dr. Morgan's carport had always looked like a tornado victim cyclone or the mess resulted from a continuing search.

Since no one had shown up to arrest me yet, I returned to the house to work through the murder.

If Dr. Morgan was seated at the kitchen table with whoever killed him in the chair opposite, the body either remained in the chair after death or fell to the floor near the back wall.

Then, the body was moved out of the house through the side door.

The distance from the chair to the exit was about ten feet; from the exit to the car's trunk maybe another fifteen feet.

Logistically, moving the body to the door shouldn't have been too strenuous. He could have dragged Morgan along the floor. I squatted for a closer look between the Spanish tiles. Although the grout was already a dark brown, something had stained it in the right locations. Could have been blood. Maybe a cooking spill. The crime lab would apply sophisticated tests to find out.

The hard part would have been moving the body from the

kitchen floor into the trunk of the car without being seen. Had to be done at night. The area was much too open for daylight skullduggery. This was an affluent neighborhood, though. Maybe the neighbors worked away from home during daylight hours.

In either case, it would have to be done quickly. Discovery became more probable with each passing moment.

That thought caused me to check my watch again. I'd been here eleven minutes now. Weren't Tampa PD response times a lot shorter than that?

A car trunk is at least four feet off the ground. With the advent of weight lifting as a national pastime, most people could probably manage to lift 175 pounds three feet off the ground, even without the extra strength adrenaline flow you'd have to have to kill Morgan in the first place.

But it wouldn't be easy and it had to be fast.

After he got the body into the trunk, the rest could have been done in the relative privacy of the killer's garage, assuming he had one. If not a garage, then some private location. No other way he could have bound that body in absolute confidence he wouldn't be interrupted.

So where did he get the concrete and the clothesline?

Sixteen minutes. Really? No one had reported me yet? Perhaps Morgan's Tampa neighbors were less nosy than I'd assumed.

Another pass through the house. No clothesline. But through the bedroom window I saw a storage shed in the back yard and dashed out there for a quick look.

Nothing inside the shed. Behind it, though.

Eureka.

Broken grey concrete patio stones under the trash cans. Six

missing. Small enough and light enough for easy handling and heavy enough to weigh down the body. And who would notice them missing after the homeowner died? This had to be the source of the concrete weights.

But finding patio stones of just the right size that wouldn't be missed is a lot of luck to count on. The killer had to be someone who knew he'd find those materials easily available. Meaning someone very familiar with the house.

Nineteen minutes since I'd parked Greta in the carport. Still no sirens. Huh?

I felt sure I'd found everything knowable from Morgan's physical surroundings. But I wouldn't get another chance.

I dashed back inside for one more look around.

Something else bothered me about the scene. Such a mess. But something not right about that mess. What? I couldn't put my finger on the problem. It was there, though. I could feel it.

Twenty-two minutes. Good grief. What the hell was Tampa PD doing?

I hurried to Greta; snatched the disposable camera from her miniscule glove compartment. Snapped quick pictures. Kitchen, dining room, living room, master bedroom and den. The pictures would distort the scene, but better than trusting memory for the details.

Something wasn't right here, and I resolved to let my unconscious work on what that something was.

Twenty-seven minutes. Pushed my luck as far as I was willing to go.

But when this was over, I planned a long chat with Ben Hathaway.

Dropped the film off for overnight developing on the way home.

CHAPTER TWENTY-FIVE

Tampa, Florida
Saturday 2:15
January 23, 1999

RUNNING LATE. STOPPED BY to pick up the developed film
and stuffed it in Greta's glove box with all the other essential
junk I had in there. No time to examine the photos now.

I'd invited Dr. Carolyn Young to Great Oaks. Easier to play
my home course. Less thinking required, more time for my
planned inquisition.

We'd agreed to meet at the clubhouse at 2:30 p.m. when the
course would be nearly empty and she could, as she put it, help
me improve my game. Dressed like a golf magazine
advertisement in pink and green, she stood tapping her pricey
spikes on the pavement out front when I dashed up.

"Sorry—"

"Never mind. We've loaded your clubs. Shoes, too. Let's
go," she said. Strode toward the cart.

I didn't dare take a minute to pee.

Carolyn Young might have been 55 years old, but she sure didn't look it. If her smooth skin, firm breasts, and great legs were the result of modern medicine, I wanted some. I suspected her patients felt the same way. A perfect advertisement for her plastic surgery practice.

She commandeered the wheel; "I'm in charge" attitude apparent in every movement. Nothing about her was tentative. No idle chit-chat, either.

When we arrived at the first tee, she instructed, leaving no room for negotiation.

"Take the first shot. I'll check your swing."

After my respectable tee shot, she said, "Your swing isn't bad. You're too tense."

Gee, ya think?

She pulled her driver from her bag and stood over the tee wagging her butt. "Loosen up. Let the club do the work. Watch me."

In an easy, relaxed way, Carolyn knocked the snot out of that golf ball. Amazing hit. A good twenty yards farther than my lie. I'd thought maybe she played golf with Marilee Aymes every week to salve a guilty conscience. Not sot. Marilee was a good golfer, but not that good. Carolyn must have let Marilee win. Also amazing.

But why?

After the first three holes, Carolyn had given me enough suggestions for this lifetime. Some were helpful, but most were pure harassment. If she'd constantly harped like this with Morgan, no wonder he'd dumped her gorgeous ass.

On the fourth hole, I watched my ball sail ridiculously right, over the creek and onto the fairway on the other side.

Carolyn waited behind the wheel, hand tapping impatiently,

one foot on the accelerator and the other on the brake. "Come on. Don't dawdle."

I strolled to my bag and placed my club deliberately. Took my sweet time.

"Enjoyed meeting Fred Johnson when I substituted for you last week," I said before sidling up to my seat. "He's overshadowed by Grover in their partnership, don't you think?"

My butt barely touched the vinyl before she'd lifted her foot from the brake and the cart jumped forward. I grabbed the side rail and held tight.

She drove the cart at breakneck speed along the paved path, over a fat snake, *ka-plomp*, *ka-plomp*, and never slowed. I looked back; the snake slithered off, undead, as we sped across the bridge, over the creek, and beyond.

She replied, "Grover has a big personality. It's too bad he's not as good a lawyer as he fancies himself."

"He gets some awfully big verdicts, and he always seems to have the most high profile cases in town," I shouted over the wind whistling and the protesting whine of the cart's gas powered engine.

"Maybe. But Fred is the successful one. He picks the winners. You only have to be around them together to figure that out."

Was she calling me stupid now, too?

Carolyn drove right up to her ball, jumped out of the cart and grabbed her nine iron. She set up, took her shot, landed on the green and jumped back in the cart, all in less than two minutes. Mashed the accelerator and sped over to my ball, stomped the brake and threw me forward.

"Do you think they make these things with seat belts?" I

asked as I got out of the cart slowly, and tried to shake myself out so I could concentrate to beat her lie.

"Sorry," she said.

In a pig's eye.

You can learn a lot about a person by the way they act on the golf course. Polite? Play by the rules? Short temper? Clubs in the lake? Like a trial, it's a microcosm of life. Carolyn Young was impatient, fast. And very good. In golf and in life.

Tested my theory.

Slowly, I studied the angle of the ball to the pin like a newbie. Laid my club on the ground and walked back to check the direction of the ball.

She fidgeted like a kid needing a pee.

Yep. Speed was her ally. Her tactic was to rush me, get me frazzled. She'd be on her best game and I'd be off mine. Fat chance.

After I hit, I strolled back to the cart, wiped the dirt off my club with my towel, and took my time. Then I moseyed to the passenger side, climbed in, and hung on.

Again, she mashed the accelerator before I settled into the seat, and drove about 20 miles an hour toward the green. Maybe this was a specially jazzed cart, customized for her need for speed?

She said, "I've known Grover for years. He's always been an insufferable chauvinist."

"Is he old enough for that?" I asked her.

She laughed. Jerked the cart to a stop. Jumped out. Grabbed her putter.

"The biggest problem he has," she continued talking during her putt while the ball rolled seven feet, curved left and fell into the cup, "is how many law firms he's been booted from. He stays with each one as long as they can stand each other. A nasty divorce follows. Your turn."

She collected her specialized kryptonite ball from the cup and stood to one side, positioned to gloat.

I stooped down, laid my club from the ball toward the hole, took a couple of practice swings. I could see her tapping her foot and fidgeting, getting more annoyed by the second. Some people just have no patience.

She continued to talk while I belabored the putt. "Generally, he gets asked to leave. Too many junior lawyers complain about the way he treats them; too many lawsuits against the firm for discrimination or harassment or whatever."

She wanted to demand I hurry, but she kept quiet.

Finally, after delaying a good five minutes, I hit the putt.

My ball rolled ever so slowly right toward the hole and stopped about six inches short.

"That's a gimme," she said, hopefully.

"No, no. I insist. I'll putt it in," I replied and plodded through the whole procedure again. Wondered how long she could hold her temper; and what she'd do when she lost it.

"But he has the magic touch with juries and whenever he loses one position, he gets another. For some reason, as offensive as he can be to his friends and neighbors, juries love him," I told her.

My second putt tapped solid, the ball rolled the final six inches smoothly, and dropped in.

Carolyn didn't see my little victory dance because she'd turned to retake the cart.

"Maybe," she said, speeding to the next tee. "If a cynic might say jurors are stupid. Truth is, Grover's highly manipulative; he can talk a banana out of its peel. A few million dollars from unsophisticated polite southerners is easier for him to get than a winter cold."

We lurched to a stop. Again, she jumped out, set up, and hit her tee shot a country mile on a par five, 509-yard hole.

She watched her ball land safely in the fairway before she resumed the constant chatter. This, too, was a tactical distraction. Gamesmanship, not sportsmanship. All the more curious because she could beat me easily playing appropriately.

She asked, "Have you ever heard the story about how he got his first million?"

Continued my setup. Pretended to ignore her. Whacked the ball well enough. We moved to the fairway.

She said, "Grover was three years out of law school. He defied his bosses. Accepted a plaintiff's case, after his request was refused. Handled the case at night, on weekends. When he couldn't get a quick and hefty settlement, he took the case to trial. The jury gave him what the defense attorney wouldn't. Awarded five million dollars to the family. Grover got fired the moment the verdict came back. And made the headlines as the youngest member of the million-dollar club. All in the same instant."

"You admire him for that?" I asked.

"Hell, no." She'd hit her second shot another 200 yards with her three wood and stood aside.

When I duffed my next shot, she snorted under her breath before she rushed away.

I wondered if Carolyn Young knew the rest of Grover's story.

Grover didn't hold on to that first verdict. He'd settled the case at a substantial discount to avoid the loss on appeal. But he'd made his reputation as "the people's lawyer." The next day, he hung out his shingle at the corner of Kennedy and Tampa Street and attracted more business than he could handle. He joined the Trial Lawyers' Association and rapidly became its rising star. He took on case after impossible case and won every time.

Or so it seemed.

Truth was that he lost as many cases as he won; settled quickly at steep discounts; hid his losses and denied any existed.

By the age of thirty-five, Grover was a multimillionaire. And then he decided he needed respectability, which he couldn't get from a random jury selected from the motor-voter registration rolls.

Grover joined another prestigious firm and married a state senator's daughter in a splashy wedding at St. John's Church followed by a splashier reception at the Tampa Commander's Palace. They promptly delivered four children in five years, including a set of triplets. He seemed conventional for the first time, perhaps, in his life.

And respectability proved too much for him.

Maybe the burdens were too heavy, or the fish bowl too transparent. He began using drugs and traveling with a faster crowd.

When George and I arrived in Tampa, Grover had been divorced three times. His children didn't speak to him. And he was in the process of rebuilding his fortune as he'd created the original one: taking on lost causes.

How much of this did Carolyn Young know or care about? Her antipathy originated elsewhere, I felt sure. But what had caused it? Carly?

Time to find out. I'd had enough. I felt a sprained ankle coming on, from a hard twist somewhere during the next three shots.

"Why are you taking referrals from him on explant surgeries, then?"

I'd meant to offend, shove her back a few notches.

Haughty toned reply. "Because I'm a surgeon and his clients are patients." Eyes narrowed. "I suppose Marilee Aymes has been talking about how much money I get for the work." Nostrils flared. Snorted.

Not a particularly attractive habit. "She mentioned it."

"I'll bet. Marilee seems to think a doctor should donate her talents for the good of mankind. Making money on the practice of medicine is sinful in her book." Carolyn's tone was nasty now. "If I'd inherited money, maybe I'd agree. As it is, even Michael Morgan didn't leave me his shares in our company. I'm not apologizing for making money while I can, Willa. Last I heard, your husband was a healthy capitalist, too. It's no crime."

She'd finally raised my blood pressure with her condescending words about George.

"You've got a few years to make money yet," I snapped at her, looking around for a convincing place to stage my minor accident.

"True, but this explant business won't last forever and I'm planning to make all the hay I can while the sun shines." She sunk another fifteen-foot putt.

The sand trap to the right of the next green was a good spot for an ankle twist. I deliberately hit my ball there and headed over. While she had her back to me returning to the cart, I fell down and yelled as if I'd landed at the bottom of the Grand Canyon.

Of course, when I devised this plan, I forgot she was a doctor. She didn't buy it for a minute, but she seemed as glad to quit as I was.

I took the driver's seat, ignoring that I'd claimed a right ankle sprain.

"Does Grover refer many explant patients?" I asked.

"Yes, but not as many as his partner, Fred Johnson. I could make more money if I took referrals from Johnson."

"Why don't you?"

Her venomous retort could have killed alligators through her breath. "I wouldn't do business with Fred Johnson if I was starving to death. That man is a snake and anyone who doesn't believe it should have talked to Michael Morgan."

Whoa! Jump back!

She really was a ruthless bitch. Good to know. Wise to avoid.

The Clubhouse was straight ahead. Very little time left in captivity. *Make the most of it, Willa.*

"You've mentioned Dr. Morgan several times today," I said, trying to act like I'd just noticed. "Did you know him well?"

"I knew Mike Morgan better than anyone did. We were planning to be married." Quietly, fighting for composure. Her chin quivered and eyes filled. She took a couple of deep breaths and wiped her tears. Theatrics? I didn't think so.

"I had no idea, Carolyn. You must be devastated. I'm so sorry." I said, with real sympathy.

If she had loved Morgan, maybe everyone was being too harsh. But I knew this would be my only chance to ask her, so I softened my tone and pressed on.

"Do you have any idea who killed him?"

"I'm sure Ben Hathaway will tell you that there were enough suspects to fill the Tampa telephone book. But a woman scorned is most likely."

"I've heard Dr. Morgan had a number of affairs," I said,

letting my voice trail a bit. "Who might have been jealous enough to do such a thing?"

"I've thought about that a lot these last few days, Willa. I've developed a narrow list. If I was a betting woman, which we know I am, I'd look for one who stands to gain the most now that he's gone, and that obviously wouldn't include me."

Obvious answer. Hathaway had said the same thing.

Trouble was, Carolyn Young might be the only woman who knew Morgan and didn't profit by his death.

Had she orchestrated that, too?

CHAPTER TWENTY-SIX

Tampa, Florida
Saturday 4:45 p.m.
January 23, 1999

DOG TIRED, PREOCCUPIED, READY for a break that included a tall glass of something very cold, I called to George when I entered our flat. "Are you home?"

"In here," he called back from the living room.

I lifted my foot to step across the threshold and stopped abruptly, foot still in the air, when George yelled, "Bup, bup, bup!"

Across the divide, George stood hands on hips, feet braced, iced tea in hand, examining his efforts. A carpet of black ink on 8.5 x 11" white recycled copy paper, twelve by sixteen feet, placed in the center of the living room reached almost to the threshold. He had moved the furniture aside to accommodate his giant newspaper article mosaic as it grew beyond Harry and Bess's favorite rolling rug.

"What are you doing?" I asked.

"This stuff is fascinating. I started laying out your articles chronologically on the kitchen table, but I ran out of room, so I moved them to the floor."

"Okay. But what is it?"

"A chronological display of everything you pulled off the computer." He said this with more pride than the accomplishment seemed to warrant.

I'm sure I seemed less than grateful for his creation, because that's how I felt. I needed a shower to get the sand out of my hair, and a fresh set of clothes.

"I can see what you've done here, but so what? I've read those articles until I can practically recite them verbatim. They don't solve Morgan's murder or tell me where Carly is."

He smiled, unperturbed. "You may be the lawyer, Willa, but you have no head for numbers and you're missing the obvious. Read these in the order they were written, not in the order they were printed, and they give you a more accurate picture. This way, it's easier to see that one reporter is responsible for more than half the stories, too. And guess who that reporter is?"

George seemed so proud, I was sure the author must be a Pulitzer Prize winner, at least.

"I give up."

"Robin Jakes," he said, looking like the cat who'd consumed second helpings of Big Bird for lunch. "Look here," he said, pointing again and again. "And here. Here. Here. See?"

How did I not notice that? Because I skipped the fluff like dates and bylines and headed to the meat, that's why. Bad habit.

Robin Jakes is a good friend of ours from Detroit. A perfect resource; one that never would have occurred to me.

"That's not all. Look at the development of these articles," he maneuvered around the edges of his paper carpet; coaxed me onto the floor with his enthusiasm and an insistent pull on my leg.

"George, I looked at the 'development' of those articles until 3:30 in the morning. If I could see some 'development' in them, I would have noticed it already."

"You don't have to be so testy. I'm only trying to help you. Look, early on, the articles are excessively sympathetic to 'the plight of the women victims of our male-dominated society which makes breast implants a desirable commodity'. But as time progresses, the articles get less sympathetic and more scientific, see?" He gestured to the relevant papers to demonstrate. "In the next group, they're discussing recent science and point out how that science supports the manufacturers, not the victims."

He had my full attention. I leaned over his bent knee on the floor so I could read the computer print more clearly. "I see what you mean. At the same time, the global settlement is about to fall apart and the major manufacturer and contributor to the global settlement goes into bankruptcy."

George nodded like a teacher whose dim pupil was finally catching on. "Exactly. Until finally, there's hardly a supportive article on the plaintiff's side. Instead, the articles are about the financial woes of the plaintiff's bar and the limited amounts being paid to 'victims'."

"And, it's only in the end that Michael Morgan's name is prominently mentioned," I said. "What do you think, George? Was Dr. Morgan about to disclose a definitive connection between breast implants and auto immune disease that would run the manufacturers out of business?"

He shook his head, unsure. "Or the opposite? Was he about to disclose no connection? The whole house of cards would come tumbling down. Either way, a large group of disappointed people would be lining up to keep him quiet."

"I think a call to Robin is in order." I said, bounding vertical, all fatigue abolished. I grabbed the phone.

"Put her on the speaker," George replied, as he leveraged his creaking knees to push himself up off the floor.

We spent an hour and a half on the phone with Robin. She told us she had been on the breast implant story since 1992. She had a special interest in the material, she said, because she'd had implants after cancer surgery and had never had a moment's unhappiness with them. She covered the story from a variety of angles as it unfolded and she had written more than seventy-five articles in the past four years under her own byline. Some had been picked up by the wire services. We didn't have them all.

Robin confirmed George's observations regarding the progress of the controversy. She told us of the hardships the corporate defendants had suffered at the hands of the plaintiffs' lawyers. She had interviewed several dozen defense attorneys who, while happy to have the work, consistently proclaimed that the science didn't support the causation theories offered to explain the women's injuries.

"What do you think, Robin?" George asked. "You've been pretty close to this thing all along. You've got to know."

Robin said, "There's no evidence here. These products are safe. No doubt in my mind."

Brief silence filled the distance between Detroit and Tampa.

I said, "What about Michael Morgan? What was his role in this thing?"

She hesitated briefly. A big, audible sigh. Then, "Dr. Morgan studied the phenomenon from the beginning. He claimed to be the most knowledgeable plastic surgeon in the country on breast implants. After he surrendered his license, he followed the controversy academically, both as an expert witness and as a defendant himself in many cases."

George asked, "You interviewed him, right?"

"Several times," she said.

"How did he seem to you?" I wanted to know.

"Varied. Sometimes was intoxicated, incoherent. Other times, quite lucid. But every time, he was absolutely convinced that he knew why some women developed autoimmune symptoms and others did not."

"Did he say why? Was it the gel? Random problems for some women? Or what?"

"Morgan said the problem wasn't caused by any of those theories. He said he knew the solution. He'd recently approached all of the manufacturers and defense attorneys. He offered to disclose his conclusions for the defense," Robin explained.

"But that never happened, did it?" I asked.

"Because of his background, all of the defendants refused to be associated with him. They said they'd rely on more legitimate research," she said.

George groaned. "I'm guessing Morgan didn't take that well."

Robin laughed ruefully. "You knew the guy, then? I met with him a few days before he died. He was outraged. Wanted to show them all up. He told me his theory and gave me a video of his presentation."

"What did you do with the video?"

"I wrote a freelance feature for *The New York Times*, Sunday Edition. After Morgan disappeared, they held it a few weeks. But it'll be published next week. I can fax you an advance copy, if you like, Willa."

We accepted her offer and signed off. I gave George a proper thank you kiss, and headed to the shower when he trudged down to the restaurant for the Saturday night dinner crowd.

Cuddled up with Harry and Bess. Read the fax four times. Well written, but too many information gaps. And no video.

So I made a plane reservation on a six-thirty flight the next morning.

Then, I called Kate's son, Mark, for an early lunch. No answer. Again.

CHAPTER TWENTY-SEVEN

Tampa, Florida
Sunday 5:30 a.m.
January 24, 1999

AWOKE TO ANOTHER GLORIOUS January day, with dawn
in its infancy and ambient temperature fifty-five degrees.
Carefully slipped away from my sleeping husband and ducked
into the shower. Postponed my morning Java; I'd pick up a latte
at the terminal. Sunday morning meant light traffic all the way to
Tampa International Airport's short-term parking lot. Smooth
sailing along the surface streets, timing the traffic lights, and I
arrived eight minutes after leaving our driveway; so quick, my
hair was still slightly damp.

Parked Greta near the blue elevators, grabbed the
photographs from her glove box, rode down to the third floor and
hustled to slide between the tram's closing doors. No way to
speed up the tram ride, but when it stopped at Airside D I dashed
to the Northwest Airlines gate. The gate agent barely looked up
when she accepted my first-class boarding pass. Walked aboard,

plopped down in 2A, snugged my seatbelt, and checked my watch.

Elapsed time: twelve minutes. Not a personal best, but not bad. So far, the trip was working out as well as I'd planned.

A little extravagant to travel first class for my two hour and fifteen minute nap to Detroit, but worth it to skip chatty vacationers, screaming and seat-back kicking kids, and cranky businessmen crammed into coach. During my years in private practice constant travel had generated a limitless supply of frequent flier miles close to expiring anyway. In those days I seemed never to sleep anywhere except on airplanes. Back then I'd nod off before my plane left the gate. No more.

Today, I watched the departure show unfold as it normally did until takeoff. Twenty-five seconds after lift-off I'd completed my prayers and for the first time since August 16, 1987, failed to drop into immediate REM sleep for the duration of my flight.

The normal nap schedule had been stamped into my brain by the crash of Northwest Flight 255, the deadliest sole-survivor crash in U.S. aviation history and the first airline disaster I'd personally witnessed.

An unforgettable disaster and equally indelible miracle.

On Sunday night, August 16, 1987, flight 255 was bound for Phoenix. My flight was scheduled to depart thirty minutes later.

I'd changed my travel plans the day before. A second deposition had been added to our docket. Instead of a quick trip out to Phoenix and back on 255, our team now planned to start in California and then hit Phoenix on the way home to Detroit. I'd watched 255 load passengers at the gate, still angry that I wasn't one of them because my opposing counsel had forced a second day of travel into my jam-packed schedule.

Flight 255 pushed back at 8:32 p.m., right on time.

Light rain drizzled outside, but storms were moving our way. Everybody needed to get out before the storms delayed everything to a snarled mess.

The DC-9's engines started easily enough and 255 taxied to runway 3C, my runway, awaiting clearance for takeoff. The plane ran an abnormally long takeoff roll, almost all the way to the end of the runway, before it lifted off.

But thirteen minutes after push-back, at exactly 8:45 p.m., 255 rotated skyward for takeoff. And something went horribly wrong.

The plane never gained altitude.

Never soared.

It lifted less than fifty feet off the ground. A series of quick disasters followed.

Flight 255 rolled left and hit a light pole, severing a portion of its left wing.

Rolled right, hit another light pole, another, and the top of a building.

Belly-flopped into flames.

Bounced and skidded a wide fiery ball along Middlebelt Road dropping burning sections and killing two motorists on the ground in its wake.

After twenty seconds, Flight 255 slammed into the I-94 expressway's eastbound overpass and exploded like a giant bomb flooding heat and smoke, destroying by impact forces and fire.

Only one passenger survived. A four-year-old girl seated in 8-F, traveling with her brother and parents. She was found still belted into the seat, 35 yards from her mother. She suffered broken bones and burns, but pictures featured a big pink hair-bow and purple nail polish and a beloved brown teddy snugged under her left arm. *The Detroit Free Press, The Detroit News* and countless national media described every conceivable detail about the "miracle child of Flight 255."

Twenty seconds can be a lifetime. For 156 people one hot August Sunday evening, it was. But for the miracle child and me, twenty seconds defined our lives.

The girl was reunited with relatives and lived a devout life, I'd heard. I often thought about her and everyone who died that night.

After pushback I watched my fellow passengers and imagined 255's travelers spent those last thirteen minutes getting settled, organizing blankets and pillows, opening books and magazines. On my flight, mothers comforted children and nervous fliers relaxed grips on the seat's arms when the plane safely left the tarmac and continued to climb. On 255, passengers must have done much the same, too briefly.

For the first twenty-one seconds after takeoff on every flight, I pray.

Once airborne this day, my fellow passengers relaxed. Babies no longer cried with earaches, conversations resumed, couples squeezed loved ones, opened their books, closed their eyes. Window-side passengers admired the view.

Flight 255 went down twenty seconds after liftoff; normally, after twenty-one seconds, I do, too.

But not today.

Today, sleep was pushed aside by the riddle I couldn't seem to solve: Who killed Michael Morgan?

CHAPTER TWENTY-EIGHT

Tampa, Florida
Sunday 7:20 a.m.
January 24, 1999

AT THIS POINT, THE possibilities seemed endless, even if I discounted all my personal acquaintances. I ran though the list.

Any lawyer involved in the breast implant litigation, on either side, would certainly have a motive to keep Morgan's threatened great solution to the health issues from ever being published, if Carly's theory of the litigation were true.

Ditto, the "victims," manufacturers, and the doctors making bundles on expert fees.

Somehow, though, I thought the murder a little too vicious, too devious for a purely professional motive. The killer took extraordinary steps to keep his work secret. Only luck and the low tide caused Morgan's body to be discovered.

Morgan was reported missing. The police would eventually have inspected Morgan's home and found the obvious evidence of murder, but with no physical body a charge and conviction was unlikely.

No, simply killing Morgan was not the goal.

The killer meant to make Morgan disappear. Forever.

Bad luck, not stupidity, had thwarted the killer's achievement.

Not a detached professional motive, then, but a personal one.

Methodically, I considered each person I knew to have an axe to grind with Michael Morgan. I took out my yellow legal pad, filled now with notes, facts, thoughts on the case. I wrote down each of the possible suspects on two pages, leaving room for notes after each name.

Forced myself to consider each one in turn.

Eliminated Carly immediately.

Carly didn't kill Morgan; I wouldn't consider the possibility. She had no motive. If she'd discovered her company's products were faulty, she could have resigned. She didn't own MedPro, after all.

Nor did she have the capacity to kill.

Carly had always been difficult and often impossible, and I do subscribe to the nature theory of childhood development. Even so, I wouldn't believe any of Kate's children capable of murder. Never.

Which led me to consider MedPro's two remaining founders: Dr. Zimmer and Dr. Young.

Zimmer was least likely. Too old and frail to kill Morgan in his home and spirit his body off to the gulf.

An accomplice? Possible.

But Zimmer worried excessively about death by heart attack. He'd quit golf because he feared the stress might kill him. He wouldn't risk the physical and emotional stress of murder on his weakened ticker. Certainly not simply to avoid *potential* financial ruin when he held only a *partial* interest in MedPro.

Sadly, no. Not Zimmer. I crossed him off my list.

The next name seemed to come alive on the page, tapping its feet, dashing to the finish line, shoving everyone aside, declaring itself the winner.

Carolyn Young.

Yes. Definitely a killer candidate.

By all accounts except hers, Morgan had used her. And discarded her like so many others. She admitted she never got over him. That sounded like a good motive for murder, but it wasn't the only one she had.

Carolyn Young was an owner of MedPro. Marilee Aymes claimed Carolyn was willing to commit theft to obtain that ownership. She also sought to protect her very lucrative explant scam and expert witness fees. The end of the litigation would make a sizeable dent in her earning power. For Carolyn Young, killing Morgan would have been both personal and professional.

I wanted to believe it, but I didn't quite.

Maybe if she hadn't made such a public spectacle of herself at his funeral? That day, it seemed to me, she really did love him still.

Not crossing her off, but I kept going down my list.

Considering the strengths and weaknesses of each suspect in the same way, I covered Marilee Aymes (very angry, capable of lifting the body, a good shot?), Victoria Warwick (woman scorned?), Sheldon Warwick (reelection bid tainted by wife's affair with Morgan?).

Paused. Sheldon Warwick is a proud man. He wouldn't be pleased by Tory's affair. But murder? Everybody knows Tory's a flake. If it never affected him before, no evidence the knowledge pushed him to kill this time.

Christian Grover (a definite possibility), Fred Johnson (the same motive as every other plaintiffs' lawyer on the planet), O'Connell Worthington (ditto on the defense side), even Cilla Worthington (you've got to be kidding), Kate (now you're really getting silly).

I still had several names to cover, but the flight attendant tapped my shoulder and asked me to put my seatback in its full upright position for landing, and the captain slowly lowered the L1011 onto the runway at Detroit Wayne Airport. Passengers did not applaud, but we should have.

One major advantage to flying first class, besides interesting flying companions and comfortable seats, is that first class is always at the front of the plane. While my fellow passengers accumulated overstuffed bags and waddled up the aisle, I dashed out into the frigid jet way and immediately realized I'd forgotten my parka.

January above the Mason Dixon line. How absurd.

Instead of renting a car, I turned my pink tropical wool blazer's lapels up, hustled to the taxi stand and stomped around to generate warmth in the sunless damp while I waited for the first available heated cab.

"The Renaissance Center, please," I said between chattering teeth, naming the city within a city now synonymous with the best of Detroit.

He looked at me like I'd have to repeat myself in Arabic before he'd comprehend, but after a while the taxi headed east onto the rebuilt I-94 entrance ramp toward Detroit. The only trace of Flight 255 was the black marble memorial surrounded by blue spruce trees on Middlebelt Road.

About twenty-five minutes later, I winced at Joe Lewis's oversized black fist positioned at the entrance to downtown Detroit. Joe Lewis was a great native son, but why the artist couldn't have presented a more flattering and welcoming sculpture of the man was a mystery.

The temperature sign at Comerica Bank declared fifteen degrees without the wind-chill factor, which would bring the "feels like" temperature down another ten to twenty. *Shit.*

The taxi driver pulled into the driveway between the chiller berms, stopped in front of the RenCen's main entrance, collected his forty-five-dollar-plus-tip ransom, and released me.

Briefly, I looked up. The Renaissance Center, brainchild of Henry Ford II, was built to revitalize Detroit's economy. Designed by an Atlanta architect and opened in 1976, it resembled a collection of five giant silver cans separated from the rest of the city by a concrete bunker. The center cylinder, at seventy-three stories, housed the claimed tallest all-hotel skyscraper in the western hemisphere.

Lingering to admire was impossible. No matter. I knew every inch of the place.

Frigid cold chased me inside the icy architecture where the indoor temperatures were marginally higher. Chillers inside the berms used Detroit River water to heat and cool the building. Slight miscalculation. River water, like the atmosphere inside and out, was near frozen in winter.

By 1980, completed and occupied, the RenCen was memorable for three truths: Gleaming buildings reflected Detroit's decline too brightly. The cylindrical labyrinth was impossible to navigate even with a blueprint and a guide. And the post-construction fight was the first lawsuit of my career. I defended the case for eight years before we moved to Tampa.

Now Detroit was more decrepit than ever. Locating restrooms inside the cornerless RenCen buildings remained impossible and the construction lawsuit continues without me.

I rode the glass elevator facing the Detroit River and Canada up forty-five floors to The Renaissance Club at the top of Tower 400. Breathtaking view. Made me almost nostalgic for the city where I'd practiced law for eight years.

Almost, but not quite.

I shivered again in the cold elevator; wrapped my arms around myself. How had I ever survived here?

Robin Jakes waited in the club's lobby, fashionably attired in a heavy wool pantsuit, closed shoes, and a turtleneck. She was a bit shorter and wider than I am, but when she greeted me with a warm hug, I bent and too enthusiastically embraced, clinging for body heat.

Seated at a window table, hot coffee poured, caught up on family matters, I held the cup in both palms like a warmer and prompted, "So tell me what your articles didn't say about Michael Morgan."

Robin's crooked chagrin seemed genuine. "He was a curious guy. Brimming contradictions."

Cold waves emitted from the glass walls, raising gooseflesh over every inch of my skin. Was there no heat in this entire building? I jiggled my legs under the table.

I asked, "How so?"

"Brilliant, arrogant, but charmingly charismatic. A parade of lovers, but serially monogamous, he said."

"All female? The lovers?"

She tilted her head, as if the question hadn't occurred to her. "I never asked, but I'd guess he was two-thousand percent hetro."

I nodded. "What did you talk about?"

"He used to ask me why women latch onto every screwy idea that comes along for improving their physical appearance."

"Not what I'd have expected from him," I said.

She folded ringless fingers with short buffed nails together on the table between us. "He raved for hours about how women spend billions of dollars on makeup and clothes to enhance their outer appeal, and billions more on drugs, creams, and injections."

"What about surgery?"

"That, too. Then he'd move on to eating disorders and the American woman's preoccupation with excessive thinness. Women die, he'd say, but others are not deterred."

"Curious rant for such a womanizer, don't you think?"

"I do. I did. But he seemed possessed, almost." She mocked his tone and cadence while wagging a pointed finger at me. "Health is one thing. Exercise and proper nutrition for health reasons is sound thinking. Prolonging the joy of living is everyone's right. But bulimia, anorexia, plastic surgery, removal of ribs, tattoos, body piercing. These are abominations, mostly preying on women, primarily frivolous and some seriously harmful. You are a beautiful woman. Don't do things like that."

The waiter warmed our coffee and delivered soup. I wondered if I could put my frozen feet in it.

CHAPTER TWENTY-NINE

Tampa, Florida
Sunday 1:35 p.m.
January 24, 1999

ROBIN ADOPTED TWO VOICES now, hers for questions and Morgan's for answers, like an audio book. "And the men, I asked him. What are they doing? He said, 'They wear oxford cloth button down collar shirts from ages eight to eighty, from his mother's selections until his undertaker chooses.' Then he'd wave his hand to flip through the next bit. He said, 'With brief respites in the teen years for obnoxious T-shirts and middle age for red bikinis.'"

She chuckled at the image these last two apparently conjured up.

I was half listening and shivering, and otherwise thinking that Carly had delivered a variation of this same speech not too long ago. She must have heard the rant from Morgan, too.

"Morgan made more than one fortune exploiting this supposed wealthy-woman's neurosis," I said.

Robin teased, "And slept with them all before, during and after. That's what made him interesting to interview. Sex and attraction is an endlessly fascinating topic. Haven't you read the bestseller list lately?"

We ordered more coffee, and she salivated when our waiter presented the desert tray featuring six different bowls of ice cream. Even the smell made me colder.

I lit up a Partaga. I think better when I'm smoking and there's a fire stick in my hand.

Robin ordered a double scoop hot fudge sundae. Maybe burning off those extra calories raised her body temperature or something.

"The point is that what Morgan said got me to thinking about the issues, and that's how I sold the piece to the Sunday *Times*. Whatever causes the behavior he described, breast implants might be the poster child for the condition."

"What do you mean?"

"Well, think about it," she said between spoonfuls of the frozen sundae. "A more chauvinistic product has never been marketed. Yet millions were sold, and most implants were beloved—no, more like worshiped—by women. Even after the potential side effects were publicized and access restricted, women manipulate FDA rules to get implants." She'd finished the sundae and pushed aside the dish. "Why is mammary fat worth all that pain? Maybe even death?"

"You'll be nominated for a Pulitzer, Robin. The article is well done. Maybe we can talk more on the phone when I get home?"

"Oh, sure. You've got a three o'clock plane, right?"

I nodded. "What's on the video tapes?"

"The Morgan video is running on "Dateline" Thursday night.

I brought you a copy. You can take it with you." She handed me a blue plastic box.

"What's in the shopping bag?"

"I've got about twenty hours of raw footage. I talked to him on every conceivable subject over a period of weeks," she placed the bag closer to my seat. It contained more than a dozen similar blue boxes. "I thought you might want to see all the tapes. Get Frank Bennett to play them for you."

"Why?"

"Commercial tapes. They can't be viewed on your home equipment."

Robin paused as if to confirm something to herself before she pulled one last box out of her briefcase. She pulled a five dollar bill from her pocket.

"You're still a lawyer, aren't you, Willa?"

What was she getting at? I paused. Slowly, responded, "Yes."

"You told me once that you'd be my lawyer if I ever needed one. Do you remember that?"

"Well, yes, but—"

"Take this five dollars." She handed the bill to me and I took it without thinking. "You're my lawyer now. Whatever I ask you to keep confidential, you can't disclose without my consent."

"Well, not exactly—"

She handed the red plastic box across the table. Held it a moment too long before she released it to me.

"The taped presentation Dr. Morgan wanted to make to the manufacturers. He gave it to me in confidence, but now that he's dead…"

Her voice trailed off.

I put the five dollar bill in my pocket and opened the box. A black tape. No label. No identifying marks. Maybe fingerprints or DNA could be lifted from it or the box?

Snapped the box closed again.

Glanced up and met her steady gaze.

"Do you really want to give this to me? I might be required to turn it over to authorities. Are you okay with that?"

"I don't know who else Morgan showed it to. I haven't disclosed it and I'll take your word that you won't either. Not unless you ask me first."

I worked through the likelihood that I'd be required to give up the tape. No matter. I absolutely wouldn't give it back without seeing it.

A fact Robin had counted on.

"Red alert, huh?"

I slipped the red box into the bag with the others.

She laughed, "It's a bombshell, all right. We've known each other a long time, Willa. You won't disclose the tape without my permission. If I can't trust a judge, who can I trust?"

Indeed. She didn't know the CJ.

"You know as much about the evidence as anyone at this point, Robin. Do you agree with Morgan's theory?"

She tapped her index finger against her empty ice cream bowl. After four beats, she said, "I've heard enough theories to fill the Library of Congress. Suffice it to say Morgan believed. I guess I don't expect it to be what he liked to call it."

"Which was?"

"'The Silicone Solution.' He believed his solution would end the lawsuits and give women their peace of mind again. He thought businesses could go back to making good products that women wanted to buy. But his is just a theory. Like the others. Could be true. Maybe not." She shrugged.

"If you don't believe it, then why do you care if I show the video?"

Robin said, "Watch everything first. Then, if you feel you want to share it with someone, ask me first. I'll probably agree. I've kept copies; already sold copyrighted stories. You'll have to let Frank watch with you anyway. I trust him, too."

She and Frank have been working the Michigan/Florida connection for years.

We rode down together in the elevator, smoothly gliding through 400 feet of cold, gray January sky.

Robin placed one hand on my arm to draw my attention.

"One last thing, Willa, that might be important."

"Yes?"

She took a deep breath and for the first time, seemed reluctant. The elevator continued to slide. Robin stalled. "Now that Morgan's dead, I've been feeling guilty about not reporting this sooner but he didn't want me to, so I respected his wishes. I'm not even sure it's true or that he would want me to tell anyone."

She sounded unsure, tentative. Very un-Robin like.

The elevator stopped at ground level. My flight was due to depart in ninety minutes. I'd need to hustle.

"Robin, I've got to go. Right now. I'll treat this like everything else we've discussed. I promise. What is it?"

She hesitated briefly. I pulled my arm away. "Robin—"

She sighed, said, "You'll see on the tapes that Morgan and I got quite friendly after a while. He was coming on to me, I think more out of habit, you know? It's how he related to women."

"Yes," I drew it out to encourage her to hurry it up.

"But he started to tell me things. About his life. Stuff I don't think he would have told me otherwise. You know, how many affairs he'd had, how he wished he'd had children, things like that."

"Okay."

"Everything is on the tape. I never talked to him off the record."

"Robin, look. I'm sorry. I cannot miss my plane. Walk with me."

She trekked by my side a few steps before she stopped again, took another deep breath. "Okay. Well, one of the things he said. He was being blackmailed. For more than ten years."

Not such a secret. He'd told Carly the same thing.

"Did he say why?"

"It started when he agreed to settle his first wrongful death case. There was a confidentiality agreement. He denied liability." She hesitated.

"But?"

"He knew he'd killed that patient."

Wow. Way to bury the lede. I stopped pulling away. Gave Robin my full attention.

Asked, "I take it someone else knew, too?"

She nodded. "Morgan paid for silence."

"How much?"

"Three million dollars. Or more. He was a little vague on the total."

I whistled, low and slow. Three million reasons to kill.

Made sense if Morgan had been the perpetrator of blackmail, not the victim.

Why would the blackmailer kill the golden goose?

Unless Morgan was threatening to stop paying. Then, maybe it made sense.

"Did he tell you who the blackmailer was?" I asked her.

"You'll find the conversation. I don't know which tape. May be a couple hours in, though."

"Robin, I've really got to go now. I'll call you from home." I pulled my arm away.

"Just be careful, OK? Blackmailers kill, too."

I returned her quick hug and promised to keep in touch.

Jogged to the taxi stand lugging her shopping bag filled with videotapes and hoped I'd have time to buy a duffle at the airport.

Waited to catch a cab, totally unaware of the biting cold.

CHAPTER THIRTY

Tampa, Florida
Sunday 3:50 p.m.
January 24, 1999

ON THE RETURN FLIGHT, I got my list of suspects out again and I had more to think about. If Morgan was being blackmailed, and he'd paid over three million dollars over the years in what the novelists call "hush money," where did he get it? He was a successful doctor, I'm sure he made a good living for his time, and he had written more than one successful textbook. But he'd had more than a little trouble with lawsuits, drugs, and high living. He made some money from his ownership interest in MedPro. Still, even one million after tax dollars would be hard to come by.

I pulled out the photographs I took of Morgan's house. I looked at the kitchen, the blood on the wall, the position of the table and the door. I looked at the living room again, examining the strewn furniture and books. I remembered that something about the house bothered me when I was there and I tried to look at it again in my memory, with the pictures to help. I visualized the scene, then looked at the picture of that part of the house. I kept looking at the pictures and visualizing the rooms. Suddenly it came to me. I had it. It wasn't what I'd seen, but what I hadn't seen that had bothered me.

I thought about every private home I've ever been in, including ours. Had I ever seen one so obviously lived in as Michael Morgan's with absolutely no personal photographs at all? I couldn't think of one.

So where did Morgan's personal photographs go? And why? Did they include the killer? Or the reason for the murder? Too many questions, and too little information. But it was an angle I hadn't considered before, and I knew Hathaway hadn't either. I wrote the word "Pictures" in capital letters on the top page of my yellow pad.

Another thing was the blackmail. Everything I knew about Morgan's finances would fill a thimble but I just couldn't make it add up to a few million extra dollars to pass to a blackmailer after taxes, or even more unlikely, outside the IRS. Where had that money come from? Maybe he got the money the same way he paid it out, in blackmail. I liked the idea, but I had no evidence to support it; unless it was in this bag of videotapes I'd practically had handcuffed to my wrist since Robin gave them to me. I wrote "Blackmail" on my legal pad, too, as if I'd forget it.

I got back from Detroit about 6:30 at night. I hadn't had a chance to call George to tell him about my conversation with Robin, so he didn't yet know about the tapes. When I got home, the first thing he told me was that Grover was being held for questioning in the murder of Michael Morgan. George had called Ben Hathaway and told him we believed Grover had some knowledge of Carly's whereabouts, so Ben agreed that we could

come down to the station and observe him question Grover
through the one-way mirror. Grover had refused a lawyer. What
did he need one for? And even if he did need one, he'd never
admit it.

Ben believed Grover had been blackmailing Morgan.
Morgan's bank statements showed several large payments to
Grover's partner, Fred Johnson, over the last four years. Ben
wanted to believe the money went to Grover but if Grover knew,
he wasn't saying.

George drove us to the Tampa Police Station at about 10:30
p.m. Grover was in the interrogation room and we could both
watch and hear. He consistently denied any knowledge of Dr.
Morgan's new research conclusions. He knew Dr. Morgan was
working on a solution to the breast implant autoimmune disease
issues and, he claimed, that's why he'd refused to allow Morgan
to be deposed in any of his cases.

He said he had not seen Dr. Morgan for several months
before Morgan died and had no idea that he had reached any
definitive conclusions. Grover admitted to being under financial
pressure over the loans he had taken out to finance his breast
implant cases, but he denied any involvement in Morgan's death.
He said he was going to be an even richer man when his cases
settled. Why would he need to blackmail Morgan?

After an hour, Ben Hathaway came out and told us he would
be keeping Grover for further interrogation the rest of the
evening, but, unless something new came up, there wouldn't be
enough to arrest him. George and I went home after Hathaway
promised to call us if an arrest was made.

On the way home, I told George what Robin had said
about the blackmail. "What I can't piece together," I said, "if
Johnson was getting the payments, as the bank records

showed, why didn't Ben detain Johnson instead of Grover?"

"Too simple, I guess. We'll have to watch the tapes. The more interesting question is, where did Morgan get the money to pay Johnson?"

"I've been thinking about that. The only thing I can figure is that Morgan blackmailed someone else to get it."

George seemed to consider that for quite awhile before he said, "Yes, and there are so many possibilities. All those rich women with their secrets. Any evidence that Morgan kept a record of what they all told him? And what they might have paid to keep him quiet?"

It was an issue I hadn't considered. What if whoever trashed Morgan's apartment was looking not for "The Silicone Solution," but for a record of blackmail payments? Wouldn't that put a different spin on things? Things are not always what they seem, I had learned over and over in this investigation. But this time, I thought we'd been the victims of deliberate misdirection.

When we got back to Minaret, we walked into the lobby and there was Carly sitting on the couch. As soon as she saw us, she ran toward us, sobbing hysterically. She kept saying, "You've got to help me, you've got to help me" over and over and over.

We took her upstairs and managed to get her calmed down. Between sniffling and hiccupping, she managed to tell us the problem. "Christian's been arrested. They think he murdered Dr. Morgan. You've got to help me get him out."

I shook her, hard. It startled her into a less histrionic pose, but only for a moment. "What do you mean?" I asked her. "Grover's not been arrested, he's being questioned. Maybe he killed Dr. Morgan. And if he did, he'll be charged."

"Oh, Willa!" and she began to sob all the harder. "Christian didn't kill Dr. Morgan. We can't let him be charged with murder."

"How do you know he didn't do it?"

"I know him. He couldn't have done it. Anyway, I know who did. That's why I've been hiding. It wasn't Christian," she said while tears continued to pour from her eyes at about the same water volume as the Naguchi fountain in front of the Convention Center.

"Then who did kill Dr. Morgan?" I asked her, fully expecting her to name Johnson or Young or even Aymes.

"O'Connell Worthington."

"But that's not possible!" I said.

"That's preposterous!" George said simultaneously. We both sat down heavily on the couch.

"Maybe," Carly hiccupped, "but true. I saw him outside Morgan's house that night. I went to see Morgan. I had convinced MedPro that he'd found The Silicone Solution and it was good news for us. I wanted to tell him they'd meet with him. It was what he wanted, and I knew he'd be happy." Her nose was streaming at the same rate as her eyes and George gave her his handkerchief. George might be the only man on the planet who still has a freshly washed linen handkerchief at all times.

CHAPTER THIRTY-ONE

Tampa, Florida
Monday 1:00 a.m.
January 25, 1999

"I CIRCLED HIS BLOCK a couple of times because there was a car pulled up on the side of the house and I didn't want to meet anyone there, or," and she looked a little sheepish, "interrupt him if he was busy."

We all knew what she meant.

"Anyway, on about the third pass, I saw Mr. Worthington leaving the house, pulling off a pair of surgical gloves. He dropped a gun into his pocket." Her breath caught. She gulped air. "I left right away. But I've been afraid he saw me. I think he trashed my apartment."

I sat dumbfounded. George was, too. No one said anything for a long time.

Not that I believed her. O'Connell wouldn't have committed murder.

Nor would I allow Carly to accuse him. Probably seeking

to divert attention from Grover, a much more likely suspect.

"Why didn't you tell me this before?" I asked her, quiet steel in my tone.

Carly looked down at her hands. Seemed to have difficulty answering the question. She'd twisted George's handkerchief into a thin rope, and then pulled it as if she could shred the linen into pieces the way she'd done with her paper napkin that first day.

A dark stain spread over her neckline, wet with tears. She refused to meet my gaze.

"I told Christian."

My temperature rose about ten degrees. George laid a calming hand on my shoulder. He should have covered my mouth.

Sarcasm. "Because he's such a *trustworthy* man, I suppose?"

Two hiccups. More nose blowing.

She whispered, "We've been secretly living together for about a year. Don't feel left out. No one knew."

George's hand on my shoulder squeezed hard. Not as good as duct tape over my mouth, but I got the message.

"Okay," I said, drawing out the word into three syllables.

"Not about Morgan's research. I wouldn't tell Christian that." More sniveling. "But about Worthington. He said no one would believe me. Worthington's reputation is impeccable. Except for my relationship to you, which isn't even legal, I'm a nobody. I'd had an affair with his nephew, which he disapproved of. Why would anyone believe me?"

I'd have politely disagreed, but why lie?

Carly nodded. "See? Even you think so. Christian was right."

She took an enormous amount of air into her lungs and rushed the rest. "And we thought they'd find his body quickly and forensics would prove Worthington did it and then I wouldn't have to say anything at all."

She began crying again, but this time her tears flowed silently. We waited while her wave of tears passed. She blew her nose one more time.

"But then, they didn't find the body and when they finally found it, they didn't know who it was. The time dragged on and on. I got so stressed I couldn't function."

George asked, "What were they looking for? In your apartment?"

She smiled, albeit weakly. Reached into her pocket and pulled out a computer disk. "I'm not sure, but I think he was looking for this."

"What is it?" George and I asked at the same time.

"I think it's Dr. Morgan's solution report. I think it lays out all of his data and conclusions. He gave it to me the last time I saw him."

"Why?"

"He said someone was trying to kill him, but I thought he was kidding."

George frowned.

"He wanted you to hide this in your apartment?" I asked.

She shook her head. "He asked me to have it encrypted. We have sophisticated equipment for that. Thwarts intellectual property theft."

"I see," George said.

Carly seemed on firm footing now, discussing her work instead of murder. "If it checks out, and I've convinced MedPro to analyze it, Morgan said his solution vindicates all of the defendants. He planned to put an end to this litigation. Stop the bleeding, he called it."

She looked up and met my gaze, much stronger. She'd found firmer footing. Seemed almost okay.

"We may be the evil empire," she smiled, "but we're striking back."

After a few moments of silence, Carly said, "So what should we do now?"

It was well after midnight. I was dead tired. Not in the mood to traipse to the police station again. Hathaway wouldn't release Grover on the strength of a statement from his lover, even if George and I vouched for them both.

Robin's tapes beckoned.

Let's be honest. I wasn't about to accuse O'Connell Worthington, Tampa's most prominent legal figure, of something that couldn't be proved. CJ was on my back over a parking place mix-up. I could only imagine what he'd do to me after I accused his brother-in-law of murder.

No, I wouldn't act on Carly's story without more.

I admit my ego was involved, too.

I'd been with O'Connell Worthington almost every day during the trial, and never guessed he'd recently murdered a man. He appeared less distraught than Carly did now. In fact, his work defending his client had been excellent.

He believed in the manufacturers' cause. Worthington wouldn't suppress evidence proving his clients were right. Carly's theory there made no sense.

Beyond all of that, I didn't trust her. She'd been withholding information from me all along. Why take her at her word now? Wouldn't that make me an even bigger fool?

But then I remembered Worthington's temper tantrum the

day of the Bar meeting. And his opulent surroundings.

Maybe money corrupts absolutely.

But for O'Connell, the code of honor he lived by was strong.

No, I didn't believe he killed for money. No matter what Carly thought she saw.

She waited for my answer.

I stood, stretched, yawned.

"We'll see Chief Hathaway in the morning, but not tonight, Carly. Let's get some rest first. It'll be a brutal meeting. We'll need all the strength we can muster," George said.

She agreed to wait, but she wasn't happy about it.

"You can see Hathaway without us, Carly. Or you know where the guest room is. I'm exhausted," I said.

She pouted all the way to her room and slammed the door. Her petulance made me feel better because it felt normal.

George and I fell into bed.

During the night, I either dreamed or hallucinated Morgan's murder over and over, like a tape loop.

Never did I see O'Connell Worthington shoot Morgan. I couldn't visualize it; couldn't rationalize it, either.

O'Connell was small and slight, not to mention old.

He could have shot Morgan, sure. But no way he could he have moved the body into the trunk of his car.

O'Connell's car? White BMW. Not dark blue sedan.

I couldn't make it add up. When I stopped trying, I must have finally dozed off. But not for long.

After a couple of hours, I gave up. Padded to the kitchen. George was already there with the coffee, looking more exhausted than I felt.

"Can't make the facts fit. Even if he *would* have done it—which I don't believe—he *couldn't* have done it. O'Connell couldn't have removed and dumped the body. He's not big enough; strong enough."

"Adrenaline can do that," George reminded me.

"I don't believe it. The effort would have killed O'Connell, too." I plopped my head in my hands, bleary eyed and wired.

George looked no better. We were on the same mental wavelength, though.

He said, "Unless he had help. If he didn't do it alone."

"A conspiracy? How could he trust *anyone* to keep quiet about such a thing?" Lifted my head, swigged the last of my coffee. Took my cup to the pot for a refill. The pot was empty. I started a fresh one.

"Maybe it's time to look at those video tapes Robin gave me. I'll bring your coffee if you'll set up. The red box is on top of the television."

George grunted; left to get the television in the den organized. None of the other tapes would play on our home equipment. For the rest, we'd ask Frank Bennett to use his editing booth at NewsChannel 8.

The coffee brewed, I carried both cups toward the low sound emanating from the tapes. When I reached the perfect vantage point, I saw the television screen filled edge-to-edge with an older, male version of Carly Austin's face.

I dropped both mugs of coffee all over George's favorite of Aunt Minnie's wool antique rugs.

"God Damn it, Willa! What's the matter with you?" George jumped up, ran to gather wet towels to soak up the coffee before stains grew dark and permanent.

George pushed the "mute" button on the remote. No sound distracted.

I stood transfixed.

Morgan's blue eyes sparkled, as Kate said, just like Carly's. His red hair was identically curled. His complexion was ruddy where her skin was flawless, but that might have been from age or drink. His smile was hers, and so were his teeth. Even the nose, although he could have afforded a more substantial one.

Why didn't I know this earlier?

Morgan. Carly's father. The best explanation for her fixation on him.

Anything less would never have captured Carly's attention to the same extent.

So many clues. Why hadn't I figured it out? I'd seen photographs of him, certainly, but always black and white. I'd never met him. Yet, I should have known. I felt like an idiot.

George returned with his wet towels, saw me still staring at the television.

"What the hell?" he said.

I grabbed his arm and pointed his gaze toward the screen.

"Look, George. Look at him. Who do you see?" I whispered.

"Michael Morgan, I presume," he said, mocking the old "Dr. Livingston" routine. "But if he upsets you that much, I'll turn him off."

He collected the remote and did just that.

George still didn't see it.

I guess if you didn't know, maybe it wasn't so obvious, and I felt a little less like the loser in the old "I spy" child's game: One child picks out something in plain sight and the others try to find it.

Having a good grasp of the obvious is a positive character trait.

I'd always believed I possessed it.

CHAPTER THIRTY-TWO

Tampa, Florida
Monday 4:30 a.m.
January 25, 1999

WHY WAS MY AWAKENING so jarring? I'd tired of
Carly's quest long ago. Partly, I thought her unrelenting
quest disrespectful to her mother. Now, I didn't know what to
think.

George said, "Are you planning to fill me in here?"

So I related the entire tale. What Kate had told me about
Carly's father, and what I had already known.

"It's him. Michael Morgan. Carly's sperm donor," I said.

"That's not possible."

"It's the only possible explanation, George. I've eliminated
every other possibility. Look at the guy."

I punched the remote, left the sound muted. George watched
Morgan talk, move, gesture.

Distractedly, he said, "The resemblance is uncanny."

No kidding.

Of course he was Carly's father. Otherwise, why put Carly in his will?

He asked, "Does Carly know?"

"She must," I said. "But if not, should we tell her? Or should we confront Kate?"

That idea did not appeal to me. At all.

We hashed it around for awhile before we punted. We'd watch the tapes, then decide.

Carly knew what Morgan looked like. She must know more. Interesting that she'd never mentioned the resemblance, if that's all it was.

I picked up the phone. Dialed.

"Who are you calling at this hour?" George demanded, watching the video still.

He picked up on the third ring. "Frank. Willa Carson here. I need a favor."

Maybe, if he hadn't had that crush on me, he'd have refused. But I'd never called him before dawn. Once a news man, always a news man.

"Robin Jakes suggested I call you."

Instantly alert he replied, "Oh?"

I explained what we had, what we needed.

He said, "I'll meet you at the station in fifteen minutes."

We left Carly asleep in the guest room. Where would she go, after all?

As promised, Frank had set up the editing booth with three chairs and minimum fuss. He knew when to accept a gift horse. Altruism had nothing to do with his decision.

"Start with this one," I said, handing him the edited tape airing later in the week on national television.

"Dateline's" familiar format featured guest journalist Robin

Jakes' interviews with Morgan, interspersed with commentary and reportage about him and his theories, as well as history of the "breast implant crisis."

George smirked. His oft repeated low opinion of the media was that nothing short of a "crisis" was deemed worth covering beyond a ten second sound bite.

Morgan's voice was deep, resonant, commanding. I imagined him crooning in the ears of countless women. No doubt he displayed a certain charm. Good physical condition. If he suspected his killer, overpowering him would have required significant size and strength, as I'd suspected.

Someone he knew, then. Someone he would sit down with at his kitchen table voluntarily. I'd been hoping that theory was untrue.

The story contained several sequences of Robin and Morgan walking around Tampa; along the Bayshore, at University of Tampa, outside his home, sipping coffee con leche at Cold Storage. These sequences were filmed on multiple occasions. Wardrobes, weather, background vehicles and pedestrians varied. The overall effect was of in-depth investigation.

Morgan declared, "I know why some patients get sick and others don't."

Robin asked, "You've researched women with implants who've developed nonspecific auto-immune symptoms, such as rashes, fatigue, joint pain, memory loss and the like?"

"Extensively."

"And what did you discover, Dr. Morgan?" Robin said.

"Quite simply stated, the silicone solution." He didn't seem smug, although the words on a transcript could be read as condescending. "And no one will listen to me."

"We are listening now. Millions of women and their families

are concerned here, Doctor. What is the answer? Why do some women get sick? Allergies? Randomness?" Robin pressed.

His expression and tone were serious, "I'm sorry I can't tell you, and you knew that before you asked. I've explained that we'll reveal the answer at the right time. But I've told someone. And I've provided a sealed copy of my presentation, in case something happens to me before I can present the data in the right context."

Robin leaned in, crossed her forearms, reaching out physically and emotionally. "You've finished your work and prepared a presentation. Why are you unwilling to tell us now?"

His voice shook a bit. "I'm telling you that I know and that's as far as I can go right now. People know I've been researching. There are people who don't want me to find the answer; don't want to know the answer. But I do. And now the world knows I've done it. You might say this interview is life insurance."

Seemed more than a little paranoid, but if Robin challenged his stated fears, the questions must have been left on the cutting room floor. Carly said Morgan told her he'd been threatened. Was that true?

In all, the report was fair and complementary, but was primarily a chance for the regular "Dateline" staff to rehash the breast implant controversy and give a new twist to the story. Aside from revealing Carly's paternity to me, it hadn't told me anything new, but Frank seemed intrigued.

"Put this one in next," I said, handing Frank the tape Robin thought contained the blackmail conversation.

"Robin said this one is about six hours long, and the conversation we're looking for is about half way through." While Frank and I set up, George collected cappuccino, bagels and cream cheese from somewhere. We set to the food like a pack of hungry wolves.

"Okay, maybe three thirty-three?" Frank asked, running the digital counter to that spot.

"She didn't know precisely, but sure. Let's start there," I said.

Robin and Morgan were seated in his living room. I recognized it from my visit to the house, and from my pictures. But the image was disoriented. In Robin's video, all the furniture was upright and the room was arranged as it should be. I took the remote from Frank; manipulated the video until I found a wide-angle shot of the room.

Stopped.

Pictures.

On the piano, to the left of Morgan, were three photographs in frames. Fuzzy. Photos of Morgan and three different women.

"Can we zoom these shots, Frank?"

"Sure. We're all about video around here. Hang on a second."

He pressed some buttons for a few moments, then stepped back. "How's that?"

Bookended disaster.

The first photo was normal. Morgan in black tie, snuggled close to a formally dressed Carolyn Young. She looked beautiful, as always. But also happy.

A fourth picture was Morgan standing between Cilla and O'Connell Worthington. Again dressed in formal wear.

The two center photos were nudes.

Frank restarted the tape.

I felt almost like the night I watched my first plane crash.

George said, "Wow."

Robin spoke angrily. "Mike, during that malpractice case, you knew you were negligent. You operated on a patient while you were drunk. The patient died. How could you possibly think that wasn't your fault?"

Morgan pressed back, heated defense to justified outrage. Blue eyes bulged, face crimsoned, nostrils flared.

Nature or Nurture? The old debate.

But anyone who watched this video and knew Carly at all would see Morgan was her sperm donor without a doubt. DNA not required.

"The woman died. It happens. No proof whatsoever that I did anything below the standard of care," he snapped tough. "Causation, causation, causation. Look, if I'd operated with my feet, pickled to the gills, and she lived, no one would have complained, would they? Besides, I've paid for that mistake. About three million times."

He didn't seem to realize the import of what he'd said, but Robin did.

She followed up quickly with the next question. "What do you mean? The settlement to the family was only $50,000 and the hospital paid, not you."

Morgan responded rapidly, without planning. "That's what the hospital paid her husband, not what I paid the lawyer."

"You mean, the lawyer's forty percent fee?" Robin seemed puzzled, but her instincts told her she was on to something. She went with her instincts.

Morgan snapped back. "No, I don't mean the goddamned fee. I mean the money I paid that bloodsucker Fred Johnson to keep quiet about it."

Fred Johnson?

Grover's partner.

The one whose bank records reflected receipt of Morgan's blackmail payments.

"I spy." Again.

I felt pretty stupid.

We watched more of the unedited interview, getting a feel for Dr. Morgan. Seated beside me, George was drawn to the rest of the tape. Frank, too, seemed glued to the screen, calculating. Probably seeking a method to persuade me to release these tapes for "Live at 5" tonight, but I couldn't worry about that now.

Robin never asked Morgan where he got the money to pay the blackmail, but I figured there could only have been one source. He must have been blackmailing the women he'd had affairs with and passing the money through to Johnson. The married ones would have paid for silence.

But how did he do it? What leverage did he have?

All this time we'd assumed Morgan was murdered because he knew something about the breast implant controversy that his killer wanted to keep quiet.

What if that wasn't the silence motivating his killer?

What if his killer was concerned about another of Morgan's secrets?

We tried to ditch Frank, but he wasn't having it. Now that we'd involved him, he stuck to us like glue. We were finally able to shake him by telling him we were going home to sleep, but we'd call him the second we woke up or if anything at all happened.

Courtesy would keep Frank at bay for about four hours. After that, we'd have to come up with trained Dobermans.

CHAPTER THIRTY-THREE

Tampa, Florida
Monday 7:15 a.m.
January 25, 1999

WHEN GEORGE AND I got home, Carly was still down for the count. We'd consumed too much caffeine and too much tension to sleep.

We put Morgan's report in the computer and read it before we did anything else.

Carly had unencrypted the whole disk allowing us to review the entire document.

The Silicone Solution report was long, complicated, and technical. Written for peers, not the general public like us.

I read through it a couple of times, skimming most of the medical jargon and the scientific recitations, which didn't mean much to me anyway.

Morgan said he had been a member of the medical staff at Mid-Florida University hospital in Tampa and on the faculty for several years back in the 1970s and 80s. Later in his career, the

University allowed him to return to teaching after he'd lost his license to practice medicine, mainly because he promised to bring in grants and do a great deal of research.

He said grants to study the effects of silicone on the human body were easier to get. When the FDA declared a moratorium on breast implants, several of the larger manufacturers immediately donated money for research grants to prove the implants were safe and effective. Morgan's grant was funded by MedPro.

He summarized his research, including the disproved allergy theory.

The report contained tedious details, but the bottom line was no such allergy existed.

Given how ubiquitous silicone is in products I use every day, I was glad to read as much.

However, like the accidental discovery of the glue that didn't stick leading to the invention of those ubiquitous un-sticky note pads, Dr. Morgan said he found something significant instead. He called his answer "Morgan's Syndrome."

Morgan said it's only been within the last century that the immune system has been recognized as the single major determinant of health and disease.

His scholarly and scientific explanation seemed to boil down to this: the immune system is a sophisticated scanning device that searches out and eliminates anything foreign.

When the immune system is compromised or absent, it fails to detect and destroy bacteria causing diseases and allows the body to attack itself, like AIDS.

Morgan described exciting new work in psychoneuroimmunology: the relation of the mind to the body's immune system.

He said recent studies proved conclusively that the brain and the immune systems talk to each other and are interdependent.

Morgan said emotional conflict undermines physical health and absence of stress promotes health.

Oversimplifying, Morgan's conclusion was that the "victimizing" of women by their own lawyers and the media, coupled with unscrupulous doctors willing to make a misdiagnosis without scientific support and to prescribe treatment, along with the hysteria around the supposed ill effects of free floating silicone in the body, had resulted in a psychoneuroimmunologic illness: Morgan's Syndrome.

"In other words," George said, "after all that, Dr. Morgan's great Silicone Solution is that they think themselves sick. How did you say Kate put it? You get what you expect to get."

He stretched and moved to the veranda seeking daylight.

I wondered who would have killed Morgan for that?

CHAPTER THIRTY-FOUR

Tampa, Florida
Monday 8:05 a.m.
January 25, 1999

PSYCHONEUROIMMUNOLOGY: THE SCIENTIFIC STUDY
of the mind/body connection.

So much of the last century had been devoted to the study of
how the human brain works that theories abounded.

From Freud's study of "hysteria" and psychological
dysfunction to Csikszentmihaly's studies on human happiness
and optimal experience, an astonishing number of theories had
been explored.

Physical examinations of Einstein's brain have been going
on since it was retained for study after his death.

Goal setting and visualization are now de rigueur not only
for athletes, but for salesmen, doctors, even day care providers.

Our popular culture has intuitively believed that attitude can
cure cancer, although it's never been proved.

Imagine the impact on all of society if Morgan's theory had

been proved by the scientific method. This would not only be The Silicone Solution, it could be the beginning of a solution to all illness and all achievement.

Man could truly control his own destiny. It would stir more moral debate than cloning, put physicians out of business, cause the gross national product to soar.

And the theory would make the scientist who popularized it immortal as well as rich.

Morgan's solution was so simple that, like the concept of ulcers caused by virus, and colds caused by germs, it would take years before the world would accept it. It would be controversial and next to impossible to prove empirically.

But Robin was right, too. Morgan's theory wouldn't end implant litigation. Too many had too much at stake for that.

No.

The Silicone Solution itself was worth killing for, but it just didn't feel right to me.

Trust your intuition, Kate says.

Greed is a common motive for murder, sure. But this murder was powered by passion.

Before removing the disk from the computer I looked at its directory structure and tried to decipher it.

Everybody has their own way of naming computer files, and some of his I could figure out.

"Rpt.dr1," "Rpt.dr2," were easy: drafts of his reports.

"Cronin.pat" and "mem.pat" were a little tougher, but when I called them up on the screen, they turned out to be lists of patients participating in Morgan's study who had received Cronin and MEM type implants. "Cronin.rup" and other similar files contained data on patients who claimed their Cronin type implants ruptured, and so on.

I examined the entire disk, reviewed files I couldn't figure out by their names. Everything was related to his report, and once I figured out Morgan's system, I would normally have skipped the rest.

But I decided to be thorough rather than impatient, just this one time.

As much as I like to believe in divine insight, or brilliant flashes of genius, I'm sorry to report that thorough, like slow and steady, wins the race.

Eventually, neck screaming through tense muscles, I found it. Buried in the sub directory containing files labeled ".pay": A list of women who had paid Morgan, amounts paid, and when. His very own accounts receivable list.

The total was staggering: enough to pay Frank Johnson's blackmail and then some.

Most of the women in town old enough to have known Morgan in the biblical sense were listed.

The amounts didn't seem reflective of net worth; had they paid more or less depending on how valuable silence was to them?

Some had paid only a few hundred dollars once. Others had paid installments for longer than home mortgages amortized. For some, Morgan's blackmail scheme seemed to be as perpetual as Foucault's pendulum as long as he was alive to collect it. I doubt it could be an asset of his estate. That is, unless someone planned to take up where Morgan left off.

I copied the disk twice for safety; hid the original and one copy in my locked box of discs.

Then, I erased the "pay" files from the copy I put in my pocket to give Chief Hathaway.

No reason to splash these names all over the *Times*. If Tory

Warwick, Carolyn Young, Cilla Worthington and even Kate had paid to keep their affairs with Morgan quiet and never complained, I couldn't see that any valid purpose would be served by disclosing their business now.

The amounts each paid were curious, though. You'd think one of the wealthier women would have been the biggest contributor.

Still, his biggest depositor must have hated him for years as he slowly drove her into poverty. I could imagine her rage, her embarrassment, the scandal of it all.

I'd been right.

This was a murder of passion.

But how to prove it, that was the question.

As I walked out of the study, the house phone rang again. I figured it would be Frank, no longer content to talk to the answering machine, like he had the last three times he called.

"Willa Carson here," I said.

"Chief Hathaway is here to see you," the downstairs hostess said.

"Send him up, please."

I went out to the veranda to get George and checked on Carly. Unbelievably, she was still sleeping.

Hathaway sat in what George had begun calling "the Hathaway chair." He came right to the point.

"We released Christian Grover. Not enough evidence to charge him with murder or blackmail," he said. "We'll keep looking."

"Of course," George said.

Hathaway asked, "Have you found Carly Austin?"

Bad timing. The words were barely out of his mouth when she walked into the room. Hathaway flashed a glare my way. We might all find ourselves in trouble if we were hiding suspects.

"We might be able to help you there, Chief," George told him, dryly.

When you're caught with your hand in the cookie jar, it doesn't help to claim you're looking for the vacuum cleaner.

I said, "It seems Carly has been hiding at Christian Grover's house because she believes she saw the man who murdered Michael Morgan."

Braced myself for the explosion, but it didn't happen.

Maybe Grover had said something to get his own ass out of trouble, or maybe the chief just took one look at Carly and realized that she could never have completed the coverup alone. Surely he considered whether she and Grover did it together. Two people could have managed it. Morgan wasn't that big.

Before Hathaway could get too worked up, George said, "Why don't you tell the chief who killed Morgan and how you know that, Carly."

And she did.

When she finished, I provided the disk in my pocket, along with a short summary of its contents.

Neither George nor I believed her conclusions but neither one of us said Carly was wrong.

Carly saw O'Connell at Morgan's house that night. But O'Connell didn't kill Morgan; he was there to help the killer dispose of the body.

Ben permitted Carly to leave. I've seen slower moving jets than her exit. True love was a powerful motivator, I thought sourly.

We brewed more coffee; I laid out my plan and they both liked it.

We agreed to implement tomorrow.

I didn't promise my plan would draw a valid confession, although both O'Connell and I knew who had killed Morgan.

My arrogance, and too much television, made me believe that under pressure he would name a killer who would never be charged otherwise.

If I hadn't been so tired I'd have recalled his *élan* since the murder. Maybe then I'd have avoided the horrible final scene.

CHAPTER THIRTY-FIVE

Tampa, Florida
Monday 5:30 p.m.
January 25, 1999

I SET IT UP carefully. I'd be spending half an hour alone with a nasty tempered man who was an accessory to murder.

I don't know whether it's easier to kill when you've got nothing more to lose, but I wasn't interested in testing the hypothesis.

Unlike Dr. Morgan, I've never had the patience for science.

My clerk scheduled our meeting for 5:30, after the trial day. My bailiff would be close by. Security in Federal Buildings is tight since the Oklahoma City bombing. I was sure he wouldn't be able to bring in a gun or a knife, and I also thought I could probably take him if I didn't let him sneak up behind me again. Long enough for the bailiff to arrive, anyway.

Belt and suspenders: I scheduled Ben Hathaway for 5:45. Clever, eh? That's why they pay me the big bucks.

O'Connell arrived ten minutes early. I made him wait five

minutes past his appointment time before I allowed my secretary show him in. Business as usual.

When he walked in, he looked around the room as if he was expecting someone else to be there.

I said, "O'Connell, please, sit down."

Waved toward one of the green leather chairs. I didn't need the elevated platform under my desk to enable me to tower over the normally nervous chair inhabitants. But I occupied the office my predecessor had decorated it. He was only about five feet tall, and I'm sure you've got your own ideas about little men with a little power.

In this instance, though, I confess that I felt more confident being a foot taller than I otherwise am.

O'Connell looked up at me from his chair. It put him a little more off balance, unsure.

"Judge Carson." He nodded.

Was he that cool, or reverting to forty years of training?

He said, "Good of you to see me. What can I do for you?"

Smooth.

But I had no intention of allowing him to take over this time.

Put two people in a room who are used to having complete control over their lives sometime and watch what happens. It's a little like two male lions in the same cage. Right now we were circling. He watched for clues.

He hadn't dared to ignore my "invitation" with a case currently in trial in my courtroom. But he wanted to know why I'd summoned him here and he wouldn't ask twice.

I let him simmer a while longer. "Excuse me one minute while I review this order, O'Connell. I'll be right with you."

One of my former partners used to sit in a room with one other occupant in complete silence. Nature abhors a vacuum, he would say. Pretty soon, most people will talk to fill up the silence. O'Connell Worthington was too old and too crafty a player to chatter without purpose. But the silence worked its magic. He began to perspire; a little damp above his upper lip, but it was definitely there.

"Too warm in here for you, O'Connell?" I asked him, letting him know I'd noticed.

"I'm fine, Judge. Thank you."

He clearly wasn't fine.

I was winning round one, and we both knew it.

"O'Connell, I asked you here because I need a little advice." I said, after ten more minutes of silence, putting the order I'd been revising to one side.

He crossed his legs and put his arms on the chair's arms. Giving advice was a role he was all too familiar and comfortable with; I sensed him relax.

I said, "I heard something and I'm wondering how I should handle it. I thought you might be able to help me."

Ah, the irresistible damsel in distress.

"I'd be delighted to help you in any way I can, Wilhelmina. What is it?" Gallant, chivalrous O'Connell asked me.

He smiled.

He struggled to look normal.

But he wasn't.

I looked directly into his eyes. "I know who killed Michael Morgan."

What had I expected? Tears? A breakdown?

His poker face was perfect. Not a twitch.

He didn't say anything.

He seemed unconcerned about whether I knew who the killer was; calculating whether I could prove it.

Lawyers know: if you can't prove it, it didn't happen.

A fine sheen of perspiration now covered his face.

I kept silent, waiting him out.

After a while he cleared his throat and said, "Are you sure?"

Up until that moment, some part of me had doubted Carly's word, doubted Morgan's blackmail story, doubted those damn pictures on the piano.

I wanted O'Connell Worthington to be what I had thought he was. An honorable gentleman, an ethical lawyer with a lovely wife and beautiful family.

Like I'd told Carly, some "perfect" lives only seem that way to outsiders.

Now I knew O'Connell was none of the things I had believed him to be, and it saddened me more than I'd expected.

He *was* at Morgan's house that night. He *did* put the gun in his pocket, and he *was* driving a large, dark sedan. I could feel it. This time, Carly was right.

But I was also right: he wasn't a killer. He couldn't be. My judgment just couldn't be that wrong. Again.

I said, "Yes, I'm sure. I've had testimony from an eye witness."

"Who's the witness? Are you sure he's credible?"

"She. I believe her; and I've had quite a bit of experience with prevaricators."

I'd kept a steady eye on him as we talked.

He'd started to squirm, but you'd have to know O'Connell to notice it.

He slowly pulled out his monogrammed linen handkerchief and wiped his brow. Silly, but my thought was that George isn't the only man who still carries one. O'Connell re-crossed his legs and held onto the handkerchief in his left hand, settled himself more evenly in the chair.

He was stalling, testing me. How much did I know? The best defense—deny, deny, deny.

My intercom buzzed. "Judge Carson, Chief Hathaway is here," my secretary said over the speaker, right on cue and loud enough for Worthington to hear it.

"Ask him to wait, Margaret, thank you." I continued to look at Worthington. "What should I tell him, O'Connell?"

He cleared his throat, twice, before he got it out. "I'm sure your witness is lying, Wilhelmina. Why don't I volunteer to represent her?"

"I've always admired you, O'Connell. When we first arrived in Tampa, you sponsored us at the club. You supported me when I was nominated for my appointment. It was largely because of you that the other big firms in town endorsed me. Your work with the bar has been exemplary. You have been 'Mr. Ethics' to every young lawyer in Tampa."

This was one mournful moment and I allowed my voice to convey the sadness I felt. Not an accusation, but a realization.

He started to fold into himself, diminished by his guilty knowledge. I'd reminded him of what he'd thought he was; what all of us believed him to be. He was remembering the plaque the Hillsborough County Bar Association gave him just last fall naming him Lawyer of the Year. His ego wall covered his entire office. Forty years of life in the law, all gone now. He felt his world collapse.

In the end, his training didn't desert him. He sat tall and proud, held his head high, and said, "Please invite Chief Hathaway in, Judge Carson. I'd like to surrender myself to his custody."

That statement wasn't enough for me. I craved confirmation. "Sure, but just one more thing I'd like to know. Why did you search Carly Austin's apartment and what did you hit me with?"

His chest puffed up with indignation. "I have no idea what you're talking about. I've never hit a woman in my life, including you." He could still be regal when the occasion demanded.

So we called in Ben Hathaway, and O'Connell surrendered.

But he hadn't confessed, and I knew he wasn't Morgan's killer after he was arrested any more than he was before.

Then, feeling like I owed Frank Bennett, I called and told him O'Connell had surrendered. He could cover the story in time for the 11:00 news.

Maybe now that Carly was out of trouble, I could leave the investigating to the professional investigators. Wishful thinking. Again.

CHAPTER THIRTY-SIX

Tampa, Florida
Thursday 5:00 p.m.
January 28, 1999

THREE DAYS LATER, GEORGE and I shared an outside table at the Sunset Bar. He studied next week's menu; I stared at the calm waters of Hillsborough Bay, marking time, now and then rubbing the sore spot on my head and wondering who bopped me with that bowling ball.

"Head's up," George murmured. Unfortunate choice of words. "Hathaway's at the bar."

"Ummm," I said, lowering my lids to avoid eye contact. What I thought was, *"Finally."* Maybe if I ignored Ben, he'd go away. Maybe the whole mess would go away. I'd read Morgan's research several times, but his theories were short on details for erasing screw-ups through mind control.

No luck. Felt the opposite chair groan when Ben plopped his heft onto the seat; heard him slurp a long pull of Ybor Gold out of the frosted mug.

George said, "Good afternoon, Ben."

"In what universe?" was his sour reply.

"Couldn't agree more," I confirmed a little too enthusiastically.

Crunched my eyelids tighter, still focused on eliminating Ben as the personification of my errors. Not working.

I said, "I can't tell you how sad I am that O'Connell Worthington's in jail."

He should have been out by now. Learning my heroes have clay feet might not be the most disappointment I can experience in life, but its right up there with discovering my own stupidity in other respects.

Truth to tell, I was more disappointed that Christian Grover wasn't in custody instead of O'Connell. Not only because I liked Grover less (a lot less), but because Carly liked Grover too much. Grover would cause indigestion around the Thanksgiving Dinner table for years to come.

Definitely not a peaceful thought.

Tried again to focus.

Ben said, "Stay tuned."

George responded. "What?"

Hathaway slurped and swallowed and slammed his empty mug on the table. "We can't prove Worthington actually killed the guy. His lone confession won't cut it with a jury of his peers. I expect him to walk, if the State Attorney bothers to indict him."

"What do you mean?" I hoped I'd managed the perfect note of curiosity.

Ben Hathaway's creative crime solving skills were weak; he'd taken way too long to realize he'd arrested the wrong man for murder.

But it was my fault. I'd misjudged O'Connell Worthington.

When I set him up, I'd expected him to save himself by naming Morgan's killer.

So far, I'd been dead wrong.

"Well, we can't find any trace of a murder weapon, although we've checked the house and his office. He drives a white Cadillac, but his wife drives a black one. Neither vehicle contains any trace of physical evidence in the trunk or anywhere else. And we just can't figure out how he'd have physically been able to move the guy, tie him up, and dump him in the gulf. Dead bodies weigh a lot more than you think."

No kidding. It took three days to figure that out?

Ben ordered a second beer, gulped again. "There's no physical evidence of any kind linking Worthington with the body. The problems with the case go on and on. Sloppy crime, but the cover-up is as close to perfect as anything I've ever seen."

He drained the second mug, set it down softly. Delivered what he'd come here to say. "The big problem is now that Worthington's dead, we'll never know who killed Morgan."

What did he say?

I popped my eyes open and stared.

"Dead?" George and I said simultaneously.

"Suicide. In his cell a couple of hours ago. I thought you'd want to know."

I was speechless. And responsible. My head dropped into open palms, fingers splayed through my hair, rubbing the sore spot harder, pressing the pain.

After a few moments, George asked, "How did it happen?"

Ben stood, crossed arms over ample belly, leaned against the deck rail, ignoring the old wood's groan. "Investigated too many cases over the years himself, I guess. He knew what to do. He tied his socks together and climbed onto the sink. He tied one end of the socks to the bars on the windows and the other end around his neck. Stepped off. That was it. If he'd been a bigger man, he would have pulled the bars off the window. But he was so slight, they held."

Tears pooled in my eyes. How could O'Connell be dead? How would I ever live with myself?

George took my hand, squeezed tight.

"He was a proud man, Willa. The shame. Tampa's a small town that way. He'd have felt an outcast in a home he once owned." He squeezed my hand tighter. "Really, what else would he do?"

George meant to comfort us all but his words failed.

My stupid idea put O'Connell in jail. He wouldn't have been there otherwise. He'd still be alive.

Now two men were dead and the killer, I believed, still free.

Although I wasn't so sure it mattered anymore. At some point, enough has got to be enough.

O'Connell paid for Morgan's murder. A life for a life. Carly was out of the woods, I had dodged the impeachment bullet.

I needed to let it go. But could I?

CHAPTER THIRTY-SEVEN

Tampa, Florida
Thursday 5:45 p.m.
January 28, 1999

SUNSET TONIGHT WAS PROJECTED for 6:07 p.m. Now, the huge orange ball lingered near the horizon, glowing around Ben where he stood propped against the rail, head bowed. O'Connell had stood precisely there many times. Was it possible he'd never do so again?

Squeezed my eyes shut to hold tears in check; felt the hot trickle on my cheek and brushed it away. Crying would be done in private.

Ben had raised his gaze to mine when I'd controlled myself well enough to look again. When he spoke, I glanced away immediately.

He said, "I hate to ask you this, but would you come with me when I tell his wife?"

"Pricilla doesn't know yet?" George asked.

Ben wagged his head slowly, side to side. "Someone she

knows should be there. She's bound to take it hard."

I definitely did not want to witness when Cilla learned O'Connell was gone; I could tell George didn't, either.

George stood, pressed my shoulder. "Willa, you'll want to wash your face. Let me get my jacket, Ben. We'll be right back."

George held my hand and we went upstairs to make ourselves somewhat more presentable. I don't know why we felt we had to look composed to deliver such terrible news, but we did.

George drove and Ben followed in his own car. Behind us, orange sun fell below blue horizon as we crossed our bridge onto the mainland.

We held hands for the three-mile trip to the Worthingtons' Bayshore mansion. Absently, George stroked my palm with his thumb pad. I remembered happier visits; balls and cotillions, old-fashioned parties; Cilla's southern charm and O'Connell's courtly manners. None of this could I voice and retain composure.

George parked in the circular drive. We emerged from his Bentley into the breezy dusk as Ben Hathaway drove up.

He joined us, touched my arm gently, patted George's shoulder, straightened his own posture and buttoned his jacket.

"Thank you both for doing this," he said, quietly, as if he couldn't have faced Pricilla alone. Ben was a cop. Delivering bad news was a part of the job. But our mission tonight was different.

No matter what had come before, from this point forward, Ben Hathaway would be counted among our friends as long as he would have us be so.

Three abreast, feeling nothing like crusaders, we trudged the long driveway and reached the front door much too quickly.

Ben rang the bell.

The housekeeper opened the door as she had a thousand times before.

George said, "Good evening, Mrs. Beason"

"Mr. and Mrs. Carson. Was Mrs. Worthington expecting you?" Lucille asked.

Ben replied, "We'd like to see Mrs. Worthington, if we may."

Lucille must have been curious, but she was impeccably trained. "Certainly," she said. "Please come this way."

She escorted us into the old-fashioned parlor where Worthingtons had greeted guests for more than a hundred years.

"Mrs. Worthington will be right down" she said, as if we were welcome visitors. She departed, leaving the door open. I heard her footsteps on the stairs.

A few moments later, from the second floor, the housekeeper's screams reached our ears. George and Ben ran up the staircase toward Lucille's screams.

I reached the master bedroom seconds behind George, but light-years too late.

Lucille Beason's face was buried in George's shirt while he made vain attempts to calm her.

Ben stood beside the four-poster where Cilla reclined fully clothed in the dress she'd worn to Michael Morgan's funeral.

Ben checked Cilla's carotid artery for a pulse while deliberately punching buttons on her phone with his left thumb. He made no effort to resuscitate. He responded to quick questions, finally saying, "No need to hurry."

The room was high ceilinged and spacious. Front windows overlooked Hillsborough Bay, and I could see our home, Minaret on Plant Key, clearly.

Cilla had been born in that bed, as all four of her children had been. It was there she'd slept with O'Connell for forty-seven years. Maybe she just couldn't sleep there without him.

Had Cilla killed herself because she knew her husband was dead? Or had she thought to prevent him from suicide? Or had they planned joint suicide? We'd never know.

Two envelopes and a wrapped package rested on Cilla's dressing table. I slipped the envelope addressed to Carly and the small package with my name on it into my pocket.

The other envelope was addressed to Ben Hathaway. It contained a full confession, executed and notarized by O'Connell Worthington, a gentleman even after death.

O'Connell provided the hard evidence of his guilt that Chief Hathaway had been unable to find. Motive: O'Connell said he'd killed Morgan because Morgan's theories were timed to insure his financial ruin. Means: He'd included a purchase receipt showing his ownership of the murder weapon. But he said he'd thrown the gun into the Gulf at the same time he'd thrown in the body. Opportunity: Well, we had Carly's eye-witness account for that. He apologized for the inconvenience.

EPILOGUE

CHIEF HATHAWAY MARKED THE Michael Morgan murder closed. O'Connell's firm was for sale, half a step ahead of foreclosure after having over-extended their lines of credit for breast implant litigation. His written confession contained lengthy details of his downward financial spiral, meant to persuade doubters of his guilt. Hathaway and the State's Attorney accepted.

O'Connell and Pricilla had been the epitome of our society for fifty years, as had their families before them. Public disgrace was more than they could bear.

I chose not to challenge O'Connell's bluff.

The Worthington's joint funeral was standing room only. Everybody, including me and George, Kate, the Warwicks, Carly and Grover, and the rest of Tampa, was visibly saddened.

Bill Sheffield told us his bank had been providing Worthington's financing. The firm declared bankruptcy; lawyers scrambled for new jobs.

CJ occupied in the family pew, sobbing like a child at the death of his only sister and his life-long friend. Would he be more antagonistic toward me, or less, because of the role I'd played in their deaths?

When he couldn't pin it on Grover, Ben Hathaway gave up and charged Fred Johnson with blackmailing Morgan. Johnson was disbarred, convicted and ordered to make restitution to Morgan's estate. No one's figured out what to do with the money. The legal wrangling will likely last beyond our lifetimes.

The package Cilla left for me on her dressing table before she died contained her diary and the four missing pictures from Morgan's piano. The two nudes were Morgan and the very young, very beautiful Pricilla Worthington. Glory days?

I only read three sections of Cilla's diary.

First, the passage describing the coincidence placing both of us in Carly's apartment. She'd been searching for Morgan's disk; panicked when I showed up. She said she'd never hit anyone on the head before, and thought she'd killed me, but was glad she hadn't.

Me, too.

Not a bowling ball, though. She'd used a Steuben vase. Good to know. Maybe a bowling ball is softer.

The second segment, her account of the night she killed Morgan, contained few surprises. After I'd discovered her name on Morgan's list of accounts receivable and recognized her nude picture captured in Robin's video, I'd suspected her. Saving her reputation, the rest of her money, and her husband was plenty of motive. Under the circumstances, many women would have done what Pricilla did. When O'Connell surrendered, my suspicions had been confirmed.

The final pages outlined her plan to kill herself. Sooner or later, she said, Hathaway would have found the evidence to arrest Morgan's killer even after her husband took the blame.

Pricilla knew O'Connell Worthington III would never have allowed his wife to be charged or convicted. Her death, she thought, would set him free.

Before she died, had she known she'd waited too long to save her husband?

A few days after the funerals, I had lunch with Carly at Minaret. Gave her Cilla's letter. I watched her read it, and watched her cry.

Dear Carly,

I'm sorry, dear, because he was your father. He didn't deserve a fine daughter like you. You're better off without him.

He did deserve to die. When I first knew him, he was kind and caring. But he changed. Maybe it was the drugs, or the women, or the success, or the failure. I don't know why. He became cold, greedy. The world is better off without him, too.

Much too late, I learned he didn't love me, that I was only one in a long line of women. I broke it off immediately, and then spent the rest of my life trying to buy his silence. He demanded money for years. He took everything but our house. O'Connell never knew. I never wanted him to know, but it took every cent of my inheritance to keep Morgan quiet.

It was the video. He recorded our affair. Others, too. He threatened to show those tapes unless I paid him. I burned every last one after he died.

I paid the money he demanded and other women did, too. I might have paid him forever. But he wanted to destroy O'Connell. That, I would not allow.

Pricilla Worthington

Carly cried for a while after losing her father. Maybe it

helped that he wasn't a father worth crying over, but I'm not sure.

Unfortunately, Carly seems quite fond of Grover. Maybe her brothers can handle that catastrophe-in-the-making. Mark's been promoted and is moving his family to Tampa. Kate, the grandmother, is thrilled. Jason called from Washington last night. He said he'd been in Romania for a couple of weeks and wanted to catch up on the boring stuff happening at home.

George and I enjoyed nightly sunset cocktails. Early February breezes were soft, skies cloudless blue, and the temperatures near eighty. My feet rested in his lap; he massaged achy toes gently. Harry and Bess splashed each other in the salt water.

"How much do you love me," I asked him one night, eyes closed, totally relaxed.

"More times than you can count," he replied softly.

"Would you die for me?"

"You mean like Romeo and Juliet?" I could hear the smile in his voice.

"No." I said. "Like Cilla and O'Connell."

THE END

ABOUT THE AUTHOR

Diane Capri is the *New York Times*, *USA Today*, and worldwide bestselling author.

She's a recovering lawyer and snowbird who divides her time between Florida and Michigan. An active member of Mystery Writers of America, Author's Guild, International Thriller Writers, Alliance of Independent Authors, and Sisters in Crime, she loves to hear from readers and is hard at work on her next novel.

Please connect with her online:

Website: http://www.DianeCapri.com
Twitter: http://twitter.com/@DianeCapri
Facebook: http://www.facebook.com/Diane.Capri1
http://www.facebook.com/DianeCapriBooks

If you would like to be kept up to date with infrequent email including release dates for Diane Capri books, free offers, gifts, and general information for members only, please sign up for our Diane Capri Crowd mailing list. We don't want to leave you out! Sign up here:

http://dianecapri.com/contact/

LEE CHILD

THE REACHER REPORT:
March 2nd, 2012

...The other big news is Diane Capri—a friend of mine—wrote a book revisiting the events of KILLING FLOOR in Margrave, Georgia. She imagines an FBI team tasked to trace Reacher's current-day whereabouts. They begin by interviewing people who knew him—starting out with Roscoe and Finlay. Check out this review: "Oh heck yes! I am in love with this book. I'm a huge Jack Reacher fan. If you don't know Jack (pun intended!) then get thee to the bookstore/wherever you buy your fix and pick up one of the many Jack Reacher books by Lee Child. Heck, pick up all of them. In particular, read Killing Floor. Then come back and read Don't Know Jack. This story picks up the other from the point of view of Kim and Gaspar, FBI agents assigned to build a file on Jack Reacher. The problem is, as anyone who knows Reacher can attest, he lives completely off the grid. No cell phone, no house, no car...he's not tied down. A pretty daunting task, then, wouldn't you say?

First lines: "Just the facts. And not many of them, either. Jack Reacher's file was too stale and too thin to be credible. No human could be as invisible as Reacher appeared to be, whether he was currently above the ground or under it. Either the file had been sanitized, or Reacher was the most off-the-grid paranoid Kim Otto had ever heard of." Right away, I'm sensing who Kim Otto is and I'm delighted that I know something she doesn't. You see, I DO know Jack. And I know he's not paranoid. Not really. I know why he lives as he does, and I know what kind of man he is. I loved having that over Kim and Gaspar. If you haven't read any Reacher novels, then this will feel like a good, solid story in its own right. If you have...oh if you have, then you, too, will feel like you have a one-up on the FBI. It's a fun feeling!

"Kim and Gaspar are sent to Margrave by a mysterious boss who reminds me of Charlie, in Charlie's Angels. You never see him...you hear him. He never gives them all the facts. So they are left with a big pile of nothing. They end up embroiled in a murder case that seems connected to Reacher somehow, but they can't see how. Suffice to say the efforts to find the murderer, and Reacher, and not lose their own heads in the process, makes for an entertaining read.

"I love the way the author handled the entire story. The pacing is dead on (ok another pun intended), the story is full of twists and turns like a Reacher novel would be, but it's another viewpoint of a Reacher story. It's an outside-in approach to Reacher.

"You might be asking, do they find him? Do they finally meet the infamous Jack Reacher?

"Go...read...now...find out!"

Sounds great, right? It's available. Check it out and let me know what you think.

So that's it for now ... again, thanks for reading THE AFFAIR, and I hope you'll like A WANTED MAN just as much in September.

Lee Child

Made in the USA
Middletown, DE
10 January 2020

82939358R00189